# BLOOD ORCHARD

S.D. Hintz

S.D. Hintz

SECOND EDITION

Blood Orchard

Published by Aristotle Books

This book is a work of fiction.
Names, characters, places, and incidents either are the product of the author's imagination or are used fictitiously. Any resemblance to actual persons, living or dead, events, or locales is entirely coincidental.

*for Ashanti and my parents,*

*thanks for encouraging my madness.*

S.D. Hintz

# CHAPTER ONE

### Six-month-old triplets kidnapped, bloodied

Coren Raines shook his head and folded the Tribune into a coffee cup coaster. He had moved in two days ago. Everything seemed perfect. He was forty-five miles from his ex-wife and his rambler was camouflaged by wetlands. He was in the middle of BFE, an ideal foundation for a fresh start. Yet those facts alone failed to smear the bold print. Onward, Illinois had made the headlines.

The crime had rocked the small town. While violence was commonplace in Chicago, Onward was alien to such misdeeds. The mayor posted advisories for everyone to secure their homes and keep an eye out for suspicious activity. The kidnapper was at large and the authorities lacked a solid lead. The tight-knit community had unraveled like an old scarf.

Coren switched on his laptop. The headline haunted him. Images scrolled through his mind like a Halloween screensaver: a crib beneath a shattered window, the mother bawling beside a bloody sheet.

"Jesus."

Coren reclined in the chair and clasped his hands behind his head. The workday was destined to be unproductive. He stared at the oceanic desktop background, straining to clear his head.

He stood and stepped away from the laptop. The spare bedroom was filled with unpacked boxes. He knew that was the remedy. Manual labor always lifted the weight on his shoulders. Maybe after a few hours of housework he could return to his full-time job.

A rasping rumble and clanking swelled through the open living room window. A vehicle was pulling up the driveway. Coren wondered for a moment if it was his lawyer, and then squashed the thought. The divorce had been finalized weeks ago. Maybe it was the mailman, or one of those cookie-carrying Girl Scouts.

Coren crossed the living room and peered between the curtains. His heart somersaulted. A navy blue Crown Victoria with tinted windows parked sideways, blocking in his Suburban. Maybe it was a reporter. They had swooped into town like buzzards starving for a morsel of news. Although the car looked as if it was better suited to a private detective or FBI agent.

Coren sighed and let the curtains fall into place. He nibbled his thumbnail. It had to be the FBI. A triple kidnapping had stained the streets two blocks down. The authorities were bound to interrogate their small population. Luckily, he had been a resident for a mere two days. There was no way in hell he was a suspect. Though in the back of his mind that was what worried him. He was the freshman on campus, number one on the dean's list.

Three raps rattled the front door. Coren gulped and unlocked the deadbolt.

A man in a khaki uniform opened the screen door. He towered over Coren by six inches. He was barrel-chested with broad shoulders and a clean-shaven face. His gold badge, bullet tie clip, and belt buckle engraved with a "P" glinted in the searing sun. He pocketed his Gargoyles, and then removed his Stetson. He was bald as Lex Luther. He regarded Coren with bloodshot eyes.

"Mornin', Mr. Raines. Sheriff Pritchard. Mind if I have a word?"

"Not at all. Come in."

Pritchard stooped inside and crossed the living room. He slipped out a red handkerchief from his shirt pocket, like an amateur magician trick, and dabbed a bead of sweat on his brow.

"I'm sure yer well aware why I'm here." Coren nodded. "Then I'll save ya the small talk. Where were ya last night, Raines?"

"Here."

"Of course ya were." Pritchard scanned the living room. His glare fixed on the coffee table. Strewn across the glass were two unopened bills, a letter opener, and an issue of Consumer Reports. "Where else would ya be? It's not like ya've been downtown. Ya haven't stepped outside of this dump. It's damn suspicious, if ya ask me."

Coren raised his brows. He bit his tongue as a retort tickled his vocal cords. He reminded himself that he was in the presence of Onward's sheriff, the last person he wanted to piss off.

Pritchard picked up the letter opener and eyed it. "So, what do ya do all day, Raines? Ya don't work in town."

"I telecommute." Coren fidgeted, glancing around for a household task. He needed to busy himself. He shuffled his feet. "Stock trading."

Pritchard dropped the letter opener and snatched the envelopes. He squinted at the plastic windows. "An e-nerd, huh? You guys are always six eggs short of a dozen."

"Excuse me?"

Coren's forehead began to sweat. Pritchard seemed like the kind of cop that never left empty-handed, regardless of his suspect's innocence. He surely had a backhoe for the dirt he dug up.

Pritchard crumpled and tossed the envelopes. "Stocks my ass. The only thing yer tradin' is yer soul."

"I think you need to come back later with a warrant."

Pritchard advanced. He made a pistol out of his thumb and forefinger and shoved it in Coren's face. "I am the warrant! I'll stay as long as I want, ya hear me? I'll turn this dump upside down if I'm so inclined!"

Coren backed against the wall. Pritchard loomed over him like a grizzly bear. He reeked of baby powder and cigarette smoke. Coren clenched his teeth, wide-eyed, certain Pritchard was going to clock him. Instead, the sheriff slapped on his Stetson, retracted his flesh pistol, and then blew the barrel's invisible smoke.

He barged past Coren. "I'm startin' to think yer stewed, Raines. Ya been drinkin'?"

"Coffee." Coren lingered in the living room while Pritchard stormed the kitchen.

"Irish?"

"Cream."

"Ya kiddin' me?"

Pritchard picked up Coren's coffee cup and sniffed it. As he set it down, his eyes locked on the makeshift coaster. One word circled with a brown stain jumped out on the folded newspaper: **kidnapped**.

Pritchard grimaced, and then scowled. "Where'd ya get this?"

"The paperboy. Why? Is that evidence, too?"

Pritchard snatched the coffee cup and hurled it. Coren ducked as it flew over his head, thudding on the living room carpet. Pritchard yanked the newspaper off the table and tore it in half.

"Ya think I need a reminder of this? They're everywhere! I can't go two steps without 'em askin' me 'bout the Trammell triplets!"

"I'm sorry. I'll throw it away."

"Shut up! Just shut the hell up! Yer lookin' guiltier by the second!"

"Because I have a newspaper subscription?"

Pritchard marched over to the desk, plopped down before the laptop, and opened the Internet browser. Coren's jaw dropped. He had to get this psychopath out of his house. The maniac was hell-bent on scoring him a criminal record.

Coren rushed the desk as Pritchard accessed a search engine and typed "adolescent boys." "Hey! What the hell are you doing?"

Pritchard whirled and aimed his flesh pistol. An earthworm-like vein pulsed in his forehead. "Freeze, Raines! Don't make another move!"

Coren ignored the ridiculous order. There was no way in hell Pritchard was downloading a virus into his computer, let alone pornographic pictures of children. The psycho cop had crossed the line, and his imaginary gun couldn't freeze water.

Before Pritchard could punch the "Enter" key, Coren lunged for the power strip and yanked the plug. The laptop blinked out. Pritchard leapt up and kicked Coren in the ribs.

"I told ya to freeze!" Pritchard grabbed the laptop and shoved it off the desk. It crashed on the linoleum. "Now I've got ya! Concealin' evidence! What else ya hidin' from me?"

Coren groaned and rolled onto his back. He winced as a sharp pain shot through his chest. His right rib cage was either bruised or broken. He watched Pritchard walk into the kitchen, pause at the sink.

"Looks like I found what I came for."

Pritchard grinned, baring his yellow teeth. He grabbed the balled up dishtowel on the counter and reached into the sink. Dishes clattered as he removed a bloody steak knife. Coren instantly regretted breakfasting on sirloin and eggs. Pritchard withdrew a Ziploc freezer bag from his pant pocket and sealed the evidence. He chuckled as the blood smeared the plastic.

A crackle followed by a shrill squelch twisted his grin into a glower. He grabbed the walkie-talkie from his gunbelt.

"Pritchard."

"Sheriff? -eputy Marten here. -e've got a vulture on the swoo-... reporter...-ack and blue motorcycle...-outhbound on Main Street."

"Copy that, Marten. I'll head 'em off."

Pritchard reattached the walkie-talkie. He then reached into his pant pocket and withdrew a handful of shiny badges. He replaced the one on his shirt, stuffed the rest in his pocket, and stared down at Coren.

"Yer under my microscope, Raines. I'll have yer head if ya did this." He overturned the kitchen table and left the living room.

The front door slammed. Coren groaned as he sat up. He grabbed the desk, gritting his teeth, and pulled himself to a standing position. He stumbled forward and plopped down on the chair. It spun right ninety degrees.

Coren stared out the smudged window. He was surprised Pritchard neglected to excavate the backyard, seeing how he was a stickler for evidence. The guy was a time bomb.

"Christ."

The more Coren reflected on his peaceful morning smoldering to hell, the more his ribs ached. He suddenly wished he had cleared the breakfast dishes. Who knew steak and eggs yielded accusations? Even if he had eaten shredded wheat that morning, Pritchard would have found a shred of evidence for his Ziploc.

Coren slouched and sighed. The last time he had a thorn in his side he walked away. If he did that now, Pritchard would call an APB. He had to stand his ground. Pritchard would return soon enough, probably without knocking.

Coren needed to fight off the bully, as if it were fifth grade all over again.

*****

After icing his ribs for an hour, Coren mustered the nerve to lift his T-shirt. The right side of his torso was purplish-blue. He decided to forego the hospital and rely on home remedies. Nurses and doctors would only interrogate him. He had his fill of police involvement for the day. Pritchard was surely on the triage speed dial.

Steadying a tumbler of gin and juice, he stepped out on the ground level deck. He set his drink on the splintered floorboards, then sat on the Adirondack chair. He closed his eyes, popped two Advil in his mouth, and brought the glass to his lips.

*What a day.*

He wondered if getting his ass kicked would qualify for workers' comp. He smiled as he considered emailing the details to his boss. What did it matter anyway? E-Conomi ran itself. As long as customers bought and traded currencies, stocks, and bonds, he would get paid regardless.

Coren opened his eyes. He gazed through the railing. Man, he had a lot of work to do. The backyard was a gardener's nightmare. The grass was shin-high, half-dead, and riddled with dandelions. The sole elm needed a pruning ten years ago; its branches drooped to the ground like a willow's. A large chunk of rusty, corrugated metal glinted along the tumbledown worm fence. A crumbled, cobblestone well with a caved-in rustic roof stood in the middle of the yard. A large crow was perched on the lip. It flapped its wings, cawed, and then knocked a cobblestone loose into the well as it took flight.

Coren sighed. The yard made the rambler worth every cent of the ninety thousand dollars he had paid. Like most new homeowners, he had visions of grandeur. The entire backyard would be transformed into a Japanese garden by fall. In his mind's eye, he saw a seven-foot tall waterfall flanked by bonsai trees. Wood bridges spanned a guppy pond. A latticed pavilion stood at the end of a pebbled path. Maybe he would even keep the well, spruce it up with a pantile roof. Once he had his Garden of Eden, he had a feeling that he would be spending more time outdoors.

He regarded his tumbler, through gin and glass. He felt better already. His head had cleared and the side ache subsided.

His thoughts dawdled on his ex-wife Deborah. She was a pharmacist and marathon runner. She would have scolded him for chasing two Advils with a screwdriver. Her face would have been as red as her lipstick the moment he told her he was taking a sick day to sit around and get plastered. She would have handed him a typed list of chores for each room in the house, all the while ranting on how she expected them to be done by the time she came home. Then she would have dropped by at lunchtime to check on his progress. What had he seen in that woman, besides her athletic physique? He felt sorry for the guy she had cheated on him with. He was shackled to a ball and chain that held the key to a padded cell.

Coren drained his glass, leaned his head back. It was funny how gin whisked away his worries. The Pritchard incident seemed surreal, almost as if it was a dream. Still, he made a mental note to fortify his property. He needed a security system. Or an eighty-pound pit bull.

Coren closed his eyes and smiled as images of Pritchard being chased by a rabid dog down the drive lured him into sleep.

*****

A high-pitched scream had Coren sitting up wide-awake. His heart hammered, triggering a pang in his ribs. He snapped his head in every direction.

He was alone.

The breeze carried the sound of rustling leaves and the lingering scent of the screwdriver. But he had heard the scream clearly. It had seemed deafening and then faded out like a 1980s pop song.

Coren stood, kicking over his glass. He walked to the deck railing. His gaze roved the backyard. A robin chirped on the fence accompanied by a staccato of crickets within the wetlands. All else was quiet and still.

Coren shook his head. Maybe that pesky crow had cawed overhead. Or the wind had rocked the hunk of scrap metal. He had dreamt the scream, plain and simple. He struggled to recall his morning nap, but drew a blank. Now he knew why Deborah had forewarned him about combining ibuprofen and alcohol. There were probably side effects, such as nausea, dizziness, and imagined screams.

Coren's mind wandered back to Pritchard. He was a bundle of nerves because of that nutjob. His shoulders were tense and anxiety rushed like adrenaline through his veins. He had a feeling that was the first of many bad dreams to come. He needed a stress reliever besides gin before he shriveled his liver.

He turned his back on the yard, looked at his watch. It was 9:30AM. There were dirty dishes to wash and towers of boxes to unpack. Accustomed to Deborah's weekly chore lists and eager to ease his tension, Coren picked up his tumbler and headed inside.

S.D. Hintz

# CHAPTER TWO

Coren had the dishwasher loaded in ten minutes. The confiscated steak knife prodded his conscience - the bloody blade smearing down the side of the Ziploc. Even though he was a model citizen, the thought of Pritchard conducting DNA tests on his belongings made him feel like a criminal.

He picked up the torn newspaper off the dining room floor. The coffee-stained headline glared at him. He read about shootings and beatings everyday in the Tribune, but they were forgotten by the time he turned the page. Crimes against children, on the other hand, especially ones close to home, weighted his shoulders like a backpack.

*Ya think I need a reminder of this?*

Coren crumpled the newspaper and fed the trashcan. Pritchard had exploded at the headline. The sheriff was probably virgin to high-stress situations. After all, what serious crimes were committed in small towns? Cow-tipping? Trespassing? Surely nothing that compared to a bloody kidnapping. Coren figured it made matters worse that Pritchard knew the townies personally. That might explain why he flew off the handle at Onward's new resident.

Coren picked up the laptop and set it on the desk. He plugged it in, flipped the power switch. The CPU blinked and flashed, then the flat screen blipped to life. Satisfied that the computer was unscathed, Coren switched it off and folded the screen. He was playing it safe. He would stash it somewhere inconspicuous in case Pritchard made another house call.

He passed through the living room, glancing at the bay window. He wondered if Pritchard had him under surveillance. The house was probably bugged with mote-sized cameras watching his every move. He needed to think of a way to keep Pritchard at bay without looking guilty. He could build a gate, although it would take a good week and he needed to secure the property by tomorrow morning at the latest. He would have to think hard on it over a liquid lunch.

He entered the spare bedroom, second doorway on the right side of the hall. Three pyramidal piles of boxes occupied the three corners. Yellow daisy wallpaper – a hideous décor Coren planned on removing – brightened the one-window room like mustard on a hot dog. Until now, he had ignored the room. He had glanced at it during the showing with his Realtor, but that was the extent of his scrutiny. At the time, he had thought it a sufficient storage closet. After all, it was a spare bedroom, what use would he have for it?

He set the laptop on a taped box labeled "Hardware" in permanent marker. He looked at the adjacent pile. The three groups of boxes represented various rooms of his previous house. The tower his laptop sat on was from the garage, which his new house lacked; there was merely a gravel parking space for his Suburban. He decided he would unpack those boxes last.

The pile in the left corner belonged to the kitchen. He looked away as thoughts of Pritchard haunted him. That left the middle pyramid. He lowered the topmost box labeled "Photos." He grimaced and unfolded the flaps. Gold-framed pictures of Deborah were scattered within, dumped carelessly like a deck of bent playing cards. His eyes locked on an 8" x 10." The married, clean-shaven Coren held Deborah around the waist beside a palm tree. It was their Hawaiian honeymoon. They had loved each other then. The island scenery and the exchanged "I do's" gave them fairytale hopes that they would live happily ever after.

He wondered if he would fall in love again. He was thirty-six years old. He had a feeling that once he was over-the-hill he would plummet off a cliff. Most women steered clear of divorcees. Dirty laundry was a chore to clean.

Coren grabbed the permanent marker from the windowsill and scribbled out "Photos." He wrote the word "TRASH" on the flap. He then dropped the box on the floor. He smirked at the sound of crunching glass.

He looked to the tilted tower. The wall caught his eye. In the midst of the urine-yellow garden, a long thread of wallpaper curled out like a pig's tail. Coren was a bona fide thread-puller. If a string dangled from his T-shirt or pant leg, he was quick to snap it. In his eyes, fraying conveyed a cheapened appearance. It made him look as if he wore hand-me-downs. He grabbed the thread that sprouted from the flower petal and tugged it. It tore the wallpaper downwards as if it was perforated. He let the elongated string slip from his fingers.

He leaned over the boxes and opened the wound with his fingers. He frowned. He had expected to see plaster or off-white paint beneath the wallpaper, but instead there was silver. He ran his finger down its smoothness. It was cold steel.

"What the heck?"

*Why is there steel beneath the wallpaper? Unless the previous owner patched up a hole with whatever he had handy. Or are all the walls in the house made of steel?*

He stepped into the hall and knocked on the wall. It was as hollow as a squirrel's home. It was definitely made of plaster.

Coren returned to the spare bedroom and approached the tear. He grabbed the snag with both hands and pulled. It tore toward him with ease and opened a gleaming wound down to the floor. It was all steel.

Intrigued, Coren shoved the piles of boxes aside and worked the wound. With each strip he ripped off, more steel was revealed. Five minutes later, he stood in the center of the room and stared at the glimmering wall as if it was the hull of a UFO.

*****

The Crown Victoria jumped the curb and screeched onto Main Street. The sirens wailed and the red and blue lights whirled in a blur. Pritchard took a final drag from the Marlboro and flicked it out the window. He then grabbed the CB and barked in a plume of smoke.

"In pursuit of a black and blue Harley! Suspect is male, black leather jacket, blue jeans, blue helmet. Remain on standby! I repeat, remain on standby! I don't want any more vultures hawkin' us!"

Pritchard floored the gas pedal. He hated reporters. They poked their brown noses into police business and asked stupid questions. They were viruses that plagued him everywhere he went and sweated him like a sauna. He would pay for an opportunity to bust one of them up.

The Crown Victoria bore down on the speeding Harley. The suspect turned, flipped the bird, and opened the throttle.

Pritchard activated the nitrous oxide. "Yer mine!"

He sped after the Harley down the deserted Main Street. He was glad that downtown had been shut down and lacked eyewitnesses. He had a feeling the pursuit was going to end nasty.

The last thing he needed were the townspeople seeing him in a bad light.

The Harley's needle was buried. The Crown Victoria closed the gap as the brick shops dwindled away. The suspect looked over his shoulder, realized the sheriff's intent, and shook his head.

The Crown Victoria's bumper rammed the Harley's back wheel. Pritchard grinned as the suspect lost control. The Harley skidded in a spray of sparks, caught the gravel shoulder, and then plummeted into the drainage ditch.

The Crown Victoria screeched to a halt. Pritchard cut the sirens and stepped out. He approached the shoulder, pocketed his sunglasses, and looked down into the ditch. The Harley's engine smoked and died amidst the knee-deep sewage. The suspect stumbled through the murk, then collapsed on the reedy bank. Pritchard drew his firearm and descended the ditch. No reporter was going to breach his posse and get away with it.

"Freeze, ya hear me? Freeze!" Pritchard used the bubbling Harley as a bridge. He stepped on the bobbing leather seat, submerging the handlebars, and crossed the rippling slime.

The reporter turned over and rested on his elbows. The cop's engraved belt buckle blinded him.

Pritchard kicked him in the head. The reporter's helmet flew off and rolled down the slope, splashing in the sewage. He hit the reeds on his back.

The reporter gasped as blood trickled from his lip to his red beard. "Please. I can pay you."

Pritchard grabbed his pistol by the barrel. He swung the butt, cracking the reporter in the temple. A gash opened and blood streamed down his face.

Pritchard seized him by the jacket lapels with one hand and lifted him a foot off the ground. His forehead vein squirmed. "Ya think ya can bribe me? Do I look like a two-dollar tramp to you? *What do I look like to you?*"

"N-No, sir. I'm sorry. I -"

"Shut yer mouth! Now tell me somethin'! What's the meanin' of a posse? It blocks the road from hotdoggers like you, right? *Right?*"

"Y-Yeah. Right."

"If I catch ya trespassin' again, you'll be the next one missin'!"

Pritchard heaved the reporter into the air. He grinned as the vulture nose-dived into the slime. He holstered the Magnum and drew his flesh pistol. He blew the imaginary smoke, spat on the ground. Kicking the crap out of a reporter was liberating. He had defended his town from the circling buzzard's camera. The last thing the citizens needed was some nosy ginger peering in their windows. The kidnappings were enough to digest.

Pritchard yanked his handkerchief out of his shirt pocket and dabbed his brow. He then swapped out his badge with a shiny one and donned his sunglasses.

*****

By noon, a heap of stripped wallpaper sat like raked leaves in the center of the spare bedroom. Bolted steel glimmered from wall to wall.

Coren gaped as his mind raced. Maybe the previous owner had built a panic room and covered it up when he decided to sell the house. If that was the case and he had been some paranoid schizophrenic, then why did a broken worm fence rather than a privacy fence surround the yard? It didn't make any sense.

He turned toward the hall and approached the wood frame. He had failed to notice the absence of a door. He spotted a small silver hook protruding from the wall. He pulled it. The wall slid forward. Coren stepped back into the room and closed off the doorway. It was a sliding pocket door with a metal frame, designed to conceal the bedroom. He guessed the wall consisted of steel as well.

*Weird*, he thought as he opened the door.

He turned and stared at the double-paned window. It seemed to be the only "normal" aspect of the room. Or was it? The glass was probably bulletproof.

Coren crossed the room, flipped the lock on the window, and pushed. It refused to budge. He gave the frame another shove.

"Open up!"

The window was sealed shut. Coren caught his breath as he massaged his throbbing ribs. The room was built like a bomb shelter. He wondered what laid beneath the hardwood floor and ceiling. He assumed more steel, though he had no intention of pursuing another treasure hunt. The walls had been tiring enough. But what was the overall purpose of the room?

He needed to satisfy his curiosity. He scanned the boxes, spotted the smudged label he was searching for: "Garage (boom box)." He unfolded the flaps. The Panasonic RX-D27 sat at the bottom, wrapped up in its cord.

He set it on the floor, hoping the batteries still had juice, and turned it on. Static crackled from the speakers. He cranked the volume full blast and ran into the hall. The static was deafening and sounded as if the boom box was going to explode. Coren slammed the pocket door.

Silence.

Coren shook his head. *Wow. It's really soundproof.*

He opened the door. The crackling cacophony blared in his face. He shut off the boom box and stared at the room, uncertain what to think of the newfound peculiarity. Outside of a panic room, what else could it be? An interrogation room? The bare bones of a meat locker? An agoraphobe's escape from the suffocating world?

Coren shut his eyes. With the wallpaper peeled, the room seemed colder. The steel walls and hardwood floor chilled him to the bone as if it were an icebox. He opened his eyes as gooseflesh rose on his forearms. He backed out of the room, shut the pocket door, and shivered from head to toe.

*Must be a draft, since I tore off the wallpaper.*

The room was the ideal hideout if Pritchard made a surprise visit. At that thought, Coren knew the room would be his little secret. If Pritchard ever snooped it out, he would look even guiltier. How would he explain himself? The truth would fly like an ostrich. The room had to be hidden, end of story.

Coren sighed, regarded the boxes. He was tired and his ribs ached. He glanced at his watch. It was a quarter to one. He craved a liquid lunch. His mind was on overload and gin would settle his thoughts. He walked to the living room with shakers mixing in his head.

*****

Jay Donovan flailed in the sewage. He glared at the crazy cop trudging up the ditch. He figured the sheriff had let him off easy. He could have slapped on the cuffs and hauled him to the station house. Instead, he kicked his ass without even inquiring for a driver's license and registration. How was that for a small town cop?

Jay raised his slimy hand and wiped his face. He stepped out of the murk and collapsed on the bank. He was dripping from head to toe and reeked of week-old trash. It was a small price to pay. He was a risk-taker and sometimes he was taken to the cleaners. It all depended on how he played his cards. On this particular day, he had folded. He thought that if he blew by the cops at eighty miles per hour they would let him go. He should have known better given the widespread publicity of the crimes. He should have contemplated an inconspicuous entrance rather than acted on impulse.

"Dammit."

He stared at the sunken Harley. The engine bubbled in the sewage. He would need a tow truck. The ditch was at least five feet deep. But what was he going to do about everything else? His digital camera and cell phone were waterlogged with the rest of his belongings.

There was one option that loomed over him like a storm cloud. He could leave town. He could return to WNDY and tell his boss that he botched the story. He closed his eyes and shook his head. There was no way he could walk into that station, looking and smelling as he did, and admit defeat. He would be the laughing stock of journalism. He would rather be jailed than pass the story to another reporter.

He pulled a piece of stringy slime out of his beard, and then ran his fingers through his matted, red hair. Green rivulets cascaded down his neck. He reached inside his jacket and withdrew the soaked newspaper clipping. The ink was smeared, but the photograph of the three eleventh grade girls was still intact. The blond seventeen-year-olds posed before a tire swing, embracing one another with broad smiles as if it was the first day of summer vacation. The picture was framed in Jay's mind, but he looked at it to remind himself of the importance of dredging up the truth. He put their names to their faces from left to right. Loren was curly-haired with a cleft lip. Henna was beetle-browed with French braids. Sylvia was rawboned with ratted, split ends.

The second Jay had heard of the kidnappings, he Googled past missing children in Illinois. Lo and behold, triplets had disappeared fifteen years ago in Onward. They had vanished without a trace and the story had merely made local headlines. The general consensus was that the girls had skipped town. They were known troublemakers and had been referred to as the "Blondies", so there were no suspicions of foul play. Their cold-hearted father Paul Pritchard had been quoted as having said: 'It's a cold case with three cold fish and I'm convinced it's another one of their rebel yells.'

*Paul Pritchard.* The sheriff's belt buckle with the engraved "P" blinded Jay's mind's eye. *Pritchard! Jesus! He just kicked my ass!*

Jay's original plan of interviewing an old, retired Paul Pritchard on his front porch was out the window. He had hoped to score some juicy details, however minute, on the disappearances. The stonehearted sheriff would lend a deaf ear now, especially to a guy that disobeyed his laws. Although, there was a chance a deputy might still be hanging around town.

He gazed at the photograph one last time. He recalled the list of the girls' misdemeanors that he had extracted from the county courthouse. Loren had been caught shoplifting at a drugstore. She had pocketed bottles of nail polish, Robitussin, and Chloraseptic with the intent of getting high. Henna had been cited for assault three separate times in regards to the same girl by the name of Francine Heller, another possible interviewee. Sylvia was the craziest of the sisters. She had been charged with animal cruelty, assault with a deadly weapon, disorderly conduct, and possession of an illegal substance. It was obvious the sheriff's daughters got away with murder.

A sliver of doubt poked Jay's theory. The Blondies had been bad girls, to say the least. Was it plausible there was a connection with the recent kidnappings and their disappearance? It seemed unlikely, given the timeframe. But who would mess with girls of their reputation? Nevertheless, it was a strong lead, even if it was a coincidence that they were triplets. A few interviews would indicate whether he was pursuing a dead end.

He pocketed the photograph, and then shook the excess sewage off his clothes. Hopefully he would dry out in an hour. He turned his back on the Harley and ascended the ditch. He needed to find a payphone and call a tow truck. He also needed to call his wife and check in. Staring at the photograph made him wish he were with his two daughters; Karley and Keira were probably enjoying recess right about now. He was glad they were safe, far from the craziness that oozed from Onward.

*****

Pritchard parked the Crown Victoria alongside the curb. He scowled out the driver's side window. The Trammell house loomed over a lush, landscaped lawn. While Teresa had minded the triplets, her husband Vance had toiled to maintain the homestead. Both were loyal, hardworking citizens. Vance slaved sixty hours a week for Cartwright Construction building houses. He had even built their home in Onward. The thought of some maniac breaking into their residence and kidnapping their children made Pritchard's blood boil. He could smoke an entire pack of Marlboros and still be enraged.

He exited the car, stamped out his cigarette butt. He slapped on his Stetson and approached the front porch. The house looked as lifeless as a corpse. The screen door swung in the breeze. Curtains gusted in the wide-open windows. Brown leaves swirled in a miniature tornado near the front steps.

It had been a day since he had spoken to the Trammells. Their last exchange had been heated and emotional. Teresa had sobbed uncontrollably, hugging her knees and trembling on the porch steps. Vance had raged down the sidewalk and used his mailbox as a punching bag. Pritchard wondered how their mind states had changed over twenty-four hours.

The front door shrieked like an age-old mausoleum. Vance emerged and met Pritchard's stony gaze. His eyes were bloodshot and baggy with dark circles. His lobe-length, dishwater blond hair was a rat's nest and a five o'clock shadow outlined his grizzled goatee. He rubbed his right eye, and then tugged his half-tucked plaid shirt.

"Afternoon, Vance. Mind if I have a -"

"What the hell do you want?"

Pritchard gritted his teeth. He had the urge to slap Vance's smart mouth. "Thought I'd keep ya informed. I've got a suspect. Lives at Hodge's old place."

"What makes him a suspect? He's only been in town a couple days."

"Exactly. I paid him a visit and he played stupid. He's hidin' somethin', guaranteed."

"I got a call from Chicago Homicide. They told me they were looking at the case."

"They'll look. That's 'bout all they're gonna do. Ya see, Vance, all we got right now is missin' children."

Vance's hands trembled as they clenched the doorjamb. "Those missing children are my girls! Remember when your girls -"

"All I'm sayin' is that I'm bustin' my ass out here to get 'em back. I suggest you start doin' the same. Get a search party goin' tomorrow mornin'. Scourin' those train tracks ain't a half-bad idea. Unless, of course, ya rather stand here and pray, but that won't get ya nothin' but rain. Trust me, I've weathered these storms before."

Vance flexed his fists as Pritchard returned to his car and sparked a cigarette. The pack would be empty by nightfall, the carton by the weekend. The townspeople chapped his hide. They saw him as a one-horse town sheriff that sat on his butt and interrogated the local diner on the strength of the coffee. He would show them. Once he tagged concrete evidence on Raines, the people of Onward would respect him more than the mayor.

*****

Coren sipped a screwdriver as he gazed out the bay window. The afternoon shadows crept across the front yard, swallowing the two-tone Suburban. Swirls of dust danced along the drive. The dead lawn shivered and occasional blades were swept up in the wind, covering the front walk like fallen pine needles. The worm fence swayed as if it would collapse into splinters.

Coren's mind rode the Seagram's wave. The neglected lawn sparked firefly thoughts of the backyard. The shrill scream. The crumbled well. The lone chunk of corrugated steel. The tumbledown fence. Pritchard's blood red face.

*Yer under my microscope, Raines.*

No matter how hard Coren tried to forget, Pritchard remained in his head. *I have to do something. Cop or no cop, I can't let this guy walk into my house whenever he pleases. He's probably staking me out right now.* His gaze darted about the yard. *Oh, what the hell. Let him. He'll see I'm not going to lie down again and get my ass kicked.*

He left the house and passed the walk. The wind styled his tousled hair as it carried the shrill sound of a train whistle. Recollections bobbed like buoys in the mental wave. The last time he had seen Deborah was at the Amtrak terminal. She had been

dressed in a white power suit and black pumps with her espresso hair

cascading down her collarbone. He remembered thinking how

profanely innocent she looked, like an angel with a pitchfork behind

her back. When her hands fell to her sides, she might as well as had

the Devil's implement. She held out the manila envelope. A slight

grin curled her crimson lips. Coren accepted the divorce papers. Her

words of goodbye echoed in his head as she turned on her heels and

ran to catch the next train to Raleigh.

A throaty caw snapped his trance. He thought of the crow on

the well. The scream of bloody murder. His original plans of

fortifying the property flitted in the breeze as his feet led him around

the house.

The grass crunched like snow, a reminder that he needed to

set out the sprinklers. Boy, he had yard work to do. He was thankful

that his house was nestled far from the main road and the backyard

was out of sight. He was surprised Pritchard had not cited him for

unsuitable living conditions.

He skirted the deck. He paused as his sights locked on the

well. The caved-in roof wavered in the wind. A few chunks of cobblestone crushed the grass at the base. Coren recalled the crow taking flight moments before his eyes closed.

A caw startled him. He looked to the house. The crow was perched on the gutter, watching him. It cawed again, as if to ask: "What are you looking at?"

Coren averted his gaze, approached the well. He placed his hands on the lip. The cobblestones jiggled. If a murder of crows used it as a birdbath, it was bound to collapse in on itself.

He looked down into the circular darkness, furrowed his brow. The air was thick and musty with an odd hint of cider.

Coren took a deep breath. *Weird. The screwdriver must be getting to me.*

He tossed the last sip into the well. Yes, it smelled of apples. Maybe there were some rotten cores in the depths, or it had an endless supply of cider, the odor and taste of which he hated since childhood. Who knew what was at the bottom? He guessed the water supply had dried up. He looked to the roof. A frayed rope and rusty pail were wrapped around a chipped piece of wood.

Coren shoved the bucket. It spun around the wood support, unfurling the rope like a yo-yo. The bucket plummeted into the hole.

He reached for the rope, but it slipped through his fingers and disappeared below. A clang like an off-key gong reverberated up the well.

*Guess it's dry.*

The cobblestones beneath his palms broke loose. He grabbed the wood support. It creaked as if about to snap, but balanced him before he could fall head over heels into the hole. The debris hit the bucket at the bottom with a *thunk-thunk-thunk*.

"Damn!"

*"Oohh!"*

Coren's head snapped at the high-pitched moan. His wide eyes darted as his heart thumped in his throat.

He was alone.

He let go of the wood support.

*"Oohh! Oohh!"*

The voice was clear as cellophane. It came from below. Coren turned and squinted into the well. There was an echo to the moan, and a childish undertone. He was certain of it. But how could anyone be in the well? And how long had they been down there?

"Are…" Coren's nerves constricted his throat. "Are you okay?"

*"Oohh!"*

Coren trembled from head to toe, stumbled back.

*Get a hold of yourself,* he thought. *There's a kid down there.*

He stepped up to the well. The smell of apples wafted from the darkness. It was so overpowering that it stung his eyes like sliced onions. He blinked away the tears. His gaze locked on the opposite wall. The cobblestones were splitting.

"What the hell?"

The cobblestones failed to crumble, but a red fluid seeped from the cracks. It trickled in serpentine rivulets down the wall. Though it was impossible, Coren knew it was blood by its copious flow. Nausea twisted his stomach. His head swam from the reek of cider. Maggots wriggled from the bloody fissures in the wall.

Coren turned, doubled over, and retched. He stumbled through the grass with vomit dripping from his mouth.

*"Oohh!"*

The agonizing moan rang in Coren's ears. He collapsed face first at the foot of the deck. The stench of apples seemed to have coated his nostrils. His head pounded. His eyes streamed tears. He curled up into a ball, clutched his stomach, and vomited. He felt as if he had the world's worst hangover. He groaned as a black curtain fell over him, swallowing his consciousness whole, luring him to slip away from the sickness and embrace the sweet-smelling darkness.

S.D. Hintz

# CHAPTER THREE

*Francine Heller crossed the train tracks as the Burlington Northern rattled toward Logansport. She vowed to one day hop onto the caboose and ride the rails. The thought of travelling miles from Onward was tempting. She longed to escape the dead end roads, small town monotony, and feeling of confinement, as if there was no other place on earth to live. Most of all, she yearned to distance herself from the Blondies.*

*She slung her faded green Jansport over her shoulder and followed the windy path through the oak grove. She always took the shortcut home after school. The upside was that she avoided Mrs. Petermen's bulldog Feisty, who loved to chase eleventh-graders as if they had T-bones strung to their shoelaces. The downside was that she occasionally encountered the Blondies. She made a mental note to reroute her shortcut tomorrow. She needed to eliminate all possibilities of running into the town bullies. She grew weary of black eyes on a weekly basis.*

*The cool shade receded as she emerged from the grove. Her gaze zoomed in on Main Street. The two blocks of sun-bleached, red brick buildings loomed ahead.*

*Francine's heart beat like a drum roll. The street looked deserted. That spelled trouble. The lack of bystanders increased her chances of harassment by the Blondies. If the street had been bustling, she could have passed undetected through the crowd. Now she could only hope that the bullies were busy beating up another kid on the other side of town. She took a deep breath, certain her heart would explode, and sighed.*

It's now or never. *Her hand white-knuckled on the backpack* strap.

*Francine crossed the overgrown field that had once been Mr. Utley's yard. Since his passing, the ramshackle, taupe mobile home had been towed, leaving behind a rectangular indent of dead grass. Francine veered toward the curbside. The strange shape amidst knee-high grass, dandelions, and black-eyed Susans made her think of those crop circles she had once seen in a library book on UFO's. It creeped her out. She hurried toward the sidewalk as the weeds tickled her bare calves.*

*She looked down past her denim skirt to her blue jellies.*

*Sandburs clung to her tube socks. She picked them off one by one,*

*wincing at each poke in the flesh, and then warily headed into town.*

*Her next-door neighbors Mr. and Mrs. Emory exited Kate's*

*Bakery hand in hand. They smiled and nodded. Mr. Ratner, the*

*mailman, appeared across the street, sifting in his canvas bag of*

*envelopes. Francine's heartbeat steadied. She was relieved that*

*there were other people around.*

*She passed beneath the red-striped awnings of the bakery*

*and gazed at the storefront. Betsy Collins, the town busybody, stood*

*at the glass counter pointing at various pastries while Kate*

*wandered back and forth like an expecting father, filling an open*

*box. Mr. Adler sat at a round table near the window, his chalk-white*

*hair poking above the Tribune. The smell of donuts and coffee at*

*three o'clock in the afternoon turned Francine's stomach.*

*A green overhang replaced the awnings as she walked by*

*Wal-Drug. Beyond the bay window advertising RC Cola, the store*

*was vacant, even the pharmacy, which was odd considering how*

*many elderly people lived in town. Usually there was a line from aisle one to three. Maybe Mr. Wurtz, the pharmacist, was under the weather.*

*As Francine strolled by the adjacent shop window, Dame Apparel, an electric blue dress caught her eye. She stopped and goggled at it. It was beautiful. It was made of silk chiffon with rhinestone spaghetti straps and a starburst-beaded neckline. It screamed elegance with its high-low hemline that extended into a brush train. It was one of those dresses she had seen time and again in the movies. She looked at the price tag on the neon-lettered sign: $220.00.*

*"It's outta your price range, Smeller."*

*Francine whirled, and then backed against the storefront. The Blondies smirked before her. Loren tugged down her black Pirates cap over her serpentine curls. Sylvia twirled her shoulder-length, split ends as she snapped a wad of bubble gum. Henna furrowed her beetle brows and approached Francine, stopping an inch from her face so that her girth overshadowed her.*

*"And no one's desperate enough to ask ya to prom."*

*"Leave me alone, Henna." Francine's heartbeat hammered in agreement.*

*"As soon as you do, Smeller. Ya know this is my street. Why the hell do ya come lookin' for me?"*

*"I didn't. I'm going home."*

*"Ya ain't goin' nowhere 'til I let ya. Grab her!"*

*Loren and Sylvia seized Francine by the wrists. Henna waddled up the sidewalk and rounded the meat market at the end of the block. Sylvia skipped alongside Francine, who struggled to break free as Loren yanked her forward. At a glance, passers-by would have seen three girls holding hands in a playful tug-of-war.*

*Francine was led around the corner of the building and shoved against the wall. She was grateful her backpack cushioned the blow. She glanced left and right. The street was deserted.*

*"Gimme that!" Henna grabbed Francine's backpack by the strap and ripped it off her shoulder. She unzipped it as Loren and Sylvia pinned Francine's wrists to the wall. "This is my homework now. Find yer own to do."*

*"Put it back!" Francine hoped someone downtown would hear her. "It's mine, you fat pig!"*

*"What did ya call me?"*

*Henna tossed the backpack aside. Folders and notebooks spilled into the gutter.*

*Tears streamed down Francine's cheeks. "Why won't you just leave me alone? What did I ever do to you?"*

*"Ya called me a fat pig, that's what!" Henna clutched Francine's jaw with her right hand as she flipped out a razor blade in her left. "Now ya know what I'm gonna do? I'm gonna cut your filthy tongue out so ya don't sass me again!"*

*For a split second Francine was speechless. She trembled from head to toe as the blade inched toward her lips. Henna yanked down on her jaw and she screamed bloody murder. Henna slashed the corner of Francine's mouth, and then belted her in the gut with her right fist.*

*Francine collapsed to her knees as the Blondies released her and fled. She heard distant shouts. Blood trickled from her chin, staining the sidewalk. Mrs. Murphy dropped a bag of groceries and crouched before her. She heard pounding on pavement and glimpsed Mr. Ratner, his mailbag bouncing on his back, sprinting after the Blondies. She dabbed her mouth with her shirtsleeve.*

*Yes, she needed to reroute her shortcut tomorrow.*

*****

Jay peeled off his jacket and draped it over the payphone on the corner of Texaco's parking lot. He fished in his pant pocket, withdrew five dimes. He was still dripping wet, even after the mile walk up the road. A small puddle had formed around his Reeboks and trickled to the rusted pole of the red star sign that towered over him.

He shoved the coins in the slot and dialed 4-1-1 as he gazed at the gas station. An orange and black sign on the clouded glass door read: **Closed**. Black shades had been pulled down on the cracked front windows. Both pumps were covered in what resembled body bags. A Pepsi machine with an **Out of Order** sign on the coin slot stood to the right of the concrete building. All in all, it was a service station that served the townspeople. It was devoid of pay pumps, air hoses, and car washes. Jay was surprised it had a working payphone.

"Uh, yes, can I have the number to the towing company closest to Onward? I'm sorry? Yes, that'll be fine. Okay, great. Thank you."

A husky voice barked in Jay's ear: "Blue Tow!"

"Yeah, hi, I need a tow truck on Main Street in Onward."

"Onward? Fat chance, buddy. Place is barricaded. No way in or out. It's all over the news. You'll have to sit tight 'til the storm blows over."

"Of course. I should've guessed. Okay, thanks."

Jay hung up the phone. He was in a hell of a bind. His bike was stuck in a drainage ditch and the town sheriff had him on surveillance. The last thing he wanted to do was run into Pritchard. The maniac would beat him to death if they crossed paths again.

He needed to call his wife Jeanette. He could have her pick him up near the train tracks or some other remote location.

*No. I can't do that.*

Jay had breached the barricade for a reason. He wanted the story. He wanted to crack the case and make a name for himself. So what if he was trapped within the city limits. He had a story to cover. All he needed now was a pencil and a notepad, seeing how his camera and cellphone were lost in sewage.

He fished in his pocket for spare change. His fingers found soggy lint.

He grabbed his jacket, slipped it on, and then gazed at the horizon. The sun burned in a simmering red-orange sky. Nightfall was nearing. Worry burrowed in Jay's head. Where was he going to sleep? What was he going to eat? Downtown was shut down and the roads were blocked. The Texaco Pepsi machine was even inoperable.

Jay looked to the gas station. He wondered if there was a back door. There had to be drinks and snacks inside. His stomach growled. He was dying for a Slim Jim. Model citizen or not, he had a story to dig up and it might take days to do. He needed a place to eat, sleep, and relieve himself. Without a second thought, he headed toward the rear of the Texaco.

*****

Coren's eyelids fluttered, and then snapped open. The right side of his face was pressed against the grass, which felt like a pincushion. A puddle of vomit laced with flies had settled inches from his mouth. He was still curled up in a ball, shivering. He raised his head. The sky had darkened. The sun was a dying ember beyond the twittering wetlands.

He rolled onto his back, let his arms fall to his side. His sour stomach had faded and his head had cleared. He took a deep breath. The night air was thick with the mesquite scent of a bonfire. The hint of cider was seemingly absent.

He groaned as he sat up. His ribs ached like wildfire. Gin and Advil never sounded better.

He looked to the well. Its cylindrical silhouette resembled a bulging eyeball, or maybe even a giant apple. The latter thought flooded his head with a geyser of recollections. The cobblestones cracking. Blood trickling from the wall. Maggots wriggling out, raining into the darkness below.

Coren gritted his teeth and stood. He winced as pain pierced his side, feeling as if he had been knifed. He stared at the wavering silhouette. The raspy moan haunted his conscience.

*The kid*, he thought. *That kid's still down there!*

He stumbled into the shadows. The bonfire fog enveloped the backyard, compressing the air like a drawn tarp. He wondered who was stoking the fire pit. A twisted vision of Pritchard flashed in his head. He saw the hulking cop in sunglasses standing before six-foot flames, roasting marshmallows with a cigarette glowing in his sneer.

Coren tripped and fell onto the stone wall. He straightened as he gazed into the darkness below. A frigid gust of cider stung his nostrils and tousled his hair. His eyes burned and teared up. He shivered, staggered back a step.

*"Oohh! Oohh!"*

The little girl's cry rattled Coren. He broke into a cold sweat as his adrenaline surged. He was more scared of the fact that he was wide-awake, yearning for a sign that he was dreaming. But despite the encompassing infernal haze, his sight was clear.

"Okay. Okay, just…just sit tight."

Coren glanced at his surroundings. He wished the rope and bucket still hung. He needed something to hoist out the poor girl.

*Sheets!* he thought. *I could knot some bed sheets together and pull her out!*

He turned to head for the house, and then froze as wailing erupted from the well. He whirled and bent over the lip, peering into the blackness. The cold rush of apple air was unrelenting.

The crying grew louder, like an approaching siren.

"Don't worry!" Coren prayed the girl was unharmed. He pictured her stepping on the broken bucket and slicing her foot. "I'll be right back! I'm gonna get you out of…"

His voice trailed off and his eyes widened as bone-white flesh emerged from the darkness. A frail girl in tattered, bloodstained clothes scaled the wall. She dug her nails into the cracks and pulled herself up. She tilted her head back, wailing, tears dripping from her blood-streaked face. Her mouth glinted, gagged with barbed wire. Her curly hair was matted to her gashed forehead and looked like dead worms. Coren was rooted to the ground.

*"Oohh!"*

The girl's moans wrenched Coren's heart. He leaned over the lip and reached for her. She still had a foot or two to climb. Her trembling hands slapped at the cobblestones, fingering the cracks. Coren saw that her skeletal legs were twisted like licorice, more than likely shattered from her fall.

"Grab my hand!"

The girl clutched the cobblestones. Coren knew that if she tried to reach for his hand there was a high probability that she would slip. She slapped her palm on the next row of stones. Blood cascaded through the cracks.

"C'mon!"

*"Oohh!"* Tears dripped from the barbs in her mouth. *"Oohh! Oohh!"*

The girl's right hand slipped from the crack. The waterfall of blood ran down her left arm and the front of her clothes. Coren stepped back, and then lunged into the well. He seized the girl's wrist. She cried out as maggots poured from the cobblestone. Coren heaved her up the wall, mustering every ounce of adrenaline that rushed through his body.

"Hold on! I got you!"

He braced his foot against the base of the well. The girl was no heavier than a sack of potatoes and he hauled her over the lip with ease. She hit the ground hard, bawling, as the hot, thick scent of apple jetted from the darkness and stung Coren's face. He howled. It felt as if his skin was burning. He clutched his face, stumbled back from the well.

After about a minute, the pain subsided. Coren drew his hands from his face, expecting to see them covered in blood. They were merely smudged with dirt. He sighed. The air mass had felt acidic. He was certain his flesh was smoldering. He blinked the tears from his eyes.

The girl twitched and whimpered on the ground. She was sprawled on her stomach. Her black-and-blue legs were entwined and bent backwards. She clawed at the barbed wire in her mouth as she squirmed and struggled to roll over.

Coren knelt beside her. His heartbeat pounded in his temples. He knew he had to help her, but confusion plagued him. How was he going to move her without inflicting pain? How was he going to remove the barbed wire from her mouth? How was he going to get her the medical attention she needed? Dialing 9-1-1 was out of the question. Pritchard would never believe that he found a girl in his well. He would be booked and on trial before you could spell O.J.

"Hey." His voice quavered as he placed his hands on her arm. Her flesh was cold and callous. "I'm…I'm gonna pick you up now. We've got to get you inside. Okay?"

He thought he saw her nod, but it could have been a twitch. He slipped his hands beneath her shoulders and tailbone. On the mental count of three, he lifted her. Her whimpers heightened to moans.

"I know, I know. I'm sorry."

Coren stood and held her to his chest. He glanced at her mangled legs. He bit his lower lip as pity gnawed at him. He looked at her face, grimaced. The girl looked to be in her later teens. She had been pretty once. Now barbed wire tore her mouth when she moaned. Crimson slashes, many scabbed over, etched her round, pale face. Her eyes were electric blue and darted as if every shadow hid the psychopath that harmed her.

Coren walked away from the well. He ascended the deck steps, shoved the sliding door open with his shoulder, and carried the girl into the house.

*****

Pritchard killed the headlights and parked the Crown Victoria at the end of the drive. He shut off the engine, lit a cigarette, and then squinted out the driver's side window.

He hated the mud-hued rambler. He felt like he had to scrape the filth off his boots every time he set foot on the godforsaken property. It was common knowledge that the previous owner Ray Hodge had the worst land in town. He had heard rumors that his backyard was bone dry. He wasn't surprised that the grass was dead. No city water, no ordinances. He grinned at the thought.

He flicked his half-smoked cigarette out the window. He fished out the Ziploc baggie with the bloodstained steak knife and set it on the dashboard. He needed more evidence. The cutlery was a scare tactic, a little something to keep Raines on the edge of his crapper. If he could dig up a few more particulars, he could nail that smart-mouth to the wall. He could probably even kick his ass a couple of more times and get a lame confession out of him.

He popped the glove box and grabbed his tape recorder. He pushed "Play." The tape spun within the mini-cassette. Satisfied, he pressed "Stop." It had been years since he had to bribe someone. And Raines was a model citizen. He had a few speeding tickets, but that was it. Though he was recently divorced. That might be bait for future bribery, unless Raines didn't give a rip what happened to his ex-wife. Either way, it was one of the many roads he could follow. Most would be dead-ends, but one was bound to drive Raines over the edge.

Pritchard grabbed his night vision binoculars off the passenger's seat and focused them on the rambler. The windows were dark. The junky Suburban was parked in the same spot as earlier that morning. Raines was definitely home.

Pritchard glanced at the dashboard clock. It was 9:15 P.M. Raines could have been sleeping. Or maybe he was wallowing in depression and sitting in the darkness.

Pritchard smiled. He pocketed the recorder and stared at the clock. Raines had a wake-up call coming in an hour and a half. The town would be dead by then. Come morning, a confession might hit the headlines. Pritchard saw the Tribune in his mind's eye.

"Child Molester Confesses." He withdrew his .357, rolled the chamber. He aimed it out the window. "I got ya now, boy."

S.D. Hintz

# CHAPTER FOUR

Jay stared at the weathered back door. It was metal and warped with a sign that read: **Employees Only**. He jiggled the knob, recalling his days as a teenaged cashier at an Aurora Amoco. The women in pumps at the pumps were endless, as were the free cartons of Newports he smuggled on a nightly basis. It was no wonder his register drawer was an accountant's nightmare. He was eventually fired when the owner viewed the surveillance cameras. That memory still made him grin.

He kicked the door. "Damn."

How was he going to get in? He needed a crowbar. He wondered if the place was rigged with an alarm. He doubted it. Onward's crime rate was minimal until recently.

He scanned the cinderblock foundation. Candy wrappers and Pepsi cans littered the crab grass. There were no discarded calling cards that he could use on the back door, or a window he could break.

His gaze traced the roofline. A glint caught his eye. He walked to the far corner of the building. An iron ladder bolted to the wall led to the gutters. Jay grabbed the rungs and climbed up.

When he reached the top, he crawled onto the roof and crouched behind a rusty A/C unit. He glanced east and west. Both directions were deserted. He eyed the pebbled surface. A metal hatch glared in the waning sunlight.

*Blackjack.*

Jay shuffled across the slippery roof. He grabbed the handle and tugged. The hatch shrieked open. He let the door fall back on its hinges with a *clang*. He grimaced as an overpowering scent of cider wafted from below. He hated apples. Ever since the time when he was a child and he found a green worm in the core, he refused to eat them, let alone drink the juice. He hoped there was food besides apples in the store, otherwise his plan would be fruitless. He held his breath and descended the ladder.

When his feet touched solid ground, he reached out like a blind man and gauged his surroundings. There seemed to be shelves behind him. The room was stuffy and the reek of apples made him teary-eyed. He gagged, and then stumbled, tripping on an object. A string tickled his right cheek. He reached up and tugged it. A bare bulb blinded him.

He stood in a pantry. The ladder hung in the middle of the room. Behind him, crates of Granny Smiths buckled the wood shelves and cans of peaches flanked his shoulders. He looked down and saw that he had kicked over a box of powdered milk. He grasped the doorknob, but it refused to turn.

"You got to be kidding me."

He never knew breaking and entering could be so difficult. Of course, most hardened criminals knew how to pick a lock. He, on the other hand, struggled with turning a key the right way. His only option was to break down the door. He grabbed a crate of apples. It was heavy, at least ten pounds. He hoped it would do the trick. He lifted the crate over his head and threw it. It shattered against the door. Apples bounced and rolled at his feet.

"Oh, c'mon!"

Jay snatched a Granny Smith and hurled it. He then charged with his left shoulder leading. He barreled into the door and it gave way. He groaned as he landed hard on the speckled tile.

*Now that's breaking and entering*, he thought as he stood up.

According to the dangling sign, he had fallen down near Aisle 7. The store consisted of seven aisles and a row of coolers. Jay walked past the red shelves of Doritos and detergent. He glanced at the front window. The pumps were vacant, as was the frontage road. He looked to the front counter, then to the other corners of the store. It seemed the gas station lacked cameras and the common circular mirrors.

Jay sighed. He was twice as paranoid now that he trespassed within the Texaco's confines. He could see the story and a clip of him on the evening news: "A WNDY reporter was arrested on three counts of burglary at an Onward Texaco. Police are still looking into a motive as to why Jay Donovan only stole snacks and soda. Kara Kaminski, WNDY 11 News."

*Jesus, what would Jeanette and the girls think of me right now? I ditched my Harley, I got my ass kicked by a cop, and here I am burglarizing the local gas station.*

He opened a cooler and grabbed a Cherry Coke. He guzzled half the bottle, and then approached the counter. He eyed the candy display beside the cash register: **Reese's Pieces 2/$1.00**.

"Ooh. That's a deal."

Jay grabbed two bags of candy. He pulled his soggy wallet out of his back pocket, removed five dollars, and set it on the counter. As long as he had cash, he was going to pay for everything he took. He reached above the register and yanked out a cigarette pack from the dispenser. He tore it open and grabbed a Bic lighter off the counter rack.

He froze as Pritchard's Crown Victoria crept by on County Road 500. He dove across the counter, knocking over the racks of candy and lighters, and huddled low.

"Crap!"

He waited a good two minutes, and then peered out the window. The coast was clear. Pritchard was probably doing his rounds, ensuring that no other cracked reporters were running rampant. He was definitely crazy enough to initiate martial law. He would shoot Jay on sight if they crossed paths again.

Jay lit the cigarette and took a long drag. He had work to do. If he planned on cracking the case before Homicide rolled in, then he had to act fast. He needed a lead.

He stubbed out the cigarette and stuffed his face with Reese's Pieces. As soon as he was done with dinner, he would dig out a phone book and find Francine Heller's address. It was as good a place to start as any. Maybe she would even let him use her phone to call Jeanette. At that thought, he scanned the counter. Surprise, no means of communication in sight.

He sighed as he gazed out the window. The sky had darkened and his time was short. Night would be his best friend, camouflaging him from the patrols. He hoped Francine would answer her door. Oh, who was he kidding? She would probably turn out her lights and pretend to be gone. After all, who was crazy enough to invite someone in when a maniac was on the loose? He prayed that she was, otherwise he was back to square one with nothing to show but a pocketful of Reese's Pieces.

*****

Coren laid the shivering girl on the couch. Her gaze was hollow, lost in the ceiling. Her blue lips quivered and the barbed wire continued to gore her. She moaned incessantly as she had in the well.

Coren hurried through the darkness to the kitchen and opened his junk drawer. He found a pair of wire cutters. He then ran to the bedroom, yanked the comforter off his bed, and returned to the living room. He froze at the end of the hall.

The girl sat up. She stared into the darkness, twitching, her head jerking from side to side as if she watched a tennis match. Her moans heightened. Coren ran to her side.

"Shh. Everything's okay. You're fine. C'mon. Lie down for me."

Coren grabbed her frigid shoulders and urged her down on the couch. He covered her with the comforter, tucking it beneath her black-and-blue chin. He waved the wire cutters before her blank face.

"I'm going to cut that wire out of your mouth now. I'm not going to hurt you. I promise."

Coren put the cutters to her lips and snipped the barbed wire. It snapped off, tearing away pieces of flesh. Her bloodstained lips parted and she gagged. Coren backed away as she heaved a stream of maggots.

"Oh! Goddamn!"

He grimaced. Maggots wriggled across her bloodstained T-shirt and wormed into the couch cushions. She coughed several times, agitating the sores around her mouth. Blood trickled down her chin. Her eyes rolled back into her head and her body stilled. She seemed to slip into a deep slumber, though moaned softly. Coren considered slapping her awake, but he was paranoid of harming her even more. He watched her chest rise and fall for a few moments and decided to let her sleep. She was probably exhausted from her climb up the well, rather than dying.

Coren nudged her head up and pulled out the barbed wire. It was stiff and encrusted with blood. The girl's breath tickled his face. Coren furrowed his brow. Her breath was cold and smelled of apples. He had expected it to be hot and reek of death after the maggot incident. He leaned back and dropped the barbed wire on the coffee table. He sighed, shook his head.

*What have I gotten myself into? I have a half-dead girl lying on my couch!*

He knew deep down that she was someone's missing child. He wondered if she was a runaway, one of those kids that mustered the nerve to follow the train tracks miles from home. Then somehow she had wandered into his backyard and stumbled into the well. But how long had she been down there? She looked like a prisoner of war, battered and bruised as if she had been holed up for a good week.

Coren walked to the kitchen, flipped the light switch, and dropped the barbed wire in the trash. He winced. His ribs ached again. He opened the cupboard and grabbed the Advil. He then peeked into the refrigerator. He grabbed the orange juice carton, set it on the counter. He had earned a nightcap, and a screwdriver would be perfect for hammering the worries out of his head. If ever there was a time that he needed to think clearly, now was it.

*****

A light beamed through the bay window. Pritchard glanced at the clock. 10:26 P.M. He cursed. Raines was wide-awake and roaming the house. So much for surprising him with a pistol in his mouth. While Plan A smoldered before Pritchard's eyes, Plan B formulated in his head.

*Screw it. I'll walk up the drive and knock on the door. He won't even see me comin'. Don't need the headlights givin' him time to cover his ass.*

He holstered his pistol, exited the squad car, and gently shut the door. He reached inside his shirt pocket and activated the recorder as he followed the light of the crescent moon.

The bay window was still lit. He had a feeling Raines was fixing a nightcap. Better yet. That meant his reactions would be slow. He would be more liable to say something he might regret.

Pritchard paused before the fence and grinned. He was going to get his confession and have his name in the headlines of Saturday's Tribune. And for legality purposes, he even had a search warrant folded in his back pocket. The odds were stacked against Raines. He was a sitting duck about to get blown out of the water.

Pritchard rounded the fence. He gritted his teeth at the crunch of gravel beneath his feet. If he failed to sneak up on Raines, it would be twice as difficult catching him off-guard. He thought about crossing the lawn, but the grass was dead and would crunch even louder. He stopped at the front steps and withdrew his Magnum.

*****

Jay scratched his beard as he peered from behind a bush at the two-story clapboard house. He glanced at the lopsided mailbox with the bent flag. 628 Sangralea. That was the place. He was surprised there was a porch light on. The house looked uninhabited. It was by far the most dilapidated residence on the block and could pass for haunted in a heartbeat. The second story windows were cracked and flanked by battered shutters with broken slats. Most of the shingles were either missing or curled near the eaves, and the porch railings were cobwebbed.

Jay approached the weedy walk. *Hopefully she's not dead in there.*

He ascended the porch steps, took a deep breath, and then pressed the doorbell. It chimed once, echoing within like a rusted triangle. The door creaked open.

"Ms. Heller?"

Francine Heller stepped into the dim light. She was a pale woman of about thirty with straggly, black hair. Her small mouth was set in a permanent frown and her eyes were baggy with crow's feet. She wore a torn, nylon skirt and a stained, half-tucked T-shirt. She stepped aside.

"You're early, Detective. I'm hitting the sack in ten minutes, so you'd better make this quick."

"Ms. Heller, I'm not -"

"Did you hear me? You should be glad I didn't slam the door in your face at this hour. I'm doing you a favor."

Jay nodded and entered the house. Francine shut the door and led him down a dingy hall with a water-stained ceiling.

Jay wondered why she thought he was a detective. Was there a chance she had an appointment with one that evening? If that was the case, he had better take her advice and keep the questions to a minimum. Now that he was inside her house and she was open to an interview, he was not about to tell her he was a reporter. It looked as if it would be his first story undercover.

Francine motioned to a red armchair with a ripped cushion. "Have a seat."

He sat down as Francine reclined on a sofa and grabbed a cigarette from a cluttered end table. Jay dug out a small notepad and pen he had bought from the Texaco and eyed the room while Francine fumbled for a lighter. The slate walls were bare, the brown carpet as worn as the furniture. A single ceiling lamp cast a dim glow on the ceiling. Francine tossed the lighter onto the table and puffed her cigarette.

"Like I said, Detective, I haven't got all night."

"Right." Jay shifted in his seat. His mind drew a blank. He stuffed his right hand in his coat pocket. His finger fiddled with the contents. He realized it was the photograph. He removed it and handed it to Francine. He chose his words carefully and reminded himself that he was supposed to be a detective. "Do you happen to recall the girls in this photo?"

Francine sighed smoke, then snatched the photo. Her lip trembled as she stared at it. She set her cigarette on an ashtray.

"The Blondies," she quavered. "What's this have to do with the kidnappings?"

"I have a possible lead that the disappearance of those girls fifteen years ago is related to the recent events. Do you recall anything about them?"

"I don't want to recall, Detective."

Francine grabbed the lighter and set the photograph aflame. She then dropped it on the floor and ground it out with her sandal.

"Hey, dammit!" Jay stood, but Francine pushed him back down into the armchair.

Francine pointed at the smoldering remains on the floor. "Those whores made my life a living hell! You know what I *recall* about them, Detective? See these scars on my mouth? That was the time Henna slashed me with a razor blade. See my arm? That was the time Loren locked me in a locker while she poked me with X-acto knives through the vents. And how could I forget the time Sylvia knocked me out with a baseball bat and I woke up naked in a ditch? Now, Detective, would you mind telling me why I need to recall so bad?"

"Well, do you know where they disappeared to?"

"How the hell would I know? Let me dig out my crystal ball, Detective!" Francine snatched her cigarette, took a long drag, and then sat on the sofa. "All I know is that every time my folks told their father, nothing happened. Those girls were untouchable. And believe me, I wasn't their only victim. I just remember how happy I was when they disappeared off the face of the earth."

Francine grinned. Jay thought it sounded suspicious as he jotted on the notepad. The plot seemed so obvious. The Blondies bullied Francine on a daily basis and then they vanished into thin air. She looked guilty as sin. But how would one girl take care of the trio of troublemakers with rap sheets longer than most kids' Christmas lists?

Jay flipped the notebook page. "Where were you the day they disappeared?"

"You sound like those detectives on T.V. Hell if I know."

"Ms. Heller, they tortured you on a daily basis and then they vanished. That doesn't sound coincidental, now does it?"

"Get out of my house. Get the hell out of my house, Detective!"

"Okay, okay. I crossed the line, I'm sorry. Can you just tell me -"

Francine seized Jay's jacket collar and yanked him off the armchair. She then shoved him out of the living room. Jay clutched his notepad as he stumbled into the entryway.

"Ms. Heller, listen to me."

"I stopped listening when you started talking smack! *Now get out!*"

Francine pushed Jay outside and slammed the door. He cursed and shook his head. The journalist in him had blown his cover like an undercover NARC making a drug deal from a paddy wagon.

Stupid, just stupid.

He kicked himself for his accusations. He had entered Francine's house with hopes of another lead and instead had steered into a dead end. The porch light shut off.

Jay descended the steps. When he reached the walk, a silver Buick LeSabre parked beside the curb. Jay pocketed the notepad and walked with his head down. There were few cars driving through town and those that passed by tended to be cops. He had a bad feeling that this was the detective Francine had been expecting. And to top things off, he had impersonated a police officer. One more thing to add to his rap sheet.

The man stepped out of the car and approached Jay. He was middle-aged with gray hair and narrow eyes that sized up everyone and their pastor. He wore blue jeans, a tan polyester sweater, and a brown Bomber jacket. He scratched his mustache and flashed his credentials.

"Good evening. Detective Barter, Chicago P.D."

"Evening, sir."

"And you are?"

"Oh," Jay stammered, searching for a lie. "I'm Francine's next door neighbor. I live right there." He pointed over his shoulder. "I keep telling myself to just give her a pound of brown sugar every month. She bakes more than Betty Crocker."

Barter's eyes became slits. "Mr. Woolridge, right?"

"In the flesh." Jay shifted, itching to smoke a cigarette.

"How's business at the hardware store?"

"Can't complain. You got the time, Detective?"

Barter withdrew his cellphone, lit the display. "Quarter after ten. Hot date?"

"With Barney Miller. Hope you'll excuse me."

"By all means." Barter pocketed his phone, but held his credentials, readying them for Francine. "What time is good for you tomorrow, Mr. Woolridge? Say nine a.m.?"

"Nine it is, Detective."

Jay walked toward the house next door as Barter approached Francine's porch. He needed to slip out of sight. But how could he do it without Barter seeing him?

He gazed at Woolridge's house. The two-story eyesore had a single light burning in the upstairs window. He headed up the stone walk.

He glanced to Francine's house. Barter had his finger on the doorbell while he regarded the porch. Jay saw his chance and ducked through a cluster of rose bushes that flanked Woolridge's front steps. He heard Francine shouting at Barter as he sprinted around the corner of the house. He knew the detective would be hot on his trail before long, as would Pritchard, on the hunt with a .357 Magnum.

S.D. Hintz

# CHAPTER FIVE

Coren filled the tumbler halfway with Seagram's, and then topped it off with Minute Maid. The girl thrust forward like a catapult on the couch. Her eyes snapped open. The comforter slid to the floor. Her jaw dropped and an ear-splitting scream rang out.

Coren rushed out of the kitchen. His arm clipped the orange juice carton and it plunged off the counter, busting on the linoleum. The girl sprang onto her feet and spun as if she was playing ring-around-the-rosey, shrieking at the top of her lungs. Her mangled legs, entwined at the knees and ankles, cut her game short.

"Hey! It's okay, it's okay!"

Coren hesitated as she stumbled and crashed into the wall. The only framed picture in the living room – a watercolor of a lighthouse - dropped to the floor and shattered. He wanted to seize the girl in a bear hug and wrestle her down to the couch, but he was worried about how she might react. What if she disgorged maggots on him? He squashed the thought as she rebounded off the wall and tripped on the coffee table, landing on her back where she wriggled like a millipede. He knelt, grabbed her by the shoulders, and held her tight against his chest, as he had when she emerged from the well.

"Easy now. Calm down. It was just a nightmare. Just a nightmare. I'm gonna bring you back to the couch, okay?"

Coren stood her up. He looked at her scarified face. Her eyes rolled into her head and her jaw trembled. Her mouth glinted. Blood trickled from her nose. Coren hoped she was on the verge of unconsciousness. It would make it easier on both of them.

A loud *bang* resounded behind Coren. He looked over his shoulder.

Another *bang*. The front door shook in its frame.

Someone was attempting to break into his house. No, not just someone. He knew it was Pritchard. Who else could it be? The psycho cop had probably been staking him out.

The girl's unrelenting screams slapped Coren to realization. He clamped his hand on her mouth and dragged her into the hall. He had to hide her somewhere. Pritchard surely heard her shrieks from outside.

*Yer lookin' guiltier by the second!*

Coren cursed as Pritchard's voice haunted him. He needed to stash the evidence. But where? The bedroom? Now more than ever he wished he lived in a two-story house. A basement would come in handy. The girl swayed in his arms like a pendulum as the blood from her nose trickled off her chin. Her head cracked hard against the wall.

*Of course*, Coren thought. *The panic room!*

Had the girl not hit her head, he would have never remembered it was there. He felt the wall for the small slit, found it, and opened the pocket door.

"I'm gonna let go of your mouth. Please don't scream anymore."

He released the girl's mouth and set her on the floor. She screamed and banged the back of her head against the wall. Coren dashed into the hall and shut the door.

A *bang* followed by a slam echoed throughout the house. Coren hurried down the hall. He stared agape when he reached the living room. The front door had been unhinged and laid in the entryway. Pritchard barged inside with his .357 Magnum. Coren backed into the wall, hands raised.

"What the hell is this?"

"I heard the screamin', Raines! Where are they?"

"Who?"

Pritchard bashed him in the head with the gun barrel. Coren grunted and fell to his knees as he clutched his forehead.

"Ow! What did I do?"

"Where's the triplets? Where are they?" Pritchard pressed the barrel against Coren's right temple. "I'll blow out yer brains if ya don't come clean right now!"

"I didn't kidnap anybody's kids!"

Pritchard swung his free fist down on Coren's shoulder. Coren hit the floor face first. His jaw slammed hard and blood flooded his mouth.

"Ya just earned a lie detector test, Raines! I'll turn this place upside down 'til I find 'em!"

Pritchard tossed his Stetson on the couch. Coren paled as he recalled the maggots that spewed from the girl's mouth. He hoped they had burrowed between the cushions.

Pritchard slipped out his handkerchief while keeping his gun trained on Coren. He dabbed his glistening baldness.

"Last chance, freak. Enlighten me."

Coren spat out a molar, watched it roll across the carpet like a die.

With the swift reflexives of a gunslinger, Pritchard spun his pistol, holstered it, then crouched and gagged Coren with the sweaty handkerchief. He knotted it at the back of his head. Coren choked and heaved as Pritchard grabbed his wrists and slapped on the handcuffs.

"Ya wanna screw with me, Raines? Huh?"

Coren growled and squirmed on his stomach. His head pounded and the dull ache plagued his ribs. The handkerchief was hot and salty. Pins of pain riddled his shoulders as he tugged his wrists, scraping them against the skintight cuffs.

Pritchard yanked up his belt buckle and crossed the living room. "Any babies under here?"

He grabbed the coffee table and flipped it. The glass top shattered on the floor and dime-sized shards pelted Coren's face. He winced and turned his head.

"How 'bout behind here?"

Pritchard tore the curtains off the bay window so hard that the rod snapped in half. He tossed the beige cloth aside and it landed on Coren's legs. He turned and approached the kitchen.

"What's this, Raines? Either yer one clumsy son of a gun or there was a struggle in here. I'm bettin' the latter."

Pritchard pulled out a Ziploc freezer bag and picked up the orange juice carton. He poured out the rest of the contents on the linoleum, and then shoved it in the Ziploc. His fiery blues locked on the counter, spotting the tumbler and the bottle of gin. He snatched the glass and drained it in one gulp.

"Bet ya wish ya could've drank this, huh?" He slammed the tumbler on the counter and licked his curled lips. "That's some yuppie stuff right there. Ya always get hammered alone, Raines, or just when yer stressed out from hidin' babies?"

Coren grumbled, wriggled like a maggot. He rolled onto his back and rested his head against the wall. The pressure eased on his ribs.

His mind unloaded thoughts like an Uzi. Could he stand and make a run for the Suburban? Possibly, but it would earn him a warrant and a "Wanted" poster. So, what would happen if he remained immobile? It seemed obvious that Pritchard was either hell-bent on locking him up or kicking the crap out of him. Maybe he could cause some sort of distraction.

Pritchard disappeared around the corner. Coren guessed he was snooping around the kitchen sink again, searching for more bloody utensils.

"Ya kiddin' me?"

Coren heard the *clink* and *clunk* of cans and bottles falling on the linoleum. Pritchard was rooting through the trash.

Coren broke into a sweat. His stomach churned.

Pritchard rounded the corner with the Ziploc held before his twisted face. The bloodstained barbed wire was entangled beside the broken Minute Maid carton.

Pritchard shoved the baggie in Coren's face. "*Where are they, Raines? Talk, goddamn it! I've got ya red-handed!*"

Coren closed his eyes, and then opened them. "There's no one here but me. Do you hear any babies crying?"

Pritchard stomped his boot down on Coren's chest. Coren cried out as his ribs shifted.

"Shut up! Ya think I never met a liar before?" Pritchard pressed the full weight of his two hundred and fifty-six pounds. Coren gasped, feeling as if his lungs would collapse. "Twenty-five years I've ran this town. Yer the first piece of crap to waltz in here like yer incognito and we're immune to yer stink. Who do ya think ya are?" Pritchard retracted his boot. He shook the Ziploc in his fist. "Ya got nothin' to say? I guarantee Homicide will when this comes back from the lab."

Coren bit his tongue. His body throbbed from head to toe. He wished Pritchard would leave or put him in the squad car. He was sick of being his punching bag. Maybe now that he had his evidence he would let him heal until tomorrow.

"Almost forgot." Pritchard withdrew a crumpled piece of paper from his pant pocket. He balled it up and dropped it on Coren's chest. "Here's yer search warrant."

Coren watched the hulking sheriff disappear down the hall, tapping his skull as if attempting to rattle out a motive. It seemed he refused to leave any stones unturned.

For the first time since Pritchard's arrival, Coren thought about the girl. She was probably still screaming her head off beyond the wall. He hoped Pritchard was clueless about panic rooms. The crazy cop was smart, but it would take a seasoned detective to sniff out a hideaway like that.

Pritchard entered the master bedroom. "Let's see if ya got them babies tied to yer bed, ya sicko."

Coren heard furniture thudding and his ceramic lamp smashing to pieces. The box spring shrieked as it slammed to the floor. More rattles and bangs as dresser drawers were yanked and thrown. Pritchard stomped down the hall with the Ziploc in hand, still plumb full of the same evidence.

He crouched down to Coren's level. "So yer clever, huh? An Internet nerd like you probably schemed some secret hideout fer yer victims. Ain't that right?" Coren's eyes burned with hate. Pritchard sneered and pointed at the Ziploc. "Exhibit "B" and "C" got ya nailed, Raines. I'm on to ya like a five-cent hooker."

He seized Coren by the shoulder and yanked him onto his stomach. He tightened the handcuffs until they cut Coren's skin, then unlocked and removed them. He stood and grabbed his Stetson, concealing his glistening skullcap. He turned, drew his flesh pistol. His knuckle cracked as his thumb hammer came down while he winked in unison. He chuckled, reached into his pant pocket, and withdrew a shiny badge as he trampled the front door into the night.

*****

*She spotted the Blondies huddled by the barbed wire fence that bordered Mr. Adler's farm. The summer breeze carried their giggles like pollen and stung her eyes to tears. She bit back her frustration and composed herself. She knew they were plotting again and had no intention of letting her pass unharmed to school.*

*She clutched her backpack as she approached the Blondies. The triplets dispersed. Henna blocked the sidewalk and slapped a nightstick in her hand. Sylvia served as the roadblock and popped her bubble gum with a Swiss army knife. Loren rounded Francine as she smoked a cigarette and leered in the shadows of her Pirates cap.*

*Francine glanced up East Walnut Street. J. Edgar High was a block away. She considered her escape routes. Could she leap over the barbed wire fence and sprint across Adler's farm to Railroad Street? She had her doubts. The fence was four feet tall and would surely snag her skirt. What if she turned around and ran back home? Despite the strong urge, she was reluctant to flee like a coward. She would rather stand her ground and let the Blondies know that she was fearless.*

*Henna pointed the nightstick at Francine. "You know the drill, Smeller. Empty your pockets."*

"You took everything I had yesterday," Francine quavered.

"That was for lunch. Now I need to get my nails done."

Loren and Sylvia chuckled as they closed in. Sylvia spat out her gum and flipped out three different blades. Loren flicked her cigarette butt. She sneered as it bounced off Francine's shoulder in a shower of sparks.

Francine lowered her backpack. "Leave me alone!"

Henna waved the nightstick. "Soon as ya gimme what I want."

"You're not getting anything from me!"

Francine spun and swung her backpack. She caught Loren by surprise with a headshot, knocking off her cap. Sylvia lunged with the knife. Francine blocked the jab as she swung her backpack around. She then retaliated with a leg sweep and dropped Sylvia on her back.

There was movement in her periphery. She turned and saw her English teacher Mr. Elbridge passing by on the opposite sidewalk.

"Mr. Elbridge!" Francine whipped her backpack again, keeping Loren at bay. "Help!"

*Henna shook the nightstick at the short man in the cream dress shirt and khakis. "Get outta here! Or you're next!"*

*Mr. Elbridge adjusted his horn-rimmed glasses and ran toward the school. Henna raised the nightstick and charged. Francine swung her backpack, but Henna blocked the blow with her forearm and then cracked Francine with the nightstick. Francine dropped the backpack and clutched her forehead, suppressing a whimper as tears spilled down her cheeks. Loren shoved her to the pavement and laughed.*

*Henna snatched the backpack and jostled it in her left fist. "If I can't have this, Smeller, then neither can you."*

*She heaved the backpack and grinned as it landed in the bean field beyond the fence.*

*Francine felt a goose egg rising on her throbbing forehead. "You ugly pig! I hate you!"*

*Henna chuckled. "C'mon, girls. We don't wanna be late for class."*

*Sylvia stood and Loren grabbed her cap. They then joined Henna at her side.*

*Sylvia twirled a split end around the blade of her knife. "Next time, Smeller, I'm gonna slice you open. Nobody knocks me down and gets away with it."*

*Francine stared at the backpack through the barbed wire as the Blondies left her to cry in the middle of the street. Anger bubbled like lava in her veins. What would it take to make them leave her alone? She was at her wits' end and outnumbered three to one.*

*She shook her head and sniffled. She hated life. She hated waking up in the morning knowing that the Blondies would be waiting for her. She hated leaving school and being followed until they decided it was time to beat her up or steal her homework. She hated telling her parents about her day and listening to them yell at her for not standing up for herself.*

*She rubbed her pounding head, and then looked at her hand. She was glad it was clean. The last thing she wanted to worry about was a flesh wound. She had ten minutes until the bell rang for homeroom. At that thought, she looked up. The backpack straps fluttered with the rustling field, as if they had adapted to their new surroundings.*

*Francine stood and eyed the barbed wire. She wondered how she was going to bypass it. She needed her backpack. It not only contained her science project worth half of her grade, but also three-fourths of her textbooks.*

*She looked up the road. Walking around Mr. Adler's property for two blocks to his front door was out of the question. She had seen him numerous times on her way to school patrolling the premises with a shotgun. She guessed he was paranoid that the Blondies might vandalize his brand-new barn.*

*She knew there was only one way to retrieve the backpack. She had to scale the barbed wire.*

*****

Jay stopped and caught his breath. The last time he ran was a year ago when he had done the story on pit bull fighting. One of the snarling prizefighters had broken loose and chased him out of the pen, nipping at his heels all the way to the door. He felt as if he was reliving that day. Here he was doing the hundred-yard dash from a homicide detective.

"Shoot."

He stood at a dead end. A cedar privacy fence towered a foot above him. He knew he had to climb over it. He was not about to turn around and walk across Woolridge's front yard with a friendly wave to Barter. He reached up and grabbed the top of the fence. Splinters poked his hands as he raised himself. He held his breath as he wriggled his midsection over the top.

*I feel like I'm in boot camp.*

He dropped down on the other side. The dirt sank beneath his feet, swallowing his ankles. He stumbled out of the muddy ground with a squelch, looked over his shoulder. He assumed that he had trampled Woolridge's garden, but it sure had seemed like a fresh grave. He shook off the thought and glanced at his dark surroundings.

A clothesline draped with undergarments swayed amidst silhouetted sycamores. There was a puddled birdbath, a leaning feeder, and a scattering of pinwheels that spun in the breeze.

A strange scent stirred Jay's memory. There was a hint of apples on the wind that sparked reflections of the Texaco's pantry. He guessed that there was an orchard nearby, which would explain the gas station's surplus.

Pounding snapped Jay back into action. He envisioned Barter rapping at Woolridge's front door. He scanned the cluttered yard. The privacy fence lacked a gate. There was one way out, and that meant scaling the slats again. He hoped that his next climb would yield a solid landing. The last thing he wanted to do was dig himself out of an even deeper hole.

S.D. Hintz

# CHAPTER SIX

"I don't want any bibles, Mister! Now scoot off back to the mission!"

"Ms. Heller, I'm not a salesman, I'm Detective Barter. We spoke on the phone."

Francine's haggard face flushed like a skin scrape. Her lip curled until the cigarette butt fell to the porch. She stomped on the sparks as if they were cockroaches.

"What did you say?"

"I'm Detective Barter, Chicago Homicide." He thrust his credentials in her face.

"I'll be *goddamned*. Who the hell was in my house then?"

"Sorry?"

"Some guy just interrogated me a few minutes ago."

Barter concealed his ID and flipped out a memo pad. "Did he claim to be me?"

"Well," Francine stammered as she glanced up and down Sangralea. "No, not exactly. I assumed it was you. Who else would be knocking on my door at this hour?"

"What did he look like?"

"He was a ginger, looked like a grown up Opie. Wore a dirty leather jacket and jeans."

Barter stroked his mustache. "That sounds like Mr. Woolridge."

Francine's eyes widened and her brows raised. "Woolridge? That old coot's bedridden. Hasn't left his house in weeks. And he's bald as an eagle."

"No kidding. If you don't mind, Ms. Heller, I do have some questions for you. I'll keep them brief."

"I've had enough questions tonight."

The door slammed in Barter's face. He broke out his pad and scribbled a footnote: **Follow up**.

*****

After a moment of squirming, Coren managed to sit up against the wall. He felt like a gigantic pinched nerve. His head, jaw, shoulders, chest, ribs, and wrists throbbed in harmony.

He stared out through the front door frame as the sound of crunching gravel faded into the night. He had expected to hear an engine rumble to life. Pritchard's footfalls confirmed that the psychopath had been staking him out.

"Christ."

Coren groaned as he stood, spine straight along the wall. He thought about the confiscated evidence. Dread roiled in his gut. He was unconcerned about the bloody steak knife and Minute Maid carton. Sure the knife handle was covered with his fingerprints, but the blade was thick with cow DNA. And the orange juice carton was superfluous, a mere sticky scrap of cardboard that needed to be trashed. The barbed wire, on the other hand, was a different story. His fingerprints were all over it, as were bits and pieces of a missing girl's flesh. Pritchard had made a good point. "Exhibit C" would be the nail in his coffin, regardless if he was innocent.

He staggered through the living room, stepped over the orange pool on the linoleum. He was relieved that Pritchard had left his gin alone, besides draining his tumbler without a chaser. He grabbed the bottle of Seagram's, uncapped it, and took a swig. He closed his eyes as the alcohol warmed his stomach. He took two more gulps and felt his pain subside.

He looked down at the mess. Ants emerged from the shadows of the refrigerator, drawn to the scent like vultures to carrion. He lacked the motivation to get down on his hands and knees and scrub the floor. Any other time – say when a crazy cop hadn't kicked his ass – he would have mopped it up like the clean freak that he was.

The telephone rang. Coren jumped, and then winced. Who would be calling at such a late hour? Didn't they know that he was busy hiding a runaway while striving to look innocent? He had two guesses as to the caller. It was either Pritchard or his boss Garrison, neither one of whom he wished to speak to. He picked up the receiver and listened, waiting for the caller to speak.

"Hello? Coren?"

"Deb." He sighed and sat at the table. "Can I call you back? I have -"

"No, you're not calling me back! You don't call back when you drop me that line! Where's my box of photos?"

The panic room flashed in Coren's mind. "Huh? You woke me up for this?"

"I'm coming over to get them tomorrow."

"Wait a second!" The receiver slipped in his clammy hand. "I'll bring you the box! What time do you want me to stop by?"

"You're not *stopping* by. Roger will knock you out."

Roger. The name sparked his anger like dynamite. He hated everything about it. It was a happy name, like Jolly Roger or Roger Rabbit, and that made him spit nails.

"Well you can't come over here! I haven't even unpacked yet!"

"See you at seven, Coren."

"I told you I haven't -"

The *click* killed his retort. He ripped out the telephone cord and threw the receiver.

"Damn!"

He growled, shook his head. His house was trashed and he had a girl locked in the spare bedroom. He needed to dig out the box of photos and set it on the doorstep. Knowing Deb, she would want a tour. Maybe he could head her off and tell her he had company. Then again, if he did that, she would definitely want to enter. He rubbed his eyes and looked at the clock. He had eight hours to clean Pritchard's mess.

He pushed back from the table. *It's going to be a long night.*

\*\*\*\*\*

Jay's jacket snagged on the fence and he toppled over, landing in a sandbur patch. He cursed and hoped the commotion went unheard. He trampled the burs and looked ahead. An open field rustled in the breeze. In the distance, there was a barn with an attached silo and a dark three-story house. Barbed wire encircled the property from the line of privacy fences to the curbs of East Walnut and Railroad Street. Jay wondered if it was the only farm in town. He failed to recall passing any others on his mad dash through the checkpoint.

He crouched, pulled the sandburs off his shoes. He considered heading for the barn. Maybe it was abandoned and he could hide there for the night. It seemed risky to return to the gas station. The town was crawling with cops and there was probably an APB out on him. The barn, if it was vacant, sounded like his best bet.

He thought of Jeanette, Karley, and Keira as he stood and hurried across the field. He had yet to call and tell them that he was in a tight spot. They had to be worried sick. Jeanette would think something terrible happened to him, since he was typically home from work by 6:00pm. It was five or six hours past by now. Add another eighteen hours and there would be a missing person report filed and his face would be smiling on WNDY and every other TV station across the country. Once Barter and Pritchard caught wind of it, he would have a warrant issued for his arrest.

*Jeanette's going to kill me.*

He sprinted to the side of the barn. It was a weathered structure with clouded windows and a storm-tossed roof that sheltered half of the interior. Jay was certain it was deserted. Only a mad farmer would pen his livestock in a barn that was on the verge of collapsing.

He walked along the wall, peered around the corner. The Victorian house loomed a hundred yards from the barn and was still dark. A porch swing creaked like rotted floorboards.

Something moved near the front steps.

Jay squinted at the dark shape that bobbed in a nearby bush. The pit bull turned and stepped from the shadows. Its teeth glinted like meat cleavers as it growled, sensing danger. Within seconds it spotted Jay. He ran for the doors and the dog charged at him, barking and snarling.

A light illuminated the third story of the house. Jay grabbed the rusted handle and threw open the door. The pit bull yelped as it reached the end of its chain, yanked back like a yo-yo five feet from its prey. Jay slipped inside the barn and shut the door. He ducked into a stall and crouched behind a hay bale.

"Shut your stink hole, Collie! What's all this ruckus about, huh? I swear I'll lock you in that silo!"

Jay's body went rigid. He held his breath. The pit bull began barking again.

"*Shut your stink hole!*" The raspy voice paused. Jay heard a clack. "What? What's so threatening in there? Huh? Do we got us a trespasser? Well, let's just see if we got us a trespasser."

The pit bull growled. Jay peeked around the hay bale. The door creaked and a shotgun barrel poked inside. Jay's eyes widened. A stocky man in green long johns and cowboy boots passed the stall. His finger twitched on the trigger.

"If somebody's hiding in here, I'll blow off your goddamn head! I don't harbor no babynappers! You hear me?"

Jay's legs trembled beneath his weight. He prayed the farmer was too tired to inspect each stall. His ankle cracked above the crunch of straw. The farmer's footsteps faltered.

What happened next nearly gave Jay a heart attack. A shotgun blast rang out. Glass shattered. Seconds later, there was a second bang. Another window exploded. Jay rocked back against the wall, clenching his teeth. He was on the verge of wetting himself.

His mind ran rampant. Should he attempt to heave the hay bale at the farmer and then grab his shotgun? But what if they struggled and the gun went off? He pictured the news headline: ONWARD FARMER KILLED BY WNDY REPORTER. Maybe hiding was a better idea. If he accidentally shot the farmer, everyone would be convinced that he was the madman who kidnapped the Trammell triplets.

The shotgun fired. Glass rained down on Jay as he ducked his head and covered his ears. Another blast and a window reduced to shards.

"Well, Collie, you think I scared him off?" Jay looked up and saw the farmer walk by, and then pause at the door. "If there's anybody out here still, they best get off my land!"

The door slammed and Jay swore he heard the click of a lock. He took deep breaths, trying to slow his heartbeat, though the air was stuffy and thick with gun smoke. The pit bull barked outside, unconvinced that the trespasser was gone.

*"Shut your stink hole!"*

The dog yelped and stopped barking. Jay listened to the farmer's footsteps echo on the porch. He sat down and sighed. It was only a matter of time before the authorities received a call that shots were fired. Suddenly the barn seemed more like a crime scene than a haven.

Jay shook the glass out of his hair, stood, and furrowed his brow. Save for the straw and stalls, his surroundings looked nothing like a barn. Instead, it had the eerie resemblance of a medieval torture chamber.

S.D. Hintz

# CHAPTER SEVEN

Coren awoke with a start. A rolled up Tribune shivered in his lap. The paperboy had delivered his wake-up call, straight through the open doorway, and smacked him square in the chest.

He gazed bleary-eyed at the day beyond. It was bright, promising. But promising what? Another visit from Pritchard? A pit stop by his adulterous ex-wife who was dying for her faded photographs?

On that thought, he grabbed the newspaper, jumped up, and looked at the clock. 6:30am. He had passed out against the living room wall, exhausted from cleaning house until the wee hours. He had mopped up the orange juice in the kitchen, vacuumed the glass in the living room, and tossed the remnants of the coffee table into the panic room. His last task had been to hinge the front door, but he had instead succumbed to his drunken stupor.

He removed the rubber band and slapped the Tribune on the counter beside the Seagram's bottle. The bold headline snagged him like a meat hook. SHOTS FIRED AT FOUR IN ONWARD.

Last night swirled in Coren's head. Had Pritchard gone on a shooting rampage after he left the house? He scanned the story. It stated that four different townies had been shot at around 11:00pm. The Trammell's, of all people, were awaken by the shattering of their picture window. Harold Jeter, the janitor at J. Edgar High, nearly had a stroke when the principal's office window imploded. Ray Ratner discovered a bullet hole in the side of a Main Street mailbox. Homicide Detective Frank Barter made the "shots fired" call when a slug pierced the windshield of his LeSabre.

Coren paled at the fourth account. There was a detective in town, more than likely working with Pritchard to crack the case. That meant he would soon have another cop ransacking his house for evidence.

He tossed the newspaper into the trash. He had more important things to worry about at the moment. His ex-wife would arrive in a half-hour and he had yet to dig out the box of photographs.

His mind wandered back to the well girl. He had kept her in the panic room all night. When he had disposed of the coffee table she had been leaning against the wall, her eyes a blank stare and her mouth agape. He had tried talking to her, but she was stiff and unresponsive. He wondered if she was malnourished or dehydrated. He opened the refrigerator and grabbed an apple out of the crisper, then headed for the hallway.

He paused and pressed his ear against the pocket door. The room was silent.

*Of course it's silent, you idiot. It's soundproof.*

He mentally kicked himself, and then opened the door. The girl sat against the wall, as she had hours earlier, slack and catatonic.

Coren crouched before her. "Hey. Are you hungry? Do you want something to eat? I have an apple."

He offered the fruit. The girl's eyes rolled into her head. She seized her curly hair and tugged at it. Her eyes shut, then sprang open.

"Oh, Christ!"

Coren fell back and froze. Her eyeballs had disappeared and in their place were writhing balls of bloody maggots. Some slid down her cheeks like tears and wriggled into her mouth. She banged her head on the steel, then lurched forward and gnashed her teeth into the apple.

"Hey! Okay now! Slow down!"

She wrenched the fruit from Coren's hands and head-butted the floor, bouncing back like a Bop Bag. As she slammed against the wall her jaw dislocated with a *crack* and the apple rolled into her mouth. Coren winced as he watched the fruit bulge in her gullet like a goiter, which was then forced down like a passed kidney stone.

"No! Are you cra -"

The well girl screamed her head off. Coren panicked, hopped to his feet, and slammed the door. The girl sank her teeth into his leg. He cried out and tried to shake her loose, but her mouth was like a bear trap. He acted on instinct and gouged her eyes. The maggots poured from her sockets like sifted red rice and her head flung back. She shrieked and gasped, then shrieked again.

Coren backpedaled, colliding with a tower of boxes. The girl inched toward him, pushing with her bony arms and twisted legs in tow.

Coren's pleas were drowned out by her screams. He glanced around the room for a weapon. He grabbed the box behind him and raised it over his head. The girl stopped two yards away and began choking. Her scream was lost in a gurgle as she closed her eyes.

Coren stood still, battling indecision. Should he drop the box on her head and put her out of her misery? Or was she going to pass out as she had done earlier?

"Stay right there. I don't want to hurt you."

Coren's arms trembled. He yearned to drop the box and end the madness, but instead it was his jaw that hit the floor. The girl's torso convulsed and a round bulge rose in her throat. It glowed through her chalk-white flesh like a jack-o'-lantern. She lurched forward and gagged. Coren stumbled back and lost his balance. The weight above his head anchored him and he crashed through the tower, the box flying back into the wall.

He looked up, wide-eyed and machine-gunning profanities. The girl gagged as she regurgitated the bulge. The fruit dropped onto the floor, exuding a mixture of bile and apple juice. It blazed as the rind cracked and shed like snakeskin. The flesh beneath was blood red and pulsed. Coren's gorge rose.

The girl opened her eyes and shrieked. The fruit's flesh opened like a flower, revealing the core. A bloodstained badge simmered in a rippling red-gold pool, then melted into the floor. The girl collapsed face first and passed out.

121

Coren stared at the anomaly. He was glued to the floor, flabbergasted. What the hell was that? Had he given the girl an apple with a badge in the pit? Yeah, that was plausible. He shook his head.

He stood and glanced out the window. There was a brown station wagon parked in the drive. Coren's brows knitted, then rose in realization.

"Deb!"

*****

*Francine draped her favorite sweater over the fence. She then raised her right leg and stepped on it. The wire sagged about a foot and the barbs pierced the fabric. She focused on the backpack fluttering in the field. She couldn't leave it there. School meant the world to her. It was her ticket out of Onward. She had to retrieve her belongings regardless of the impending danger.*

*She felt the barbs poking through her shoe. She mustered the nerve and leapt. Her right foot pushed off the fence while her left leg grazed the barbs. She landed in the field face first. She grinned. The Blondies weren't going to get the best of her. She stood and winced as her shin burned. Blood trickled onto her shoe.*

*She grabbed her backpack, slung it over her shoulder. She looked into the distance at Mr. Adler's house. She had ruled out knocking on his front door to reclaim her belongings. But now she was covered in blood and needed to wash up. She couldn't risk walking into school and using the lavatory. If a teacher spotted her, she would be sent to the nurse's office and her parents would be called. The thought of being screamed at and struck brought tears to her eyes. Maybe she could sneak to the barn. There was probably a spigot where she could hose her leg off.*

*She hurried through the field, wincing every time she brushed a bean plant. She wondered how much time she had before the bell rang for homeroom. She guessed at most five minutes. She couldn't afford to be tardy again. Thanks to the Blondies, one more late arrival would earn her a suspension.*

*She reached the side of the barn and caught her breath. She stumbled, exhausted, clutching her backpack. She paused and peered around the corner.*

*The coast was clear. Though it was morning, there was no sign of Mr. Adler working the farm. She scanned the grounds between the house and barn. To the right of the porch steps a spigot protruded from the house.*

*Francine's eyes brightened and her heart pounded. All she had to do was sneak across the gap to the bushes and turn the handle. She knew there was the risk that Mr. Adler might hear the running water, but hopefully the foliage would hide her long enough to get a head start. Her plan was set. Sprint to the house, crouch down, inch the handle to the right, and then scrub her leg with the nylon strap of her backpack. She would do it in twenty seconds flat and flee like a field mouse from a snake.*

*She glanced to the front door, then to the second and third stories. Her stomach fluttered and she reminded herself about homeroom. She dashed across the yard, kicking up dirt. She felt it hit the back of her legs, probably soiling her dress, but she was more concerned about cleaning her wound. She brushed past the bushes and crouched beside the spigot.*

*"What do you think you're doing, missy?"*

*Francine whirled. She stared down a shotgun barrel sticking out of the bushes. Mr. Adler stepped from his camouflage, his green long johns concealing him like a chameleon, and motioned for her to back away from the house.*

*"Looks like I got me a trespasser. Might need a guard dog to keep all you girls off my property."*

*"Mr. Adler, please," Francine quavered. "I just wanted to wash my leg."*

*"So you thought you could steal my water? This ain't a fountain. And that looks like a barb cut. Is that how you got on my property?"*

*Francine nodded as tears trickled down her cheeks. "The Blondies threw my backpack over your fence. I didn't want to be late to school, so I -"*

*Mr. Adler lowered his shotgun. "Those three troublemakers did this to you? Wash your leg off. Hurry up!"*

*Francine ran the spigot. She winced as cold water gushed onto her wound.*

*"Those Blondies bully you like this all the time?" Francine nodded, shut off the spigot. She grabbed her backpack strap. "Hey! Use this. Don't worry, I ain't blown my nose in it."*

*Mr. Adler tossed Francine a blue handkerchief. She wiped the blood off her leg and shoe.*

*"Thank you, sir. Listen, I've got to run or I'm gonna be late for class. Sorry for trespassing."*

*"Forget about it." Hank Adler set his shotgun against the porch and scratched his stubble. "Between you and me, life would be a peach if those girls took a permanent vacation."*

\*\*\*\*\*

Jay absorbed his surroundings, rooted to the ground, like an archaeologist that had stepped into an undiscovered tomb. Medieval torture devices dangled from the rafters and occupied four of the stalls. Dark lanterns were nailed to the posts, and the walls were either tarred or painted black. One window in each direction was shot out and the night wind whipped through the barn, tossing glass and straw.

Jay had to notify the police. Not Pritchard, of course, but perhaps Barter. Someone needed to see what Old Macdonald had on his farm. He reached into his jacket and withdrew his pad and pen. He jotted down the details, such as the barn, the description of the farmer, and the number of shots fired.

He shook his head. He hoped the authorities had heard the gunshots or received damage reports. From there all fingers would point to the loose cannon in town. Of course, this was Onward, the same town that had a sheriff with a deaf ear.

*So, what do I make of all this? Is it just some farmer's sick fantasy? No. It can't be. There has to be more to it. He's trigger-happy and has a medieval museum under the town's nose.*

He shoved the pad and pen in his pocket and perused the antique collection. Some he recalled seeing on the Discovery channel and hearing by word of mouth, while others looked like the creations of an insane blacksmith. In one stall was a dusty rack, its leather straps bloodstained from past dismembered limbs. In another stall was a device Jay recognized as the Judas Cradle. Victims were racked and hoisted naked onto the triangular top, which prevented them from relaxing or falling to sleep without severe pain. Other stalls were filled with crude contraptions of head vises and iron boiling pots. In the center of the barn was a rusted hanging cage and "the coffin," both of which were used for torturing victims on public display.

Jay plopped down onto a hay bale as nausea overcame him. He strained to rid his mind of people crying out as their bodies were mutilated. What sadistic person would want to own these devices? And what did he plan on doing with them? Charging tourists five dollars to feast their eyes on the Torture Barn? As far as Jay was concerned, the farmer was a key suspect in the kidnappings.

He stood and walked toward the front. He had to leave before he retched Reese's Pieces. He nudged the doors, paranoid of riling the pit bull. They moved an inch, then refused to budge. The farmer had locked up the barn.

Jay turned and looked to the stall he had hid in. Shards clung like icicles to the window frame. It appeared to be wide enough to climb through. He pushed the hay bale beneath the sill and then knocked out the remaining glass with his elbow. He pulled the sleeves of his jacket over his hands, grabbed the frame, and lunged through the hole. He landed hard on his back and the barking of the pit bull reminded him that he was trespassing. He dashed into the field against the night wind.

*****

The Crown Victoria's brakes squeaked like a trapped mouse as it stopped beside Barter's damaged LeSabre. The detective crouched near the passenger's side door with his gun drawn. Pritchard stepped out, secured his Stetson, and then cupped his hands as he lit a cigarette. Barter rose and lowered his pistol.

"What took you so long?"

"I don't know, Detective. Maybe the fact that shots were fired at three other locations."

"Where else?"

"All over town. The Trammell's, the high school, Main Street. Glad I ain't on a hit list."

"But others seem to be. Any injuries?"

"None. Four shots in four different directions. Judgin' by the damage I've seen, includin' yer windshield, somebody's shotgunnin'."

"There's a motive, Sheriff." Barter rounded the LeSabre and holstered his gun. "The Trammell's, the school, me. It's all related to children and my investigation."

"Yer self-absorbed." Pritchard exhaled smoke into Barter's face. "Hank Adler's the only one in town with a twelve-gauge. I'm bettin' he got trigger-happy on a trespasser."

"So he shoots up town on a regular basis?"

"Shut up! I got a hunch, ya hear me? So while yer doin' forensics on yer windshield, I'm gonna find out who Adler was shootin' at. Tomorrow's another day, Detective."

"I think you ought to pay your man a visit now, Sheriff."

"Nobody's duckin' out. That's why there's a posse, Holmes."

"If no one's left town, then how many people have you questioned? I got here last night and had a word with Ms. Heller, along with a few others."

"I got my suspects, and Adler ain't one of 'em." Pritchard stubbed his cigarette on the LeSabre's hood. "And why would I waste my time interrogatin' the half-dead? Heller's a goddamn hermit. Now I'd appreciate it, Detective, if ya stayed out of my path."

"Just so we're clear, Homicide runs this investigation. I'm the new sheriff in town."

Pritchard opened the Crown Victoria's driver's side door, glared at Barter, and then waved his flesh pistol. He made a fist, cracked his knuckles. He chuckled as he climbed behind the wheel. He whipped a U-turn and sped off down Sangralea.

Barter shook his head. Onward's sheriff was a problem and could potentially harm his investigation. He withdrew his cellphone, lit the display. Pritchard needed to be displaced before he ruined Homicide's chances of pinpointing the kidnapper. If the sheriff wanted to play hardball, then Barter was down to have him ejected from the game.

*****

Francine frowned as she watched the detective and sheriff part ways. She could see the entire town from her attic window. The argument below was indication that there was little hope the Trammells would find their babies. The authorities were getting along like prison inmates and she wouldn't have been surprised if they started having shootouts. As far as she could tell, the investigation was half-assed. Besides which, the most police work Pritchard ever did was staking out Kate's Bakery.

She lit a cigarette and regarded Onward through the Zippo's flame. That was the town's fate in a week's time. That much was obvious.

S.D. Hintz

# CHAPTER EIGHT

Coren slammed the sliding door and hurried down the hall. When he reached the living room he spotted his ex-wife on the front steps, leaning into the foyer as if hesitant to enter. She saw Coren in the shadows and straightened. She brushed her brunette bangs out of her eyes and wrinkled her broad forehead. Her pink blouse fluttered as she grabbed the doorframe, and then stepped across the threshold in her high heels.

"What the hell happened here?" Deborah looked Coren up and down and shook her head. "You know what, I don't want to know. I just want my pictures."

"Fine." Coren ran his hands through his tousled hair. He had forgotten the box in the panic room. He needed to ensure Deborah stayed stationary while he retrieved it. She was a bigger snoop than a private eye. "Hold on. I'll go get it."

"So, did the Mafia make a house call last night?"

Coren ignored her wisecrack as he headed down the hall and opened the pocket door. He ran into the room, found the box atop the scattered pile, and grabbed it. He rushed out the door without a glance at the girl or the fruit mess, and collided with Deborah in the hall. She flew off her feet and hit the floor.

"Geez, Deb! I told you to hold on!"

Coren shut the door, dropped the box. He offered Deborah his hand and she slapped it.

"What? Are you hiding something from me?"

"I'm not you, *Deb*. I don't hide men in the pantry when my spouse comes home early from work."

Deborah stood and winced, rubbing her tailbone. She crouched and picked up the box.

"Screw you, Coren."

"I don't get a thank-you?"

*"Screw you, Coren."*

Deborah stormed down the hall as fast as her high heels allowed. Coren tailed her and watched her leave the house. He always thought he would be incapable of hating anyone. Ever since the adultery and divorce, however, he hated Deborah. The sight of her disinterred thoughts of her half-naked lover hiding behind the apron that stated "Shut up and stir!" Though she left with the box of photographs, certain images would be etched in his mind for life.

He walked to the foyer, raised the front door, and leaned it against the frame. He needed to secure the entrance. The last thing he needed was Pritchard barging into his house again, which in due time was bound to happen. He decided to barricade the doorway. He scanned the living room. The couch, despite its flower pattern, was heavy-duty and would serve the purpose.

Coren positioned himself at the right arm and shoved with all his might. The couch inched across the living room. A couple of minutes later it rested horizontally before the front door. His last task was to upend it. He crouched, grabbed the wood legs, and lifted. He gritted his teeth as stabs of pain racked his ribs and shoulders. He raised the couch with a guttural grunt and slammed it against the front door. He then plopped down on the floor and wiped the sweat off his brow with his shirtsleeve.

*That ought to slow him down.*

He leaned back and gazed at the ceiling. He was exhausted, but knew he had a laundry list looming over him. He mentally checked off the items.

√ 1) Unpack the boxes in the panic room

√ 2) Clean up the backyard

√ 3) Check in with the boss

Coren cleared his mind, stood with a groan. He had forgotten to add Advil and Seagram's to the list. He plodded to the Pine-Sol-scented kitchen and grabbed his medication out of the cupboard. He had definitely warped the doctoral saying "Take two and call me in the morning." In his world, it was take two ibuprofens, two shots of gin, and then call me drunk in the morning.

He walked to the deck window as he downed his medication. The rolling storm clouds swallowed the rising sun. He had a feeling that number two on the list was doomed to be postponed. The plus side was that the grass would get watered. It was long and brown enough to be mistaken for a wheat field.

His gaze rested on the well. From his standpoint, the inner wall appeared untainted and intact, though he vividly recalled it bleeding and cracking. As he reflected on last night, the events seemed more like a nightmare than reality.

*Walls don't bleed maggots! Crippled girls gagged with barbed wire don't crawl up wells! What the hell am I on? Gin never screws me up that bad. Still, there's an unconscious girl in the spare*

*bedroom. Isn't there?*

He opened the door, stepped onto the deck. Drizzle tickled his face and a cool wind stirred his hair. He drained the gin, set the glass on the railing, and descended the steps. The elm tree swayed and creaked, its branches raking the dandelions. The chunk of metal clunked against the far fence. The well's roof banged on its posts, flapping as if it would fly away any moment.

He approached the lip and stared at the opposite wall. It was clean, unbroken. He eyed the darkness below. It seemed bottomless and smelled of must and rainwater. He sniffed hard, but failed to detect a hint of cider.

*I'm smelling a well for apples and making sure it's not bleeding. Man, I'm losing it.*

The girl's moan taunted his conscience. *"Oohh!"*

He considered climbing into the well, but he was uncertain of what that would accomplish. What was he looking for? Another poster child for Mott's? Clues pointing as to why the girl had been down there? Maybe. Still it wouldn't solve his predicament. He needed to find a way to get rid of the strange girl before Pritchard or anyone else discovered her.

A caw startled Coren. He looked to the deck and spotted the crow perched on the eave. For a moment his mind conjured an image of a second girl scaling the well. He sighed, slowing his hiccuping heart.

A train whistle blared in the distance.

*The train! Maybe I could leave the girl in one of those boxcars!*

He chuckled at the far-fetched idea. The hurdle would be getting the girl to the train tracks. It would be near impossible to smuggle her into the Suburban with Pritchard staking out his house. Even if he succeeded he would then have to drive through Onward, which was crawling with cops. He didn't fancy that in the least.

Though he might be able to haul the girl on his shoulder through the wetlands to the train tracks. He never ventured beyond the backyard, but he was willing to bet he could break a path to the other side of town.

*That's the gin talking.*

He considered the laundry list. Task number two taunted him. Here he was in the backyard getting drunk and not lifting a finger. He stared at the shivering scrap metal. He wondered where it came from. It looked as if it once belonged to a shed.

Coren ducked beneath the elm and set his sights on the corrugated scrap. Something about it bothered him. Maybe it was the fact that it was the only junk in the backyard. One rusted slab the size of a van's sliding door rested against the fence.

Coren inspected it. The warped edges were sharp and reddish-orange. A streak of rust spanned the scrap from corner to corner. He reached around it, careful not to brush the edge, and pushed it forward. It slammed on the ground and gonged.

"What the -"

Coren crouched and gaped. Four small fingers riddled with black ants protruded from the grass. His gorge rose and he swallowed it as he dropped to his knees.

*Not another one. Please, not another one.*

*****

Jay awoke with his heart in his throat. For a split second he was disoriented, but then recalled climbing down the hatch of the Texaco and lying on the pantry floor, exhausted from his late night outing. He sat up and cracked his neck, which was stiff from the crate he had used as a pillow. He wondered what had startled him. Did he have a nightmare? He sure had stumbled on one in the barn.

"What the hell? We got the tooth fairy in the building?"

Jay pricked his ears. Someone else was in the gas station. The mention of the tooth fairy reminded him that he had left money on the counter.

*Crap. It's probably the owner. And I'm breaking and entering. I knew I should've found another place to crash.*

He stood and eased the pantry door shut. It clicked, sounding like a Glock cocking at a funeral. He prayed that whoever had entered the station was preoccupied. He glanced at the knob. It lacked a lock. Rather than waste his time barricading the door, he knew it was wiser to make his escape.

He climbed the ladder, popped the hatch. He blinked as drizzle pelted his face. He wriggled onto the roof and heard the door creak below.

"No, this ain't the tooth fairy. I got me a trespasser. First you wanna sneak in my barn, now my gas station! Come down here!"

Jay slammed the hatch as last night haunted him. He was beside himself. What were the chances of the farmer being the Texaco owner?

"I'll rack you, you babynapper!"

The farmer's shout echoed up to Jay as if from a manhole. He ran across the roof and descended the ladder, stumbling off the last two steps. He sprinted into the pine grove behind the station and disappeared seconds before the farmer rounded the corner with his shotgun.

*****

Hank concealed his twelve-gauge beneath the counter as the Crown Victoria parked before the storefront. Pritchard stepped out, yanked up his belt buckle, and slapped on his Stetson. Hank busied himself with counting the cash in the register.

Pritchard tipped his hat as the door rattled behind him. "Hank. How's the fort holdin' up?"

"Mornin', Paul." Hank shut the drawer and it dinged. "Carton of Reds?"

"Please. And a few questions, if ya don't mind."

"Shoot. It's not like there's a line of customers, thanks to that checkpoint of yours."

A grin threatened to uncurl Pritchard's lip as Hank turned his back and unlocked the glass case of cigarette cartons. "Were ya bustin' shots last night with that bazooka ya keep under the counter?"

"I had me a trespasser, Paul." Hank removed a carton of Marlboros and locked the case. When he faced the counter, anger lines creased his jaw. "Some stink hole was snooping around my barn. Then I come here this morning and chase him out of my store."

"Who was it?"

"Hell if I know. I barely glimpsed him."

"Then how do ya know if someone was trespassin'?"

"Collie sniffed him out last night. And he trashed my pantry."

"Hank, I ain't 'bout to interrogate yer mutt. Now who were ya shootin' at last night?"

"I told you, I don't know." He slapped the carton on the counter. "If I knew I'd tell you."

"I can nail ya on four counts of attempted murder." Pritchard unbuttoned his holster and set his Magnum on the carton. "Guess who ya almost killed? The poor Trammells, Janitor Jeter, Rat-faced Ratner, and Detective Barter of Chicago Homicide. I'm gonna search this store and yer farm fer the triplets if ya don't drop a name."

Hank stared at the Magnum. After a moment, he met Pritchard's leer with a mask of rage. His lip trembled. His voice was raspy as he spoke. "I thought I heard some reporter breached the county line and was roaming around town."

A flashback of the motorcycle chase blinded Pritchard like a spotlight. He had forgotten about the carrot top biker. Then again, he ran him out of town. He was yet another reporter hard up for a story. It was possible he had trespassed on Adler's property. As far as being a suspect, he had nothing on Coren Raines.

"I ran Redbeard outta town. But if he happened to return, where'd ya chase him off to?"

"I'm guessing he turned heel into the woods."

"The train tracks. I'll give 'em a look-see. Maybe run some drifters outta those boxcars while I'm at it."

Hank nodded and fingered his suspenders. "That'll be a flat twenty."

"On sale?"

"Today. I've got my nice hat on."

"You only got one hat, Hank, and it's bein' nice cause I got a mean streak in me."

Pritchard grabbed the Magnum and holstered it. He fished out twenty dollars, dropped it on the counter, and then snatched up his carton.

"Don't get trigger-happy on me again, Hank, or I'll have ya in the hot seat."

Pritchard walked out of the Texaco with a storm of worries flashing in his head. It was bad enough he still needed to beat a confession out of Raines. Now there was a chance he had a reporter on the loose doing personal detective work and taking pictures, probably with the intent of smearing his reputation. He had to track down that redheaded pest before his face was on the evening news.

He would pay a visit to Boxcar Alley and see if anyone was hiding out. Then he would drop in on Raines. He couldn't let that slime ball get a breather. He had to keep him on his toes and break him down. He had those triplets holed up somewhere. Onward was dead as a cemetery until the new guy showed up. He didn't buy his alibis for a second.

The slate sky flashed as thunder boomed. The clouds promised a downpour. Pritchard was glad. There was going to be buckets of blood to wash down the gutters.

*****

Barter opened his address book and scanned the residents. He clicked his pen and crossed out the names of Vance and Teresa Trammell, Ray Ratner, and Harold Jeter. None had offered solid leads. Teresa admitted that she had been crying in bed as Vance snored when their bay window shattered. Her first thought was that the kidnapper had returned, so she snatched the phone on the nightstand and dialed 9-1-1. Harold stated that he soiled his brand new Speedo and toppled his mop bucket when Principal Denman's window imploded. He assumed it was one of the students throwing rocks until he inspected the bullet hole, but he saw no one fleeing the scene. Ray had only reported the damaged mailbox, which he had noticed from his second story apartment on Main Street.

Barter sighed. He had spent two hours that morning collecting gossip. There was one other resident that he had yet to question, due to his reluctance of following Pritchard's hunches. The irascible sheriff had fingered Hank Adler as the trigger-happy townie. He supposed it couldn't hurt to cross one more name off the list.

He stuffed the address book in his jacket and climbed into the LeSabre. He turned the ignition as rain sprinkled his damaged windshield.

*Just what I need.* He pulled away from the curb and headed up Main Street.

Two minutes later, he parked beside a barbed wire fence on the corner of East Walnut Street and gazed through the bullet hole. Adler's house sat two acres back in the field. The farmer definitely had ample space to run around and blast his twelve-gauge. But what reason would anyone have to trespass on his property?

Barter withdrew his address book and scanned the list. There were no other names noted beneath Adler's. The man appeared to be a hermit, which explained his trigger-happy nature. He replaced the book and double-checked his firearm. He ejected the clip, reloaded.

He stepped out and walked to the gravel drive. He guessed that before long the potholed surface would be reduced to mud. He looked across the field. It was dying for a drink from Mother Nature.

As he approached the house, he wondered why Pritchard was so quick to discount Adler as a suspect. What was he trying to hide? He doubted that the high and mighty sheriff took his own advice.

Pritchard had a set agenda. He was focused on Coren Raines, whom he had yet to interview. But then again, Raines wasn't shooting up Onward.

He eyed the house. Though it was morning it was dark as dusk and the curtains were drawn. He ascended the porch and rang the doorbell. Maybe Adler was in his basement.

He waited perhaps thirty seconds, and then rapped on the door.

Still no answer.

Barter turned and looked across the way. The faded, dilapidated barn creaked in the gust as loud as the porch floorboards. The knotted walls swayed with the field. He was reluctant to poke his head in the doors for fear that the structure might collapse.

Then the left window caught his eye. He knew by the shape of the shards that the glass had been shot out.

He stepped off the porch and approached the barn. It was unquestionable that a twelve-gauge shotgun did the damage. He peered through the hole. His face paled to the hue of his hair. He knew at that moment why Pritchard had made Adler seem unsuspecting.

# CHAPTER NINE

The fingers wiggled.

*"Jesus Christ!"*

Coren stumbled, fell on his tailbone. The fingers clawed at the brown grass and peeled it back like a severed scalp. The black ants scuttled off the gray flesh. Coren's eyes were as wide as his mouth and trained on the exposed dirt. Earthworms surfaced, squirming between the disjointed fingers.

Coren turned and scrambled across the yard. He paused and caught his breath at the deck, shaking his head, trying to convince himself that the gin had poisoned his mind.

*No way! There's no way another kid's climbing out of my backyard! What the hell...What the hell is wrong with me?*

He rubbed his temples with his knuckles, and then squeezed his eyes shut. He was dead tired and certain it fueled hallucinations. A raindrop splashed on his forehead. He looked up the steps to the door.

*There's already one girl coughing up apples in the house*, the devil on his shoulder reminded. *Is that a hallucination, too?*

He regarded the fence. The twisted fingers were still there, clawing frantically. His Keds were nailed to the steps. Part of him wanted to return to the house and pretend that he saw nothing. His conscience, however, urged him to lend a helping hand as he had last night at the well. His greatest fear was that he would uncover another horror from the bowels of his backyard.

Thunder vibrated the deck steps and the roof of the well.

The clouds unleashed a downpour.

Coren knew he had to act fast. Should he seek shelter in the house or grab the shovel beneath the steps and dig out the groping hands? He felt like the biggest jerk in the world for considering leaving a person buried alive in a thunderstorm.

He crouched and reached between the steps. He pulled out the shovel, held it horizontally at his side.

*Here we go again*, he thought as he dashed across the backyard.

He swore his heart thundered louder than the clouds. His nerves were shot to the point where he was uncertain if his forehead dripped sweat or rain. Regret gnawed at him. He should have never moved to Onward. He felt as if he had bought his non-refundable, one-way ticket to Hell.

He stopped before the decomposed hands. The fingers bent backwards, searching for more grass to upheave. The nails snapped off one by one like Press Ons.

Coren's stomach churned. He could not stand by and watch the person suffer. He had to help. The storm was strengthening and his clothes clung to his skin. He had to squash his fear. He had to react. What made him hesitate was the paranoia that Pritchard would pop up in the backyard while he was in the midst of digging up a body. He would find himself wearing those pretty metal bracelets again in no time.

He raised the shovel in the air, then jabbed it into the worm-riddled dirt between the hands. The soil was loose, like a fresh grave.

He plunged the blade deeper. The hands reached up, stiffened.

*Oh Jesus!* Coren tossed the shovel. *I dug too deep!*

He dropped to his knees and clawed at the puddled dirt. The downpour was unrelenting, though made the digging easier. He hurled mud over his shoulder, feeling like a dog in search of a bone.

*Don't be dead. I swear I didn't mean to dig that deep. Oh, what have I done?*

He uncovered the scarred wrists and arms. The bloodstained flesh dangled like torn papier-mâché from the forearms to the elbows. They were still stiff and straight. Coren brushed against the mottled skin as he continued to dig. It was snow-cold. Goosebumps sprang up his spine.

*She's dead. I know it.*

He wondered when he had decided that the buried person was a girl.

It was the hands. The more he stared at the wispy fingers and small wrists, the more he was convinced of the body's gender.

But she was freezing! Had the rain chilled her to the bone as it had him in such short time? Or had he killed her with the shovel? Or maybe she had been dead all along and her muscles had been racked by spasms. He had heard stories of corpses rising on exam tables during autopsies.

*No!* He threw back clumps of mud, revealing a gored bicep. *I didn't kill her! She's buried in my backyard, for Christ sake!*

In his sub-conscious he knew the evidence made him look like a murderer. The fingerprints on the shovel. A girl buried in his yard with blunt force trauma to the skull. Another girl bloodied and mangled in his panic room. It was safe to say he was done for if the authorities caught him red-handed.

He froze as his fingernails raked flesh beneath the dirt. He felt as if he had been punched in the stomach. He had dug too deep again, first with the shovel and now with his hands. It seemed that the longer he strove to unbury the girl, the more he harmed her. He pulled his wrists out of the dirt. Worms slipped through his palms, dangled on his fingers.

*Maybe I should pull her out by the arms.*

The girl's hands jolted and seized Coren by the wrists. Their frigidity burned his skin. He cried out as they yanked him toward the hole he had dug. The rain had formed a small puddle and for a split second he wondered if he would drown in such a humiliating way. He struggled to tug back, but the girl's grip was overpowering.

Coren was jerked to the ground flat on his stomach. His face was inches from the rippling puddle. Was it possible that the girl was alive after all? Was she using him as an anchor to disinter herself?

The puddle splashed in his face. He blinked the mud out of his eyes and shrieked. A girl's rawboned face with hollow eye sockets emerged from the rainwater. A worm slithered out of her left nostril as her lantern jaw opened. Her skeletal head shook back and forth in spasms.

The hands pulled Coren's arms into the dirt. The mud squelched to his elbows. He was close enough to kiss the mutilated girl. Her breath was cold and smelled of cider as it hit his cheeks.

"No!"

Coren rolled to the right, twisted his body. His arms broke the girl's grip and he pulled himself free. He scrambled back from the hole, and then collapsed near the fence. The rain splashed in his face as the scent of apples drifted over him like a cloud.

*Another one*, he thought. *Another girl that looks dead, but smells like Mott's.* He grabbed the wobbly fence, stood, and stared at the hole. *I have to get her out of there. I can't leave her. Someone will find her out here half-buried.*

He approached the hole and gazed down. The girl's hands lashed out like an angry cat's, clawing at the surrounding mud. Her face was submerged and bubbles broke the surface.

Coren dropped to his knees and grabbed the girl's wrists. Her skin stung him like frostbite. The ground shifted beneath him and the hole caved in.

Coren's muscles went rigid as if the girl's body temperature had frozen him. His heart skipped, then hammered as the mud and rainwater dropped down the hole that had tripled in diameter. All disappeared in the darkness below. Before Coren knew it, his feet were planted at the edge as the girl clutched him for dear life.

Her cries echoed to the surface while her disfigured body swayed below. Coren's racing mind noted the haunting, minute details as he struggled to pull her up. Her high voice projected through her tight-lipped mouth. Her legs were stumps, severed at the knees. Her straggly, dishwater hair was stuck in the blood that had dried on the front of her tank top.

*It's another well.*

The dirt had collapsed to reveal faded brick walls. The hole seemed bottomless and the overpowering scent of cider made Coren gag. He yanked back; he prayed the girl's shoulders wouldn't pop out of their sockets. Her body was as thin and light as the last girl's, and he pulled her onto solid ground with ease.

He fell onto his back, basking in the cool rain. He looked to the girl at his feet. She wriggled and kicked her stumps as her jaw opened and shut like a fish out of water.

*No*, she rasped, and then became still, her head and limbs dropping to the sopping crabgrass.

*****

*Burl Nelson looked to the cuckoo clock above the mantle. The mechanical bird was on the verge of chirping 4:00pm. Classes had ended fifteen minutes ago at J. Edgar High. Soon the Blondies would be scaling his lattice and trespassing through the orchard.*

*He walked into the enclosed patio and scanned the backyard. The apple trees swayed in the bright sun. They smelled delicious today, having reached their mid-season peak of full bloom. If only he could quell the Blondies' afternoon appetite.*

*Everyday it was a game to them. Burl would derive some means to drive them off, but they would get the best of him in the end. In the past he had laid mousetraps in the grass, borrowed troughs filled with slop from Hank Adler which he placed at the bottom of the lattice, bought a Doberman pinscher that fell victim to Sylvia and her backpack of bricks, and even planted poison ivy around the perimeter. Nothing deterred the mischievous triplets. Instead they became more angered and determined. But what else could be done? He refused to call 9-1-1 and have their father defend them.*

*His deterrent was foolproof today. He spent his entire morning stringing barbed wire through the tall grass. It stretched in parallel lines across the orchard like a boot camp obstacle. He was hell-bent on teaching the triplets a lesson. He would handle their crimes in his court and punish them accordingly. If they whined and cried to their father, so be it.*

*He grinned as he sat on the wicker chair that faced the yard. He wished he had cooked a bag of popcorn, for it was going to be one hell of a show. He hoped there would be no happy endings or sequels. Today would be the finale.*

*The clock chirped 4:00pm. Burl's bony knees bounced. He tugged his white beard and shifted in his seat as he adjusted his glasses. Any moment the Blondies would climb the fence. He thought about running to the bedroom and grabbing the Polaroid. It was going to be a moment to remember.*

*A glint at the top of the lattice caught Burl's eye. Sylvia peered over the fence with her Swiss army knife in hand. She looked down, then left and right. Satisfied that the coast was clear, she dropped down into the backyard. Seconds later, Loren and Henna followed suit.*

*Sylvia was the first to step forward. She swiped her knife at a nearby branch, caught an apple. Burl stood and approached the screen. A few more steps and the anorexic triplet would fall flat on her ugly face. Sylvia tossed the apple to Henna.*

*"I got some apple juice fer ya, old man!" Henna cocked back her arm and hurled the baseball-sized fruit.*

*It slammed against the patio screen, splattering juice, and Burl stumbled back and toppled the wicker chair.*

*Burl groaned as his arthritis flared up his arms. The Blondies laughed and each picked an apple for an afternoon snack. Sylvia halved hers with the knife as Loren and Henna dug their nails into the skins and peeled them.*

*Henna nodded toward the orchard. "Know what we oughta do? Grab that old coot's shovel and dig up a couple of his trees. That'd serve him right."*

*Sylvia stabbed her apple. "Too bad he doesn't have an axe."*

*"He ain't that stupid, Syl, but stupid enough to leave a shovel layin' around. Go grab it, Lor."*

*"Hell yeah." Loren took a bite of her apple, and then whipped it at Burl's house. It smashed on the roof and rolled off. She cocked her Pirates cap. "Bull's eye!"*

*Loren jogged into the orchard. Seconds later, she cried out. Henna and Sylvia glimpsed her falling between the trees.*

*"Ow, God!"*

*"Aw, Lor," Henna said. "Did ya sprain yer ankle again?"*

*Loren moaned. "Stay there. That blue-hair strung barbed wire through the grass. Damn, that hurts!"*

*"Take that, you stupid tramp!"*

*Henna and Sylvia turned and spotted Burl shaking his fist at the back door. Henna's eyes narrowed and her lip curled. Nobody hurt her sister and got away with it.*

*"I'll kill ya, ya crippled coot!"*

*Loren stumbled out of the orchard. Her bare ankles bled as if she had slit them and her chin was lined with seeping puncture wounds.*

*Henna ripped off an apple and threw it. Burl ducked and it smashed the back door window. He opened the back door and glass rained down.*

*He reached into the garage, grabbed his twelve-foot tree pruner. "Come over here and do that! I'll snip off your fat fingers!"*

*Sylvia grabbed an apple and jabbed her knife through it.*

*Henna and Loren grinned, then nodded.*

*"Eat this!" Sylvia whirled and pitched the apple.*

*It spun and glinted over the tree line. Burl attempted to dodge it, but reacted too slow. The protruding blade stabbed him in the shoulder. He hollered, backing into the side of the house. He dropped the tree pruner, gritted his dentures, and yanked out the apple.*

*"You cow! You fat cow!"*

*Burl's head snapped and the left side of his face slammed into the siding. He collapsed to the grass as he felt his throbbing jaw. One of the Blondies must have snuck up and punched him. Then he saw the dented apple rolling at his feet.*

*Henna grabbed the pruner as her sisters flanked her. "So yer gonna snip off my fat fingers, huh? How ya gonna do that? I got yer pruner."*

*Burl pushed himself up. "Up yours."*

*Loren fired an apple missile and busted open his right cheek. His glasses dangled on his nose as he crumpled against the house.*

*Henna opened and shut the blades of the pruner as she inched it toward Burl's face. Sylvia hummed the theme from* Jaws. *Loren chuckled with another apple in hand.*

*Henna snapped the blades before Burl's nose. "What do ya feel like losin', old man? A finger? A tooth? How 'bout an eye?"*

*Burl glared at her, glassy-eyed. "How about you get the hell off my property! What would your father say about this?"*

*The pruner snapped shut on Burl's glasses, halving them. The lenses fell to the ground. Burl was on the verge of a heart attack. He was sure the Blondie was going to gouge out his eye.*

*Henna shook the pruner. "My father wouldn't say nothin'. And neither will you!"*

*Burl hyperventilated. "Your fa-, your fa-"*

*Loren hurled her apple and busted open Burl's right eye. He cried out as blood streamed down his face. Sylvia yanked up his beard while Henna snipped the tip of his chin with the pruner. He yelled loud enough for the whole town to hear.*

*And many passers-by paused as they window-shopped on Main Street. Many others shook their heads, assuming the Blondies were up to their bullying ways again.*

*****

Jay caught his breath as he emerged from the pine grove. He was relieved that he had distanced himself from Farmer Loony. He still could not believe that same nutcase ran the gas station. He was surprised the Texaco lacked a torture décor.

He entered a clearing. He glanced left and right, then over his shoulder. Weedy train tracks stretched in both directions. To the east there were ten to fifteen rusted boxcars, all glazed in graffiti, lined along the rails. Some were overturned with unhinged doors, while others were upright and askew entangled in milkweed, looking as if a train had once derailed.

Jay's hopes brightened. He had found a temporary shelter to replace the Texaco pantry. No one would be snooping around the tracks. He would finally have a chance to collect his thoughts and get his bearings straight. As of late he felt as if was on a wild goose chase.

He headed toward the boxcars. Lightning lit the sky and thunder cracked. Moments later, the rain poured.

Jay ran through the weeds and ducked into the first boxcar. It was bright red with symbols and profanity smeared across ghostly white letters that read **SOO LINE**. Inside, the metal floor was littered with dead leaves and cigarette butts. The air was stale and smelled of urine. Jay hoped the rain would freshen his new quarters.

He sat down on the cold floor and stared out the doorway. He expected to see the farmer rushing out of the pines blasting his twelve-gauge. Maybe the old psycho had ended his pursuit.

*So, now what?*

His news story was turning into a teleplay. He had questioned one townie and spent the rest of the time running like a criminal. He wished he was at the Texaco; at least it had a phonebook to consult. At this point, he only had his notepad.

He reached inside his jacket, withdrew it, and flipped through the pages. He recalled his conversation with Francine Heller.

*Those girls were never home, they were always hiding out somewhere.*

*Of course*, he thought. *These boxcars! Where else would the Blondies have to hide out? It would be the perfect place to lay low.*

A question he had asked Francine popped into his head: *Ms. Heller, they tortured you on a daily basis and then they vanished. That doesn't sound coincidental, now does it?*

His mind filtered through the possibilities. Had the Blondies caught the first train out of Onward? Or had Francine sought revenge single-handedly and made them disappear? The latter thought seemed unlikely, considering the Blondies' rap sheets. They outnumbered Francine three-to-one and were ten times more hostile.

Jay danced around the one quote in his notes: *I just remember how happy I was when they disappeared off the face of the earth.*

Jay stood, scanned his surroundings. He needed to inspect each one of the boxcars. He had a hunch that the Blondies had used them as a hideout. They might have even left behind evidence.

*From fifteen years ago?*

He torched the devil on his shoulder. Sure the idea was a stretch, but it gave him something to do rather than sit on his freezing butt in a hobo home. He stepped into the downpour and gazed up the tracks. A pair of headlights approached from the west. He returned to his shelter and pressed his back against the wall.

*That didn't take long.*

He had a bad feeling that the crazy farmer had hopped onto his tractor for a manhunt. He envisioned the boxcars getting plowed over one by one as if it were a monster truck rally. He shivered. The rain had soaked him and he was getting anxious. Sooner or later he would have to face Old Macdonald, regardless if he was unarmed.

He pressed his ear against the cold metal. Through the plunking rain he honed in on the visitor. It was not a tractor, of that much he was certain. It sounded more like a car.

He peeked out the doorway, and then ducked back inside. The fleeting glimpse sickened his stomach. He sank into the shadows of the far corner as a navy blue Crown Victoria pulled up to boxcar alley.

"Damn."

The farmer had dialed 9-1-1 and Pritchard answered the call. He was the only one crazy enough to track down his man in a thunderstorm. Jay's head spun through a whirlwind of scenarios. He saw Pritchard shining his flashlight into the boxcar and then bashing him over the head with it. He saw Pritchard handcuffing him to the train tracks and leaving him to die.

A siren chirped. A floodlight beamed down the alley. The car engine rumbled nearby, then groaned. Jay held his breath. He was afraid to move an inch for fear that it would echo throughout the boxcar. At the same time he wondered if he should run for it. Pritchard would be pissed if he discovered that he had remained in town.

He put his ear to the wall. The only sound he heard was the rain. He glanced to the doorway, which was curtained by a brown waterfall. If the thought of turning tail was a reality, he had better jump at the chance. Either way, he lacked a visual of his pursuer.

*Screw it! If he cuffs me, I sure as hell won't get this story out. Or see Jeanette and the girls anytime soon.*

Jay bolted for the doors. Pritchard spun around the corner with his Magnum drawn. Jay tried to stop in his tracks, but slipped on the wet floor and landed on his butt. Pritchard entered the boxcar, the waterfall cascading off his Stetson, looking as if the heavens were defecating on him.

Pritchard aimed his pistol at Jay's chest. "Don't make a move, ya little weasel!"

S.D. Hintz

# CHAPTER TEN

Barter stepped back from the broken window. He had expected to see hay bales, horses, and farm equipment. Instead he had traveled through time to a medieval torture chamber. The thought of people being punished in six-by-nine stalls sickened his stomach. It seemed Adler lived up to his reputation as the local lunatic.

*I got my suspects, and Adler ain't one of 'em.*

Pritchard's statement was a bright red flag. If the quick-tempered sheriff believed that someone shooting up town was a model citizen, then that meant that individual was crazy. Adler was a prime suspect in Barter's book. The evidence stared him in the face. He supposed there was a possibility the farmer was a collector of torture devices. The problem was that the man unloaded his shotgun last night, which cast him in a rather negative light. Who was to say he didn't kidnap babies and torture them?

The rain came down in buckets, urging Barter beneath the overhang to the double doors. He inspected the combination lock. All of the numbers except the six were scratched out. For amusement purposes, he turned the dial to six three times. He knew the farmer wasn't that stupid, but what the hell, it was worth a try.

He yanked the lock. It opened.

*No way*, he thought. *Maybe Adler's a dumb hick after all.*

He removed the lock and pocketed it for evidence. He knew it was covered with Adler's fingerprints.

Barter opened the doors and entered. The interior jabbed him in the gut. In his mind's eye he saw victims writhing and screaming in the torture devices. He thought of the Trammell triplets. Could their small bodies fit in any of the bloodstained contraptions? Maybe one. The rack. It was the only one that was adjustable. He considered the boiling pot with the frayed rope. No. The rope was too short for a baby.

Barter made his rounds with his cellphone, snapping photos of every nook and cranny. When all was said and done, he emailed the potential exhibits to headquarters. He wondered how Chief Dalton would react. He hoped he would avoid involving the FBI.

He had fingered a suspect with circumstantial evidence. Now all he needed was proof.

*****

Coren sat up. The bloodied, unconscious girl twitched beside him. He stared at her rain-splattered face. He realized she had the same striking features as the other girl, save for lacking eyes. She had the same sloping jawline and thin lips. Her hair was identical in color, though more straggly. Besides her body looking like a skeleton and having half of her legs, she was a twin. Even stranger, she was as immobile as her sister was.

*Great, now I'm starting a family in my head.*

He glanced away, and then looked back. Yes, it was the same girl, but with a different figure.

The devil on his shoulder played a harp. *That's the gin talking. Get her into the panic room. You'll see it's just another mutilated dead girl haunting your backyard.*

*She's not dead!* Coren crouched and placed his hands in the girl's armpits. *Dead girls don't crawl out of wells!*

"I'm gonna pick you up now. Okay? Here we go. Let's get you in the house."

He heaved the girl over his shoulder and dashed through the rain. Her meaty stumps slapped against his soaked T-shirt as he ducked beneath the dripping elm. Her icy breath tickled his cheek, still pungent of apples, and probably kept him sane. Had she reeked of rot he would have dropped her in the dirt without a second thought. Instead, he cleared his mind and convinced himself that he carried a sack of Fujis. And with every wet slap of her stumps it became harder and harder to ignore reality.

He stomped up the deck steps and nudged the sliding door open with his elbow. The gusting rain shoved him into the house. He kicked the door shut. As he did so, her right stump smacked him in the mouth. He nearly lost it. All he wanted to do was drop the girl, lock her up, and take a scalding shower.

He made it halfway across the kitchen when his shoes slipped on the linoleum. He fell flat on his face, watching agape as the girl rolled out of his arms into the living room.

"Oh God."

He lied on his stomach for a moment and watched her limbs spasm. He wondered if he should leave her there for the time being. The last thing he wanted to do was pick her up again. He was surprised he hadn't killed her yet. How many more times could he bludgeon the poor girl?

He scrambled to his feet and ran to her side. Her eyelids fluttered while her bony arms flopped in a cruciform position. She was still alive, in extreme shock maybe, but breathing nonetheless. He picked her up and held her out at arm's length as if she was a leaky diaper. The image of apples had been erased. Reality nauseated him. He wanted to drop her back down on the living room floor.

"Screw it!"

He rushed into the hall. As much as he loathed the thought, he pressed her cold body against his chest, cradling her with one arm as he felt the wall with his free hand. He found the inconspicuous handle and opened the door.

The girl stiffened straight as a stone pillar. Coren risked a glance. Her jaw dropped and she screamed.

*Christ, she is a twin!*

He clamped his hand on her mouth. She lurched back and wriggled through his arm. She plopped on the panic room floor and then lurched at him, attempting to squeeze past his legs into the hall. He blocked her path and tried to shove her back with his knee, but she was relentless, screaming and lunging, screaming and lunging.

Half of her body was in the room while the other half was in the hall, preventing him from slamming the door.

"Goddamn it! Get in there!"

His patience wore thin. He was reluctant to touch her since she was acting like a dog, and even more leery of getting bit. He had to do something before she got the upperhand. Her stumps kicked his shoes as she pushed forward between his leg and the doorjamb.

"That's it!"

Coren's irritation overcame his fear. He stepped aside. The girl squirmed forward and he seized her stumps. He then swung her into the room. She slid across the hardwood floor, her limbs splaying as she shrieked and collided with the far wall. The other girl - who he assumed was comatose to the left of him - belted out a glass-resonating scream as she spotted her new roommate.

Coren slammed the door, and then slouched against the hallway wall, basking in the silent shadows. This was how the house should have been. Instead it was haunted with the sweet sounds of a concentration camp.

*****

"Spill yer guts, Redbeard!"

Jay inched back across the slippery floor until he was plastered against the wall. His eyes darted from the dripping barrel to Pritchard, then to the door. He thought about hopping up and charging, but he knew his gun would discharge and he would be on the news for sure. That was all Jeanette needed to see. It was bad enough she had not heard from him in days and then to find out her husband was in trouble with the law…that would not be good. He would have to try his hardest to talk his way out.

Jay slid to a crouch and stood. "I never left town, okay?"

"Ya kiddin' me?" Pritchard pocketed his rain-spattered sunglasses with his free hand. He waved the Magnum at his bulging eyes. "Ya see these? They're in the back of my head. They follow ya like a magnet. I know what yer doin' here, boy. Yer tryin' to expose me in one of yer tabloids. Tryin' to make me look like a chump cop that stuffs his yap with bear claws and quarter coffee. Well, ya barked up the wrong tree!"

"No, that's not it at all. I just…I just wanted to -"

Thunder blasted like a bomb and the boxcar reverberated, drowning out Jay's admission. When it faded into drumming rain, he and Pritchard froze at the sound of shouting.

"Let's make one last sweep through the alley! Check every one of these goddamn boxcars, the junk piles, the underbrush!"

Pritchard shoved his pistol in Jay's face. "Don't make a move. If yer gone when I come back, you'll have a warrant and a death wish on yer head. Ya hear me?"

Jay nodded. Pritchard turned and left.

Jay walked up to the doorway and listened. Muffled conversation flitted through the gusting rain. He guessed the people were near the train tracks. Pritchard was thick-witted if he thought a reporter was going to stand around and miss a story. The warrant was a hollow threat. Pritchard did not even know his name. As for the death wish, there was no doubt in his mind he would go Bronson ballistic on him.

"Here goes."

He bolted into the storm. He was hell-bent on heading the opposite direction. The voices soon faded at his back. If gunshots had followed, he failed to hear them over the drumroll of thunder.

*****

Pritchard holstered his Magnum and rounded the line of boxcars. A search party of ten to fifteen townspeople clad in clear ponchos lingered near his squad car. Vance Trammell stepped forward and scratched his stubble. The combination of the rain and his red eyes made him look as if he had been bawling all day.

Pritchard tipped his Stetson and thumbed his belt buckle.

Vance's voice was gruff and tinged with anger. "What the hell are you doing here?"

"The same thing you are. Looks like I beat ya to the punch. I suggest ya move along. I've searched every nook and cranny of the alley and there's nothin' here."

"If you don't mind, Sheriff, we'll have a look-see for ourselves. I'd like to cross one more spot off my list."

"Then heed my word, Vance. I've done the investigatin'. Now all of ya need to take shelter from this storm."

"The only one raining on our parade is you." Vance stood in Pritchard's face, close enough to whiff his cancerous breath. "I think you have an attachment to these boxcars. Everybody knows your girls hung around these parts. And that graffiti wouldn't mean anything, now would it?"

Vance pointed at a blue-black boxcar spray-painted from hitch to hitch. The one yellow, three-dimensional word made him wince.

**Blondies**.

He locked leers with Vance. He wanted to choke him, regardless if half the town looked on. His mind's eye blinded him. He recalled the first time he caught his three daughters sniffing gasoline in his garage. That was when he had nicknamed them. They were dumb blonds from that point on. They deserved every beating he administered.

Pritchard stepped on Vance's toes. The man was the same height, but scrawny and exhausted. "Yer goddamn right that means somethin'. My girls hopped the train outta Onward. And maybe yers did, too. They could be on the black market in Montana right now."

Vance stumbled back to the search party. He shook his fist, and then uncurled his index finger. "My girls are six-months-old, Paul! They're not bullying troublemakers like yours were!"

Pritchard inched his hand to his holster. Any other time he would have pistol-whipped the loudmouth until his eyes were swollen shut; this time he reminded himself that Vance was the victims' father.

"I admit, Vance, a sheriff's daughters no doubt got some royal treatment. But no one ever touched 'em or took 'em. Their father made sure of that."

"You find my girls, Paul! You find them, goddamn it!"

Sam Emory and Wendell Wurtz seized Vance before he could lash out. Pritchard glanced back at the boxcar he had left the reporter at. Rather than look suspicious and return to the alley, he removed his Stetson and climbed into his car. He figured he had scared Redbeard enough to make him jump ship.

He withdrew his handkerchief and dried his face as the search party dispersed. Once he was certain the townspeople had vacated the alley, he would pay Coren Raines another friendly visit. The more evidence he dug up, the better the pieces to the puzzle would fit together.

S.D. Hintz

# CHAPTER ELEVEN

Barter placed his cellphone in the cup holder and turned the ignition. His conversation with Chief Dalton had been laced with praise and agreement. Thanks to his photos, he had been given the go-ahead to arrest Hank Adler and Paul Pritchard on suspicion of concealing evidence. The chief also thought it quite coincidental that a farmer had a barn full of torture devices rather than animals to feed the town, considering the circumstances.

Barter sighed. It was days like this that he wished he smoked or had less hair to lose. He had two suspects to rein in. Chief Dalton had declined FBI involvement, stating that there had been a bomb scare downtown and that it had priority over a small town kidnapping. Barter had voiced his concerns about the said individuals being armed and dangerous. The chief's words rang in his head: "You're Homicide, Detective. If you worry about your own death, how are you going to investigate the others?" He was right. He had a job to do, end of story.

He itched his mustache as he gazed across the storm-tossed field. Public records indicated that Adler owned the Texaco on

County Road 500. He would start there. He figured Adler would be easier to arrest than Pritchard. He had never cuffed another officer, but he knew it was going to be difficult.

He withdrew his pistol, double-checked the clip, and then holstered it. He was a nervous wreck. Usually he had backup in these types of situations. What would he do if he walked into the Texaco and Adler and Pritchard were both there? The odds were that neither man would go down to the station willingly. Chief Dalton had mentioned that if he was outnumbered to text a "3" and he would dispatch three squads. He was reluctant to make that call unless he had his back against the wall. He refused to give off the appearance that he couldn't handle a routine takedown.

*One at a time. I can do this. One at a time.*

"Damn."

*****

Coren stared out the deck door as he paced the kitchen. The empty glass he had left on the railing overflowed with rainwater.

*Maybe the wells will fill up with something other than crippled girls.*

He chuckled at the thought. He was going crazy, of that he was certain. The girls seemed tangible, but that was impossible. Dead bodies didn't crawl out of wells and smell like apples.

*But they're not dead! They're breathing in that panic room!*

He opened the cupboard and greeted his best friend Seagram. He needed to think things through. There had to be a logical explanation for the recent occurrences. He grabbed a tumbler, topped it off, and then took a swig with closed eyes.

What did it mean? Why were there victimized girls emerging from the depths of his backyard? And why now of all times? Had they ever come out to play *before* he bought the place?

*It's haunted, you idiot! You bought a haunted house! Why is that so hard to believe?*

He opened his eyes. His gaze rested on the laptop. It had been untouched since Friday morning. He wondered if his boss had emailed him. He ought to tell him he was taking a sick day. He suddenly had the urge to sit down as his thoughts somersaulted.

*"This is prime property, Mr. Raines," his real estate agent George Tartan had said while perusing the Disclosure Statement. "It's listed for dirt cheap, it's vacant, and a good fifty miles from your ex."*

*"The yard's a mess,"* he had replied as he paced the deck. *"What's the scoop on the owner?"*

*"Not sure. Sounds like he relocated. I guess he doesn't mind paying two mortgages."*

Coren plopped down at the desk and powered up the laptop. Did the previous owner relocate or did somebody make him move? Somebody like Pritchard.

He recalled closing on the house. All of the documents had been pre-signed and the seller's agent had said he was absent due to a family emergency. He brushed it off at the time and went about his business. Now it gnawed on him like a rat on a corpse.

Once the desktop graced the screen, he connected to the Internet and Googled Carver County, Illinois. He then clicked on their web site and pulled up the county assessors page. From there, he was able to type in his street address and access the history of past owners and tax assessments on the property.

He scanned the short list. There were two individuals listed, excluding himself. The original owner was a man named Ray Hodge. Then a month before Coren had purchased the house Hodge had signed over the title to Edwold Gentry.

*Edwold Gentry?*

Coren accessed the county records and searched the name in the database. A minute later he was informed that there were no residents with that name in Carver County. He widened the search and included the entire state. He found three Ed Gentry's. Two were deceased while the other resided in Oak Grove Manor.

*Did this guy buy the house off Ebay or something?*

Who was Edwold Gentry? And did it matter in the scheme of things? Maybe he was a relative of Ray Hodge's. Or maybe Hodge had encountered some financial problems and Gentry in good faith had offered to put his name on the title and cover the debts, and then in turn sold the house once he paid the outstanding bills. That was a far-fetched theory, but not unheard of considering the flood of foreclosures in the past year.

*So there's a different guy on the title. Big deal. What's that have to do with the house being haunted?*

Nothing. Unless one of those guys murdered two girls and buried them in the wells.

*But they're not dead! They're both playing hopscotch in the panic room!*

Realization struck him. Ghosts were not roaming his homestead. His backyard was infested with kid zombies. Which meant that at some point the girls had been laid to rest six feet under. Yet they emerged from rotten earth smelling like applesauce.

His mind replayed the image like a broken film reel. The girl swallowing the apple whole. His fingers gouging her eyes as maggots poured forth. The glowing fruit rising up her throat, then disgorging and splitting open to reveal a smoldering badge.

Coren downed the gin in one gulp, rose from the desk, and stumbled into the kitchen. He opened the refrigerator and reached into the crisper. He had several apples left in the bag he had purchased from the Texaco. He grabbed one and headed for the hallway.

The devil danced on his shoulder. *That's right, my man. Cram it in her mouth. It's the only way we can tell if she's a twin.*

Coren bumped into the wall, a gentle reminder that he was stinking drunk. He wouldn't have had it any other way. Sobriety would have him thinking that he was crazy. At least in his present state he could blame future events on the gin. He grinned at the idiotic thought, clutched the apple, and then opened the panic room door.

*****

*Francine clutched the backpack, white-knuckled, not about to lose it again and scale a barbed wire fence to retrieve it. The bell rang as she set foot on the school grounds. That was the first warning, short and sweet. The second bell always rang for an extra thirty seconds, giving students ample time to run their tails off to homeroom.*

*Francine followed the crowd of high schoolers through the double doors. Pink and blue posters decorated the entryway, reminding her that prom was two weeks away. Tears stung her eyes as Henna's barbs drowned her thoughts.*

And no one's desperate enough to ask you to prom.

*Sure, she was used to the Blondies' teasing, but hurtful words seldom lacked truth. She had her fair share of flaws that deterred even the nerdy boys from catching her eye. She knew she was overweight and cursed with her mom's crooked nose and straggly hair. She was an unpopular, homely girl who hid behind her locker door when the jocks passed by.*

*She felt wetness on her leg. She glanced down and saw that she bled again. The upper half of the gash had dried while the lower tip trickled, having caught the brunt of the barb. She still had five minutes before the second bell rang. That was plenty of time to stop*

*at the lavatory and wash the cut. The nurse's office was out of the*

*question. She didn't want to risk getting sent home and screamed at*

*by her parents.*

*She rushed into the little girl's room and set her backpack*

*down by the sink. She looked at herself in the smudged mirror. Her*

*hair was tousled and her shirt collar was askew. She turned on the*

*faucet, tore off a paper towel from the dispenser, and then dampened*

*it.*

*"I see ya got yer backpack, Smeller."*

*Francine froze, looked in the mirror. Henna emerged from*

*an open stall with a cigarette fixed in her sneer. Francine dabbed*

*her flesh wound with the paper towel. She was determined to clean*

*up before Henna cornered her.*

*Francine tossed the bloody towel in the garbage. "Guess*

*you don't need glasses then, huh? Now I know why you sit in the*

*back of class."*

*Henna slammed her into the nook of the sink and trashcan.*

*Francine winced as pain cascaded down her shoulder blades. Henna*

*held her cigarette between her thumb and forefinger and blew off the ashes, stoking the red-hot tip. Francine lurched back and hit her head on the wall. She gritted her teeth, knowing another goose egg was imminent. Henna shoved her forearm beneath her chin.*

*"How'd ya like to lose sight of me, Smeller? I'll burn yer pretty little eyes out. Would ya like that?" Henna inched the cherry closer. Francine felt the heat against her cheek. "Ya think me and my sisters didn't see ya tattlin' to Old MacDonald? Yer dead after school, ya hear me? Dead."*

*Henna jerked the cigarette back to her lips, inhaled, and then jammed it into the wall beside Francine's head. She blew a plume of smoke into her face. Francine turned and coughed.*

*Henna stepped back, retracting her forearm. Francine thought she was going to leave the lavatory, but instead the Blondie seized her backpack.*

*"Ya shouldn't leave yer stuff lyin' around, Smeller."*

*Henna heaved the backpack over the nearest stall door. Francine heard it splash in the toilet.*

*Henna grinned from ear to ear and mouthed:* Dead. *She then left the lavatory, chuckling as the door shut behind her.*

*Francine straightened up and stewed. She wanted to kill that girl. How much more could she take before she snapped and did something she regretted? No, she wouldn't regret it, but she saw herself reaching that point. The hurdle she stumbled over, though, was that the Blondies' father was the big man on campus. Any obvious means of retaliation would get her charged and booked. Any obvious means, yes. That was why she needed to be inconspicuous.*

*She massaged her shoulder as she opened the stall door. There her backpack slumped on the seat, its straps dangling in the john. She cursed and grabbed her belongings, holding them with an outstretched arm. She then sat it on the sink and dried it with paper towel.*

*She stared at the mirror. She wished that for one day she could walk the school halls in someone else's shoes. She dabbed her tears, then headed for class as the last bell rang.*

\*\*\*\*\*

*Thunder stomped across the clouds like an angry child. Francine prayed for a downpour. A good rain might postpone the game. That was how she thought of it, as a game. Unfortunately, she had yet to avoid a rout. But again, there had to be an unsuspecting way she could seek vengeance.*

*It seemed that even Mr. Adler wanted the Blondies gone. She knew, however, that she was outnumbered. How could she get the upperhand on three bullies? Maybe she could steal her dad's pickup truck and run them down. Or maybe she could gather all of the other girls that had been bullied and launch a ten-on-three attack. That might work. The problem was that most of those girls would be too discouraged to back her up. She was better off plotting on her own. Ten girls spinning their wheels would dig a deeper rut.*

*The rain teemed as Francine followed Railroad Street past East Walnut. She grinned. The odds of a safe journey looked better already, but she was still going to avoid the straight shot home, which skirted Mr. Adler's farm. She was certain the Blondies would be waiting for her that way. The thought of fetching her backpack over a barbed wire fence again riled her frustration.*

*She ducked beneath the willows that shaded the road, where the rain filtered through the canopies in a drizzle. She needed to devise a plan to catch the sisters off guard. The longer she tolerated the bullying, the greater the chance she would get seriously hurt. But what could she do?*

*Her gaze focused on the street sign ahead. It was twisted and lopsided, courtesy of the Blondies, indicating that Main Street was in the opposite direction.*

*She wondered what compelled them to act the way they did. Was it because their father was the sheriff and that was their way of rebelling? She thought so. Maybe since their father was Onward's law they assumed they had equal power.*

*She sighed as she stepped over the leaf-clogged gutter and rounded the corner. Something slammed into the side of her head. She wavered back a step. At first, she thought she had collided with a tree branch. Then she glimpsed Sylvia emerging from the woods with a Louisville Slugger. The world blurred and Francine collapsed, knocked unconscious with her head and torso in the grass while her legs splayed in the gutter.*

*Sylvia smacked her bubble gum and dropped the bat in the weeds. "Homerun! I told her she had it coming."*

*Henna seized Francine by the wrists. "C'mon! Drag her into the woods!"*

*Loren and Sylvia grabbed a leg and the Blondies lugged her limp body beyond the dense treeline. They dropped her in the brush and she rolled onto her stomach, still out cold.*

*"She can kiss her backpack goodbye." Henna peeled the straps off Francine's shoulders and slipped them through her own arms. She crouched and leaned over to Francine's ear. "Yer dead, Smeller. Dead." She stood and glared at her sisters. "Take her clothes off."*

*Sylvia spit out her gum. "Huh? I ain't queer. You do it."*

*Loren warped the brim of her cap. "What if someone sees us? We just knocked her out. Ain't that enough?"*

*Henna raised her fist and shook it at her sisters. "Strip her clothes off or I'll beat the crap outta both of ya!"*

*After a moment's hesitation, Loren and Sylvia disrobed Francine. First her sweater, then her dress, and last of all her undergarments. They tossed them to Henna, who threw them up in the branches of a willow tree. Francine's eyes fluttered.*

*"Wake up, Smeller." Henna grabbed Francine by her hair and lifted her head. Her eyes blinked. "This is what happens to smart mouths. Now stand up."*

*Francine shook her head. The cool wind tickled her flesh and she glanced down. Her eyes widened when she saw her nakedness, but the scream died in her throat.*

*"Stand her up!"*

*Loren and Sylvia seized Francine by the arms and stood her up as she thrashed. Henna smashed her fist into her face. Blood sprayed from Francine's nose. Her head lolled and her eyes rolled, then she slipped back into unconsciousness. The sisters slung her arms over their shoulders as her body slouched.*

*Henna pointed behind Loren and Sylvia, where Main Street skirted the treeline. "Dump her into that ditch."*

*Loren nibbled the cleft in her lip. "Someone's gonna see us."*

*"Since when has that stopped ya? Yer my sister. Do it! Unless yer a wuss like Smeller. Are ya, Lorie? Are ya just like her?*

*Do ya want us to beat the crap outta ya and dump ya in the woods?*

*Huh, Lorie? Ya better decide before I throw another punch."*

*"Help me drag her, Syl."*

*Henna picked up the Louisville Slugger and rested it on her shoulder, grinning as if she hit a grand slam. Loren and Sylvia hauled Francine to the treeline, paused, and then peered through the willows. Reassured that Main Street was deserted, they charged forward and heaved Francine. Her body bounced on the sandburs and rolled down the slope as blood spiderwebbed her cheeks. She landed at the bottom of the six-foot deep ditch, naked, alone, and left for dead.*

*****

Jay doubled over, struggling to catch his breath. He knew Pritchard would be calling an APB in a matter of minutes. He was uncertain of the distance he had covered, but it appeared that up ahead the woods thinned. He could make out a vague clearing through the steady rain.

*I need to find shelter and get my bearings straight.*

He needed a new plan of attack, since inspecting the boxcars was out of the question. He doubted that there was evidence left from fifteen years ago. Still, the clock was ticking. The longer it took him to dig up the story, the more Jeanette worried about him. He needed a phone.

He crouched at the edge of the clearing, and then poked his head through the branches. A deserted Main Street led into downtown. While he was relieved to be near civilization, he was paranoid that the authorities might spot him. Barter was sure to be roaming the blocks, conducting his investigation.

He glanced north and south, then dashed up the ditch and across the road. When he reached the other side he tripped on the downgrade and fell on his face at the tree line.

A rumble sounded to his right, but it wasn't thunder. He was certain a truck had turned onto Main Street. He remained still and on his stomach in the weeds. The vehicle rattled by and he looked up. He glimpsed a pickup with trees swaying near the tailgate. He had a fleeting thought of chasing after the truck and hopping onto the flatbed, where he could travel to a safer destination. That was the writer in him getting creative. Or maybe he was wearing down and thinking irrationally.

He crawled into the woods and sat against a willow, ensuring that he was out of sight. He then withdrew a bag of Reese's Pieces as his stomach growled.

*Some Boy Scout I'd make. Now all I need to do is build a fort and fire.*

He almost chuckled at the thought. He was clueless as how to fish, let alone rub two sticks together. He grew up in the big city. Roughing it to him was riding the El's and living in a rundown apartment complex. Here he was hiding from the police in a strange town with nothing but candy for nourishment. Maybe he should leave a trail in case he died of pneumonia. Then someone would at least find his body. Or they would find E.T. craning his neck for more Reese's Pieces.

A train whistle reeled him back to reality. He recalled that he was closer to the train tracks than he wanted to be. However, he did need to cross them and head toward town. He wasn't about to camp in the wilderness. He had to find a phone and a dry place to review his notes. Then he might be able to write the ending to the story.

The ground shook as the train roared by. Jay wondered if the Blondies had hitched a ride on the caboose, like he should have, and escaped Onward once and for all.

S.D. Hintz

# CHAPTER TWELVE

Barter parked the LeSabre between the Texaco storefront and gas pumps. The station looked closed. The neon "Open" sign was dark and the lot was vacant. It was possible that Adler had decided to keep the store shut down, despite the go-ahead from the authorities. After all, how many residents would wander out of their houses with a curfew in place and a kidnapper on the loose? Probably not many.

Barter tugged his sweater, ensuring that the bulletproof vest was inconspicuous. He didn't want Adler thinking he was there to start a war. He grabbed his navy blue C.P.D. cap and slapped it on. Normally, he would wear it to keep the sun out of his eyes, but today it was for the rain. He exited the car, glancing at the fractured windshield. He reminded himself that the trigger-happy man inside was responsible for that damage.

He entered the store and scanned it from wall to wall. The counter was deserted, as were the aisles and coolers. He leaned over the counter, looked below the register. There was a single gun rack beneath the glass display case of lottery tickets. It was empty.

Barter withdrew his firearm and sidestepped down a magazine aisle. He wasn't taking any chances by standing out in the open.

"*Hello?* Can I get some service up here? I'd like some scratch-offs and a Powerball!"

"What're you blind?" Barter's heart thumped. A reply had been unexpected. "If the damn sign is off, so am I! Now get out of here before I call the cops!"

*Who do you think is here?* Barter thought.

He rounded the tabloids, shoved the front door open, and then ducked back down the aisle. The door slammed shut.

"Stupid idiot! This ain't no goddamn 7-11!"

Barter peered around the rack. Hank appeared from the back of the store with a double-barrel shotgun. He craned his neck left and right. Squinting, he spotted the LeSabre beyond the rain-streaked window, but failed to catch sight of the driver.

"If he thinks this is full service, he's got another thing coming."

Hank cocked back the hammers. Barter crouched low at the end of the aisle. He eased a pair of handcuffs from his belt, careful not to clink the metal. He knew he had to surprise Adler. If he ordered him to "Freeze" the crazy farmer would probably unload on him. He had to pounce and somehow cuff him. He wished he hadn't left his Taser in the glove box.

*Just do it! Charge the guy and cuff him to the register!*

The shotgun barrel poked into the aisle. Hank approached the front door. Barter rose from his crouch and lunged. Hank glimpsed movement out of the corner of his eye and spun. Barter threw his forearm into the shotgun barrel as Hank pulled the trigger. The front doors shattered and the storm tossed the glass into the store.

"Drop your weapon!" Barter pinned Hank against the counter. His right hand clutched the barrel and shoved back, the handcuffs clanging in his fingers, while his left jammed the pistol in Hank's face. "Drop it!"

"I'll drop you," Hank said through gritted teeth, "for breaking and entering!"

"I'm Chicago P.D. You're under arrest!"

"This is Onward!"

Hank bit the barrel of the pistol, and then slammed the butt of the shotgun into Barter's groin. Barter was caught off guard. He figured Adler would surrender once he had him at point blank range. Most people would. But then again, Farmer Hank was a loose cannon and had converted his barn into a torture chamber.

Barter doubled over, swinging his pistol, and cracked Hank in the right temple. Hank swung the shotgun barrel and broke Barter's grip. The handcuffs clanked on the floor and slid out of sight. Before Barter could react, Hank clubbed him on the head with the shotgun. Barter grunted, stumbled back, and then ducked into the magazine aisle. He heard Adler reloading.

*Damn*, Barter thought. *So much for cuffing him.*

He caught his breath as the sickness subsided in his gut. His head throbbed. He thought it would have been ironic had he ended up in the pain relief aisle. Instead, he was using a rack of *Guns and Ammo* as a shield.

Hank cocked back the hammers. "So, what're you arresting me for, piggy? I ain't kidnapped any kids. I hate the whiny brats."

"Is that why you have a rack in your barn? Most farmers keep cows in there."

Hank fired. The end of the aisle exploded, missing Barter by inches, and rained shredded literature.

"That's attempted murder, Adler!"

Barter hopped up, took aim, and pulled the trigger. The first shot shattered the display case of cigarettes. The second shot hit Hank in the shoulder as he lunged to the right.

Barter stepped out. The gusting wind scattered the shards on the floor while the rain pelted his back. Adler was gone. The farmer had sought cover, though left behind a trail of blood that might as well have said "You Are Here" with a blinking arrow pointing at aisle five.

"Drop the shotgun, Adler, and come out with your hands on your head! Let's call this a day before one of us ends up dead!"

*****

Coren entered the panic room and ran his free hand through his hair, wrenching the strands on the back of his head. Well Girl #1 rocked back and forth against the wall to the left as she did spasmodic leg lifts with her mangled limbs. Each time her bruised feet slammed on the floor, she nodded, as if headbanging to a mental tune. Her sister, Well Girl #2, paced the room on her stumps, wobbling as if she was drunk, gnashing on a mouthful of hair.

Coren squeezed his eyes shut, then opened them. Had it not been for the gin, he would have been at his wits' end. He wanted to slam the door and walk away, but the cold apple reminded him of his plan.

*So, what if this girl coughs up a badge, too? What does that mean?*

He stepped forward, glanced over his shoulder. Well Girl #1 remained in her metronomic trance. He was worried she would spot the apple and lunge at him. Maybe she had her fill of cider.

His gaze darted to Well Girl #2. She failed to notice him. She continued to wobble on her stumps, her gait similar to that of a circus performer on stilts, unsteady and calculated. He wondered if he should roll the apple across the floor. He was reluctant to hand-feed her. After all, she was a kid zombie and would probably clamp her jaws on him.

His hand tensed, and he realized he was crushing the apple. He felt the sticky juice trickle between his fingers. He glanced down. Droplets splashed on the floor. The Well Twins froze. Their heads spun and jaws dropped.

*Oh no*, Coren thought, stepping back.

Well Girl #1 lurched onto her stomach and wormed toward him. Her sister staggered on her stumps, probably would have leapt if she had knees.

Coren's heart stuttered. He panicked. His first instinct was to ward them off. He turned on Well Girl #1 and swiped the apple, squirting juice in her eyes. She rolled over and howled loud enough to vibrate the steel walls. Her sister was deaf to her cries and moaned for the fruit. Coren gave her a dose of the same medicine. She clutched her eye sockets and hollered. With her lantern jaw opened wide, Coren stuffed the apple into her mouth. She snapped her blackened teeth shut like a Venus flytrap and her body trembled.

*Here we go.* Coren backed against the wall. *Now we'll really see if they're twins.*

Well Girl #2 dropped her hands from her face. Two apples pulsed in her eye sockets. Coren recoiled and banged his shoulder blades. Juices flowed from the girl's lips and cascaded down her chest. She then swallowed the fruit whole, as her sister had. It bulged in her gullet for a moment, and then slid down the hatch.

"Cough it up!"

The girl turned toward Coren and scrunched her sockets, as if squinting in bright sunlight. The apples squeezed. Coren thought she might be the first human juicer, almost grinned at the insane joke, then grimaced as the skins split and bled like fissures. Clumps of red flesh oozed from the wounds and dripped down her face, plopping on the floor.

"Jesus Christ!"

Coren looked away. He saw out of the corner of his eye that something emerged from the fruits. Two glowing points poked through the crushed openings. The apples gave birth, pushing out the gold objects. They clanged on the floor, two badges, and then melted into the hardwood.

Coren stared at the singe marks in disbelief. He was about to crouch and inspect them when the apples popped out of the girl's sockets with a squelch. They landed on the marks and exploded like rotten tomatoes.

Coren tripped over his shoes as he leaned toward the door. The girl fell flat on her face and reached for his ankles, but instead dug her nails into wood. He scrambled for the exit. He hopped over Well Girl #1, who rolled back and forth at the threshold as if she was on fire. He then slammed the door and locked the latch.

*They're twins!* He struggled to slow his heart rate. *Twins! Now what?*

"Now I need another glass of gin."

\*\*\*\*\*

Jay looked both ways before crossing the railroad tracks. There was no sign of an oncoming train, search party, or cop car. He was in the clear and relieved that he had distanced himself from Pritchard.

He wondered again why the irascible sheriff had been intent on deterring everyone from boxcar alley. Was he trying to cover up potential evidence or were the memories of his daughters unbearable? Probably the latter, though he had a hard time believing that Pritchard had a heart.

The downpour had slowed to drizzle. Jay hoped it would die altogether. He was soaked and the biting breeze racked his body with shivers. His thoughts wandered to hot cocoa, fireplaces, and tomato soup as he ascended the grassy incline. He was going to search the first yard he encountered for shelter. A shed, a deck, a doghouse, anything.

He entered the whispering woods. He knew he was headed north a couple of miles off Main Street, for the tracks ran west to east. He was bound to run into a neighborhood nestled in the knotty pines.

He paused as the grove dispersed and the trees became stunted and scattered. Withered black spruces and tamaracks replaced the firs and elms. The patchy grass faded to sphagnum and his shoes squelched with each step. Jay recognized the blooming clusters of hardhack and poison sumac.

*Oh, lovely. How'd I end up in a damn swamp?*

His gaze roved the marshy land. He considered turning back. After all, what were the chances of running across a residence on such crap property? He was probably on government acreage. He knew for a fact that wetlands were protected as if they were endangered species. He decided to walk along the outskirts in hopes of glimpsing a house.

The rattle of his last package of Reese's Pieces sparked his imagination. He should have left behind a trail. He wouldn't have been surprised if he lost his way. The more he dwelled on the thought, the more he once again saw the ridiculous parallels to E.T. He had a stash of Reese's Pieces, the cops were looking for him, and he needed a phone. An idiotic smile curled his lips as a voice croaked in his head: *J.D, phone home!*

As he trudged farther through the muck, the drone of insects and pungency of poisonous flora engulfed him. His eyes watered. His throat dried. He looked to his left. He saw that there was a greenish-yellow swamp covered in water lilies and lined with sumac in the distance. The scent of rain failed to damper nature's aroma, rather it seemed to amplify it.

Jay's head swam. His allergies flared like a rash. He sat down on a rotted tree stump and dabbed his burning eyes on his shirtsleeve. He swallowed hard, dying for an Aquafina. He blinked several times, then stared ahead wide-eyed. His blurry gaze cleared and focused on the black bank of the swamp that was still as frozen split pea soup.

His eyes narrowed. He scratched his beard. Something red fluttered in the mud. It looked like a rose petal.

No, what would roses be doing in wetlands? Maybe it was a discarded Coke can or some other trash left behind by partying teenagers, like the Blondies. The swamp would have been a perfect hideout for them. Then again, would a soda can retain its luster after fifteen years in a bog?

Jay stood and approached the bank. The swamp, its grainy film harboring insects and resonating croaks, had receded over the years. At his feet had once been the water's edge. Now the swamp ebbed five yards from the shore, providing a glimpse of its infested depths. Beetles scuttled and mayflies flitted across the sleek mud. A chunk of splintered, sodden driftwood was the playground for a trio of garter snakes.

Jay's gaze zoomed in on the red swatch. It was tattered and splotched with mud. He thought it was either a shred of curtain or shirt, both of which seemed an oddity stuck in a swamp's shore.

He crouched and reached for the fabric. He was an arm's length short, though the flies took an immediate liking to his chocolate-scented fingers. Depending on how bad he wanted to grab the cloth, he would have to step in the mud. Being a reporter and oftentimes an investigator, he yearned to extract it. It was too strange.

He stood and glanced at his shoes. The soles were caked. What did it matter at this point if they became fossilized? He stretched out his leg, plunged it in the shore. A sick squish made him grimace as his right shoe sank up to its laces. He extended his long arm and snatched at the cloth. It slipped through his fingers, rooted to the earth. Either it was long and buried deep or it was connected to something, like maybe a curtain to a rod.

*Yeah, a curtain rod. Jesus, I need a latte. Soon I'll be seeing HGTV building a damn shower stall.*

He retracted his foot, maintained his balance. He rubbed his eyes. They itched and weariness weighted his lids. He refused to let a piece of trash get the best of him. He threw his right foot forward again.

*I must be exhausted. I'm hell-bent on retrieving trash?* Jay reached for the swatch. *No. No, it's more than that. It looks like a T-shirt.*

He reached, seized the cloth, and dug his nails deep. It was anchored underground. He lunged back into a tug-of-war stance. The cloth ripped free and he landed in the mud. He looked at the swatch in his hand. It had a mud-caked button dangling by a thread. His eyes widened.

*Oh geez, there's a body buried in the swamp!*

He flipped the cloth over in his hand. Half of a tag with six bold letters was stitched in the cotton: **BOURNE**.

*Bourne?*

Jay's first thought was of *The Bourne Identity*, which was followed by a second recollection of *The Bourne Supremacy*. He stood as he felt the mud soak into his pants. He turned and walked up the shore to semi-dry land, contemplating on the cloth.

*Bourne. It's a shirt. The tag's a designer name.* Jeanette's red blouse came to mind. *Claibourne! Liz Claibourne! There's a woman buried in the mud!*

He paced the moss-covered ground, forgetting about his soiled pants for the time being. His adrenaline pumped and his hand trembled. He clutched the cloth.

*Okay, calm yourself, Jay. You don't know there's a body buried there. It could just be a shirt. Maybe somebody took a swim and left their shirt behind.* He stopped and stared at his trail of footprints. *It's a swamp! Nobody swims in a swamp!*

He recalled a story by a fellow reporter last summer. It had followed a murder mystery regarding a young woman the authorities had found anchored in an Indiana swamp. Her leg had been chained to a cinderblock and her throat had been slit. His friend's words flashed in his head like a TelePrompTer.

"She was mummified, Jay. You should've seen her. She'd maybe been in that bog six months. Of course, the methane levels are so high in standing water it snuffs out the oxygen, makes a body decay at half the normal rate. It got me thinking. The Everglades must be a goddamn burial ground."

Jay had chuckled at the time. Now it was far from a laughing matter. He had encountered the scenario firsthand. There was a mummy buried where the swamp water had once ebbed.

*You're overreacting, Jay. You have no proof that there's a grave in the mud. For all you know it could be a fossilized shirt discarded on the way to the local water hole...miles from the wetlands.*

Before he ran off searching for the nearest residence so he could call 9-1-1, he had to know for certain that the dead rotted at his feet. He hesitated as he gazed at the shoreline. If he dug up the dirt the authorities might think that he was the guilty party, assuming that there was more than a shirt to be found. He blocked his conscience. He refused to relent to his overactive imagination. He needed to find a tool to scoop up some mud pies.

He spotted the piece of driftwood. He picked it up, shook off the garter snakes, and examined it. The wood was rotted along the edges, but solid enough to break ground.

He approached the shore, planted his feet. The mud sucked at his shoes like quicksand. He wondered again if he had plummeted off the deep end, then reminded himself that his curiosity burned for satisfaction.

He stabbed the driftwood into the mud. It sank a good foot, at which point he dredged up the shore. Black soon became red. The shirt revealed itself.

At first he dug around it as he realized it was balled up. He then paused, seized the fabric, and tugged. It refused to budge.

*Okay. Time to fish it out the hard way.*

Jay plunged the makeshift shovel into the center of the bunched shirt. A *crunch* sounded and the driftwood snapped. The bright red shirt darkened to crimson, then seeped from its folds.

Jay tossed aside the broken wood. He had crushed something beneath the shirt. His initial thought was of a turtle. They often buried themselves in mud. Maybe he had pierced its shell. But why was the turtle wearing Liz Claibourne?

219

Exactly.

He crouched down and eyed the soaked fabric. It spurted discolored fluid in short streams like a broken sprinkler.

*My God, what have I done?*

He knew he should have listened to his instincts and left the shirt alone. He should have sought out the nearest house and called the police. Now what was he going to do? Bury it back up and hope the search party crossed it without a second look?

*Maybe it's just a turtle in a shirt,* his conscience reasoned. *Christ, I killed Franklin.*

The image of the cartoon character disinterred thoughts of his daughters. He was glad they were sheltered from the dark side of reporting. They often commented on the hairstyles and ties of anchors while watching the evening news. The beauty of innocence made him wonder again why he was willing to get blood on his hands.

*Because there's a body beneath that shirt!*

He reached over to a nearby bush – which he prayed wasn't poison sumac – and tore off two large leaves. He then held one in each hand and used them as if they were surgical gloves. He pulled apart the seeping folds with his index fingers and thumbs.

A yellowish-brown skull with bludgeoned snakes slithering from the sockets stared back at him. Jay shrieked, hopped up, and stumbled toward the shoreline. He doubled over and vomited on a dead shrub. He was unprepared for the moment of truth.

A body was buried in the swamp!

He ran through the wetlands with one word flashing in his head like an APB.

*Help!*

S.D. Hintz

# CHAPTER THIRTEEN

Barter trained his .38 Special on the candy aisle as he took baby steps along the blood trail. The only sound in the store was the wind howling at his back. There were no whimpers or hyperventilating. There was the storm, which seemed to be dying as the downpour weakened to drizzle, feeling like a broken showerhead on his nape.

*I know he's there, just itching to light me up like a Christmas tree. I ought to hit him from the rear of aisle four.*

"Drop yer piece, Detective."

Barter froze in mid-step toward the rack of chewing gum. The moment he had dreaded kicked him in the groin. He turned and faced the demolished entrance. He clutched his pistol as he lowered it.

Pritchard stood near the counter with his Magnum pointed at Barter's head. His Stetson was still as if superglued, unaffected by the wind. His sunglasses reflected a flash of lightning. His badge and belt buckle glinted in unison. Barter thought he looked like the Terminator.

Pritchard stepped forward. Glass crunched beneath his boot. "Drop it! Ya best start explainin' yerself. Ya got yer gun drawn and this store's shot to hell. Give me a line, Detective!"

"I have orders from Chicago P.D. to arrest Hank Adler." Barter inched back toward aisle four. He wondered where the farmer was planted. "This is my jurisdiction, Sheriff. Now I'd appreciate it if you lowered your weapon."

"I ain't lowerin' jack. Let me see yer warrant."

"No warrant. Just orders."

"Sounds like breakin' and enterin'. Looks like vandalism. Judgin' by the blood on the floor, maybe even attempted murder."

Barter brushed the butt of his gun against his pant pocket, double-checking that he had remembered to carry his cellphone. It nicked a bulge and jangled.

*Damn! Left my phone in the car. So much for backup.*

He knew the situation was on the verge of going from war zone to Armageddon. So far it seemed that Pritchard was intent on siding with Adler. He was in a stitch.

Barter felt the metal rack nudge his leg. He glanced down the aisle. It was deserted. "It's too bad your man did all this. Aside from the blood. But I guess that's why you don't shoot at an officer."

"Ya kiddin' me?" Pritchard motioned his Magnum toward the floor. "Drop yer piece and step away from the aisle. Now!"

Barter dropped his head, using the brim of his cap to conceal his eyes. Pritchard had crossed the line. He was determined to control the crime scene and cover for Adler. He was certain the psycho planned to run him out of town or jail him. Pritchard was hell-bent on a personal vendetta.

*One at a time. Pritchard first, then Adler. I can do this. One at a time.*

Barter lunged into the aisle. He glimpsed the gunfire, heard the wrench of metal. Three more shots followed. The first and second hit the floor, missing his right foot by inches. The third obliterated a Kit-Kat bar above his head and shattered a cooler on the other side of the store.

"You're under arrest, Sheriff!"

"Up yours, Chi-Town!"

Barter fired two shots, warning Pritchard to back off from the aisle. Both hit the damaged cigarette case along the wall. Cartons avalanched.

"Got ya on vandalism now!" Pritchard pocketed his sunglasses and set his hat on the counter. The situation had escalated. It was time to put the punk cop in his place. "I'd say yer under arrest, but dead men can't hear!"

Barter scrambled across littered candy bars toward the rear of the store. He felt like an open target in the aisle. He needed a shield between him and Maniac Cop.

Pritchard headed for aisle three with his Magnum pointed over his head. He towered over the racks. He glimpsed Barter's head and fired. The bullet grazed the brim of his cap. Barter rolled to the left, out of sight. He reached the end of the aisle and then dove past a cooler of Gatorade.

Another gunshot.

Pritchard was as trigger-happy as Adler was. Barter glanced back. A purple waterfall spewed from the bullet hole in the cooler.

Barter eyed aisle five. The coast was clear. He spotted the trail of blood on the opposite end. His thoughts rested on Adler for a split second. *Wherever he is, I hope he's down for the count.*

He leaned against the rack, checked his clip. Four bullets remained. He had an extra clip in his left pocket. After that, he would be empty as a siphoned six-cylinder.

"Ya might want to put those hands up now, Chi-Town."

Pritchard strolled down the aisle like a focused shopper. He didn't buy Barter's orders for arrest, but he would sell his soul the moment his Magnum tunneled through his head. *He* was the sheriff of Onward. A washed-up detective from "The Windy City" would get blown out of the water.

The glare off Pritchard's baldness spurred Barter into action. He scrambled down the row of coolers to the next aisle. He rounded the end cap and faltered, his heart rapping his rib cage.

"Bet you thought you killed me, huh?" Hank shoved the shotgun into Barter's jaw. A dark bloodstain hooked from his shoulder to his chest. "Now toss that popgun before I blow off your head."

Barter threw his gun backwards.

Hank's eyes strayed from his target. "Paul! I got the bast-"

Barter saw his chance and took it. He seized the shotgun barrels and yanked. Hank refused to let go and was propelled into him. Barter hit him like a football player, flipping him end over end. The shotgun banged into the rack of paper towels and Hank's upside down body smashed into a cooler of milk. Glass rained down and cartons toppled as he crumpled on the floor, looking as if he was frozen in a failed headstand.

Barter grabbed the shotgun and posted up, scooting back a few feet as he ducked.

Pritchard's boots crunched shards as he stepped into the row of coolers. He hesitated when he spotted Hank with the lower half of his body propped in the shattered door. Then his eagle eyes zoomed in on the handgun laying a yard from his twitching jaw.

Hank winced and gritted his teeth. Sledgehammers of pain pounded his spine. "Paul. Uhhh."

Pritchard reached down for Barter's piece. A blast deafened his ears and threw him back. At first he thought he stepped on a landmine, as insane as that sounded. Then he saw the blood spurting from his wrist.

*My hand!*

"*I'll kill ya, Barter!*" Pritchard bellowed, stumbling back into the nearest aisle. He crouched and roved the racks. Jolly Ranchers and Chex Mix surrounded him. He set his Magnum on the floor beside the puddle of blood that rippled from the steady drip. He then undid his tie and pulled it off. He braced the silk against his chest as he wrapped it around his stump. After what seemed like an hour, he made a simple knot and tightened it until it felt as if the fabric might tear. He gritted his teeth as the tie clip dug into his wound. "*Yer dead!*"

Barter almost dropped the shotgun, but then realized that he would be unarmed. He looked at Adler. The farmer was covered in glass and glared teary-eyed. He shifted and his body toppled onto the floor. He groaned and cursed as he strained to push himself up.

Barter spun the shotgun around and held it by the barrels. He then swung it and cracked Hank on the back of the head. The farmer's face smashed into the floor and his body went limp.

*One down, one to go.* Barter turned and hurried down the aisle, ducking beneath the top shelves. *Now all I need is my handcuffs.*

Pritchard stood, clutching the Magnum. His body trembled. His nostrils flared and his eyes bulged. Another cop had shot off his hand. The pain was a pinprick. His anger was an inferno. No one had ever harmed him in such a way. Cop or no cop, he was going to beat the living daylights out of Barter. Maybe he would shoot his kneecaps, then stomp him until he bled from his eyes.

He poked his head into the row of coolers. Hank was facedown in a pool of blood. Pritchard couldn't tell if he was dead or out cold. So much for his backup. He should have known the trigger-happy farmer couldn't hit the broad side of a barn.

He peered over the racks. There was no sign of Barter. He was probably slithering down an aisle like the snake that he was.

*"Yer dead Barter! Ya hear me?"* Pritchard fired the Magnum. A flickering neon sign exploded and rained sparks on the other side of the store. *"That's gonna be yer face!"*

Pritchard lowered his voice to a mutter as Hank's eyelids fluttered. "Find a piece. Yer gonna need it."

Hank nodded. He pushed himself up and leaned against the shattered cooler, groaning as the shards cut his hands.

Barter ducked beneath the sparking neon sign and found himself in the back room. There were two doors. Both were locked. He was cornered.

He gazed across the store. The floor was strewn with glass and smeared with blood. The rain had stopped, but the wind rattled the racks and plastic sale signs. *Maybe I can make a mad dash to the car and call for backup.*

He stroked his mustache as he focused on the ends of the aisles. Then he spotted it, a sliver of silver poking from beneath a rack.

*The handcuffs!*

At this point, he wondered if they were necessary. Pritchard had one hand while Adler was unconscious. It seemed like a fool's errand to make an attempt at recovering them. But what other plan did he have? He was against killing anyone unless forced to.

*Run for it! This situation's out of control. You don't want to admit you need backup.*

His conscience was right. He was a veteran officer and refused to look as if he couldn't contain a crime scene. On the flip side, his back was against the wall. He had to make a run for the entrance.

He scanned the aisles, hoping for a glimpse of Pritchard. The only movement he noticed were the rocking Ruffles bags and Borox boxes.

He stared ahead. The distance from the back room to the storefront was equivalent to a shuttle run. Although instead of grabbing an eraser during his sprint, he would snatch up the handcuffs.

He slung the shotgun over his shoulder, stole a last look at the aisles. The coast was clear. The wind threatened to blow off his cap. He ducked and ran for the doors. He imagined a starting gun firing and almost grinned at the ridiculousness of it.

Concrete popped to his left. No, it wasn't his imagination. He turned his head and saw Pritchard with his gun, aiming through the racks like a sniper in bushes.

Barter ducked even lower, but failed to sidestep the blood trail in the middle of the floor. His shoes slipped and he fell face first. Glass nicked his shirt as he slid a good yard and smeared red as if there was a ketchup spill near Aisle 5.

He clambered on his knees, clutching the shotgun barrels.

*Should've left the loafers at home.*

More shots fired, warning him to lay low. He heard two bullets ricochet and a third shatter glass followed by an electrical crackle. He guessed the hotdog machine had been grilled.

He crawled on his hands and knees toward the counter, wincing as shards pierced his palms. He was maybe five yards from the doors. Once out of the store, he'd hotfoot it to the car and dig out the first weapon he laid eyes on.

A flash of white caught his periphery. A cart plumb full of Wonder bread slammed into the counter, blocking the doors.

Barter jolted. He assumed that Pritchard was down Aisle 1. Like any experienced cop, he had sealed the premises. He knew it was time to hop to his feet and exit the building. A two-pound cart wasn't going to stand in his way. He leapt up.

"Screw you, stink hole!"

Hank lurched out of Aisle 1 covered in blood, armed with two 409 spray guns. He poised as if they were six-shooters and pulled the triggers, launching dual streams at Barter's face. Barter flailed the shotgun, but missed and knocked over the bakery cart.

Cleaning solution blinded him. He cried out and swung the twelve-gauge with a vengeance, looking like a blindfolded child trying to split a piñata. Hank stepped too close and the butt cracked him in the jaw. He staggered into Aisle 1 and crashed into the shelves.

Barter squeezed his eyes shut. They felt as if they were going to explode. His vision was a blur and his surroundings faded in and out like a home movie. He heard Adler holler, followed by a crash, but he couldn't discern where the front doors were. He paused as he felt the cool wind on his left cheek.

The moment he turned toward the exit a gunshot rang out. He hit the floor, uncertain of Pritchard's location. He rubbed his eyes on his jacket sleeve. Clarity seeped in. He saw the toppled cart smack-dab before him lodged across the shattered left door. He grabbed the wheels and shoved it outside.

He glanced back. Pritchard emerged from Aisle 4 with his Magnum trained as his stump trickled blood. Hank stumbled out of Aisle 1 with a box of matches and a single 409 gun. The farmer removed a match and struck it. He then held it before the spray gun.

Pritchard waved the Magnum left and right, as if determining which one of Barter's limbs to shoot. "What now, Chi-Town? Ya got yerself an empty twelve-gauge. I oughta blow off yer fingers for pointin' 'em."

"The FBI's on their way."

Barter inched backward. Broken glass in the door poked his spine. He tilted his head back and gazed at the sliver of slate sky as dread washed over him. He knew Pritchard had no intention of arresting him. And Adler didn't plan on saving the hotdogs with his makeshift flamethrower. He should have insisted on backup.

Pritchard pulled the trigger. The bullet ripped through Barter's right bicep. He fired a last shot. It deafened Barter's cries and exploded in the same bicep, severing his arm and spraying blood across the front of the counter. He then stepped back and nodded.

Hank let loose a stream of 409 through the flickering flame and turned the household cleaner into a blowtorch. Barter screamed and writhed. Pritchard turned and headed toward the rear of the store for the extinguisher. Hank was caught up in the moment, his eyes red and glowing like embers, careless as to whether or not his store ignited.

When Pritchard returned with his gun holstered, the extinguisher in the crook of his arm, and the hose in his good hand,

Barter was unrecognizable. The skin on his face had been melted off and his body was scorched. Had he not fired the extinguisher at Hank, the psychotic farmer would have seared the detective to ashes while his business burnt to the ground. He was glad there was no one nearby to hear the cop's screams.

*****

*Burl Nelson cranked the volume as The Safari's* Image of a *Girl crackled through the airwaves. He regarded the flatbed. The herbicide he had bought in Springfield had yet to tip over and spill on the burlap. Of course, wait until he traveled another mile and reached the uneven roads of Onward. The number of potholes made one wonder if the town had been built on a minefield. He was determined to avoid the bumps today. Last week he spent an hour sweeping the mess off the tailgate. It irked him to think how much money he had lost due to his carelessness.*

*He slowed the pickup as he passed the city limit sign on Main Street. The truck jolted and lurched. The one pothole he intended on missing seemed to have eroded since he last drove that stretch of road. He looked through the smudged back window. Both containers of herbicide had spilled open.*

*Burl pounded on the steering wheel. "Dammit! Every single time!"*

*He pushed up his taped glasses and returned his attention to the road. He was a half-mile from the railroad tracks, as if that mattered. He had hit one bump and dumped his entire product. There was no point in driving at street sweeper speed anymore. The damage was done. He shook his head, cursing until his dentures loosened.*

*His gaze veered off the road. The Blondies were crossing the tracks. They appeared to be in a heated exchange, all of their faces twisted in scowls. He was used to seeing those mischievous grins, the ones that said 'We're better than you and if you mock us we'll kill you.' He also noticed that they were in a hurry, the fat one especially, waddling faster than a frightened duck.*

What are they up to now?

*Burl decelerated as anger bubbled in his brain. Flashbacks from two weeks ago tortured him. He caressed the scar on his chin. He wished he had his pruner on him. He'd hop out and snip the fat girl's ears off.*

*The triplets disappeared into boxcar alley as the pickup rattled across the railroad ties. Burl yearned to drive down the tracks and run them over. It was too bad they were the sheriff's daughters. Otherwise he might get away with vehicular homicide.*

*He shook his head and cursed, straining to shove the bullies and their antics to the back of his mind. He had more important things to dwell on, such as cleaning the potent mess in his flatbed. His arthritis was going to love that.*

*As Railroad Street passed by on his right, he regarded the tree line of willows that dangled over the weedy downgrade. He always thought them strange, as the rest of the town was dotted with elms, oaks, and maples.*

*His gaze traced the ditch. A snapshot of a glistening glare made him ease off the gas pedal. He slammed on the brake as he realized what he stared at. His seatbelt seized him. The herbicide scuttled across the flatbed and the containers slammed into the tailgate. He undid his belt, hopped out of the cab, and rounded the bug-splattered grill.*

*He approached the edge of the ditch, and then froze. He clutched the tip of his beard and yanked out a fistful of hair.*

*"Oh, Christ, no."*

*A young girl lied on her back. Her legs were splayed in the tall grass while her head and torso were half-buried in the sewage at the bottom. Even worse, she was naked. Her forehead trickled blood down her cheeks, as did her swollen nose. Bent dandelions shivered between her armpits. Burl looked back to her slack face.*

Oh no. No, no, not the Heller girl.

*That's who she was. He had seen her the other day with her father Dean, the town drunk. He recalled that it had been early Sunday morning and Dean was on a wake and slake. The wiry, red-eyed man was dragging his daughter along the sidewalk. At first he thought that they were holding hands, but then saw that Dean clutched Francine by the wrist. He had then stopped before Burl, who was weeding his front garden, and gestured at his daughter. She approached him and asked for a bag of apples while her father turned his back and gazed at the empty street. He remembered thinking how worthless the man was and how he probably backhanded his daughter twice a week.*

*Burl ran down the ditch. The girl looked dead. Flies buzzed around her face and landed on her abdomen. Ants crawled up her forearms. He crouched and lifted her head out of the sewage.*

*"Hey!" He pinched her nostrils. She hacked and her eyes fluttered. "Hey now. C'mon. Let's get you out of there."*

*Francine came to and her eyes dazed, then focused on Burl. She moaned as he repositioned her on the incline, laying her on dry land. He then brushed the flies and ants off her skin.*

*Francine shrieked when she realized that she was naked. She looked at Burl, terrified, certain he had stripped her and was about to force himself on her.*

*"Hey! Calm down!" Burl unbuttoned his plaid. Francine squirmed and attempted to crawl up the ditch. "Christ, girl, where are you going? Here. Put this on."*

*He grabbed her by the arm and rolled her onto her back. He handed her the shirt. She sat up, groaned, and then snatched the plaid from him. She covered herself up.*

*"Did the Blondies do this to you?" Francine met Burl's gaze, then glanced back to the woods. "Hey, talk to me! Did they do this to you?"*

*Francine nodded. She and Burl looked up the ditch at the crunch of gravel and screech of brakes. Burl was certain it was Pritchard geared up to slap him with a minor infraction like driving on the shoulder or neglecting to use his flashers. Instead it was a sky blue pickup with off-white doors. The rumbling engine died and Hank Adler appeared at the top of the ditch, his stringy hair fluttering in the wind on all compass points.*

"You lose another lug nut again, Nelson?" He squinted, then his eyes widened. "Oh, goddamn, what the hell happened here?"

Burl eased Francine to a sitting position. "Help me bring her up, Hank. Sounds like she had a run-in with the triplets."

"Pritchard's girls? Again? That's twice in one day. Girl was over at my farm today washing barb cuts." Hank walked down the ditch and crouched before Francine. Anger twisted his haggard face. "Did they do this to you?"

Francine nodded, then winced and clutched her head. She groaned as tears spilled down her cheeks.

Burl grabbed her left bicep while Hank grabbed the right. "Let's haul her into my cab. We need to get her back to her folks."

"Her folks?" Hank shook his head while they turned Francine around and helped her walk up the ditch. "Dean will probably give her another beating."

"No." Francine struggled in their grip and leaned back. The gray-haired friends planted their feet and urged her forward, grunting. "No, not my folks. Don't bring me back there like this. Please, don't."

Hank felt as if he was dragging a stubborn sow. "You need clothes, girl. You're not decent. You want those bullies' father to come by and cite you?"

"I need my clothes! Where are my clothes? Let me go!"

Francine broke free, ran down the ditch, and hopped over the sewage. She then stumbled up the other side and disappeared into the woods.

Burl tugged his beard. "What got into her?"

"Probably her father." Hank grinned, but then went straight-faced when Burl shot him a glare. "Hey, she's wearing your shirt. I reckon Dean would be pissed if he saw her right now."

"I don't know about you, Hank, but I've had enough of these triplets. I'm this close to tying them to the train tracks."

\*\*\*\*\*

Coren topped off a tumbler with Seagram's, then held up the bottle and swayed it. A few shots worth sloshed against the glass. That wasn't going to get him through the night. He needed a liquor store like a clown needed face paint. He would go crazy if he had to deal with the kid zombies sober, if he was not crazy already.

He leaned against the counter and stared across the kitchen. His laptop sat neglected, who knew for how much longer. At the rate madness coursed through the house, he might never get back to business as usual.

His gaze settled on the kitchen table. It was a mess, which was surprising seeing how he had eaten little since the ordeal. Three-day-old crumbs and coffee cups were scattered across crumpled junk mail and unread bills. He lacked the ambition to clean house. What was the point? He could sanitize the place from wall to wall only to have Hurricane Pritchard make another house call.

*Unreal. I've got the Doublemint twins in the panic room rotting away. I should've let Deb see them. That would've scared her. Of course, she would've run to the police and I'd be locked in a padded cell.*

That thought raised another question. How was he going to get them out of the house? He had to haul them to his Suburban and drive to Boxcar Alley. Maybe he could drape a sheet over them and carry them out. No, that seemed too obvious. Pritchard was more than likely staking out his house.

He wondered if there was a trail to the train tracks behind his backyard. It was possible. At least then he could haul them both in a wheelbarrow through the wetlands without anyone seeing. It was a maniacal idea and would be painstaking, but he would give it the old college try if it meant getting the twin freaks out of his sight.

He walked to the deck door as he sipped his gin. He gazed across the lawn. It was undisturbed, as if nothing had crawled out. The well was intact and the ground near the hunk of scrap metal was solid. He squeezed his eyes shut.

*What does it mean? I've been hitting the gin too hard? What is it? It's like it's happening, but it's not. Man, I need to get away from this place.*

He opened his eyes. They blurred for a moment, and then focused. At first, he thought a sunspot had distorted his vision, as he had experienced many times on waking from a deep sleep. He narrowed his gaze.

Someone was climbing over the worm fence.

He killed the last swig of gin, slammed the tumbler on the table. He opened the door and let it hit the end of its track. A red-haired man with a matching beard stumbled over the rails. He landed on his hands and knees a yard short of the scrap metal.

Coren rushed onto the deck. He watched the man scramble to his feet. His tense muscles slackened as he saw what lumbered from the wetlands behind the fence.

*****

Jay's hopes had soared when he spotted the fence at the edge of the wetlands. He knew it was his salvation, that there was a homestead within sprinting distance. His brain spun around one thought: Chicago P.D. Once he found a telephone, he would call them and point them in the direction of the body. He was uncertain what it had to do with the kidnappings, but it had to be connected. There were no coincidences in the news world. There were links, motives, and alibis. Maybe the person buried in the swamp was an accomplice of the kidnapper, who had crossed the maniac and paid the price. He sure wished he had a camera.

He scanned the unkempt yard as he stumbled forth. He was positive it was a hermit's house. Everything was neglected, from the dug up lawn to the faded siding. He looked ahead. A man, who he supposed was the owner, stepped onto the deck. He stared at Jay as if mankind was an anomaly.

*Just my luck, a hermit who probably doesn't even own a phone, let alone a mower and sprinkler.*

Jay's thought processes stuttered. Should he avoid explaining himself and ask to use the phone? Should he say there was a dead body in the swamp? Was the man going to think he was trespassing since he came barreling out of the wetlands?

"I need a phone!" Jay panted as the bleary-eyed man ran down the steps. "I need to use your phone! It's an emergency!"

"In the house!" The man barged past Jay as if he was invisible. *"Get in the goddamn house!"*

# CHAPTER FOURTEEN

Hank glared at the mess before the front door. It was worse than a hog slaughter. There was a pool of blood with clumps of flesh that expanded the more Barter's blackened corpse settled against the counter. He held a grudge against guilt trips, though. The pig had shot him and deserved the fate he suffered.

"Got a mop?" Pritchard grabbed Hank's blowtorch and lit a Marlboro off the small blue flame. He grimaced at Barter's body and regarded the farmer's scowl.

"I ain't got a bucket big enough for that slop. You got a body bag in your trunk?"

"Do I look like a coroner? Yer gonna figure somethin' out, now aren't ya, Hank? I'd hate to have to charge ya with manslaughter."

"For that nutjob? He had it coming! He shot your hand off, Paul!"

"I subdued a loose cannon. You let loose on him. Now ya got a mess to clean up. Ya best bury it somewhere I'll never know 'bout. Ya hear me?"

"And what about the Chicago P.D.? Them and the FBI will be down here before you can snap."

"Guess ya better find a good hidin' spot then."

"Screw you."

"'Scuse me?" Pritchard dropped the blowtorch and blew smoke into Hank's face. "Don't cross me, Hank. Ya got yer fingerprints all over those three badges, too, don't ya? Damn right ya do. Ya owe me." He reached up with his one hand and tipped his Stetson. "If this ain't clear by sunset, I'll be lookin' for ya. I got me a wound to dress, otherwise we'll have more questions than a cracked out reporter."

Pritchard shoved the double doors. Glass fell and clinked. He walked to Barter's Buick and peered inside. The keys dangled in the ignition. The detective must have planned on his suspect high-tailing it.

He opened the driver's side door, sat behind the wheel, and started the engine. He then pulled away from the Texaco as Barter's cellphone sang on the passenger's seat.

\*\*\*\*\*

*Hank and Burl bit their tongues as Francine hopped off the tailgate and approached them.*

*"I should probably go home now."*

*The last thing she wanted to do was face her father, but it was inevitable. Regardless of her new cuts and bruises, she would have to walk into that house and pretend as if nothing happened. If she pointed any fingers or complained, she would be chastised for not standing tall. That was her father's mentality, more so when he was drunk, which was sixteen hours out of the day; the other eight he was asleep.*

*Burl twisted the tip of his beard as he regarded Francine. The poor girl was a mess. He could tell that she was sick of her daily run-ins with the bullies. "Listen, Franny. You're almost graduated, right?"*

*Francine nodded. "Next year."*

*"Tough it out. Next year you can get away from this place, go to college or something."*

*Francine dabbed her tears. "My dad doesn't want me going anywhere, Mr. Nelson. I'm stuck in this town dealing with this crap."*

*Hank scratched his stubble as he gnawed on a toothpick.
"Look here, Franny. We'll teach 'em. You need to enjoy your childhood."*

*Burl raised his bushy brows. "Nobody's teaching anybody a lesson. Revenge won't solve anything."*

*"Right. That's why you booby-trap the orchard, huh? Ain't no way they're getting away with this. Their daddy says so."*

*Francine crinkled her forehead. "Will you take me home now?"*

\*\*\*\*\*

Coren had no idea who the red-haired, Ron Howard look-alike was, but he knew that he was alive. After all, the only zombies that had been digging out of his yard were blond teenaged girls. What vexed him was the fact that the man stopped and stared at him as if he was crazy, as if there wasn't a dead girl on his heels.

He glanced over his shoulder. The man's sights locked on the open deck door and he ran for it.

Coren stopped in his tracks five yards short of the wetlands. He knew then and there that he needed another shot of gin. An obese, naked girl clambered over the fence. Her blond head dangled upside down by her blackened carotids, resting between her flabby, scarred breasts. Barbed wire bound her hands behind her back and her eyes fluttered each time her head bounced around like a tetherball. The rotted rails collapsed beneath her weight and she landed atop the woodpile.

*Holy Jesus!*

Coren watched the girl wriggle across the splintered posts onto his lawn. Her head was lodged between her chest and the ground, muffling hoarse screams. She rolled onto her back. Her head swung and landed between her thighs.

Coren spun and sprinted. He stomped up the deck steps, lunged inside the house, and slammed the door.

"That one's not getting in! No way!"

Jay stepped into the kitchen. He stared at Coren. The guy was in a panic. He wouldn't stop jerking his head, as if he was searching for an escape route or a weapon for self-defense. "What's wrong with your phone?"

"Pritchard cut the lines, that's what!"

"Pritchard's been here?"

"He's staking the place out!"

"Are you serious? Well, then do you have a cellphone?"

"Does this look like a Radio Shack?" Coren propped the 2x4 between the wall and deck door. He could see the fat zombie struggling to sit up.

"Can I use your laptop?" Jay was beyond frustrated. His face had flushed to his hair color. The guy was a raving lunatic and must not have heard him outside shouting for help. "Maybe I can send an email. Listen, buddy, it's an emergency!"

"The phone lines are down!" Coren was beside himself. He was on the verge of throwing the nutcase out of his house. How was an email going to stop the undead from chasing him? "It's frigging dial-up!"

Jay shook his head. "You got to be kidding me."

"Hand me that bottle."

Jay turned and spotted the near-empty liter on the counter. He sighed and handed it to Coren, who unscrewed the cap and killed the last three shots of gin.

"Hey!" Jay slammed his fist on the kitchen table. Coren lowered the bottle and regarded him, bleary-eyed. "There's a body buried in your backyard! I need to get a hold of the Chicago P.D."

"What are you blind? That body chased you into my backyard. The fatty's probably looking for her sisters."

"*What?*"

"There, you moron!" Coren pressed his forefinger against the glass. The decapitated corpse stumbled toward the house as her head swayed like a wrecking ball. "That dead girl you resurrected out of the swamp!"

"Wait! How do you know there's a body buried back there?"

"You're the one whose been dragging her like she's tied to your shoes!"

"Okay, okay. Calm down for a second. What are you talking about?"

Coren saw the fat girl clutch the deck railing out of the corner of his eye. He approached Jay and stood in his face. "I don't know who you are, but you led a dead naked fat girl to my house and calling Pritchard isn't going to save the day."

Jay shook his head, which swam as if a migraine was coming on. He wished he had chosen another house. This guy was drunk out of his mind and hallucinating. Or maybe he was straining to get a point across, speaking in metaphors or something. It sounded as if he was well aware that there was a body buried in the swamp. So was he angry that his secret had been uncovered?

"Listen. Yeah, I know there's a body buried in the swamp. And no, I don't want to call Pritchard; I want to call someone who isn't going to body slam me. Now how do you know there's a body back there?"

"She's standing right there!" Coren pointed the bottle at the deck door, and then hurled it. It shattered glass against glass. "She's naked, she's fat, and her head's dangling from her neck! Do I need to sketch it out for you?"

"I guess so, cause the only thing I see is your reflection."

Coren stared at the zombie on the other side of the glass. He felt as if he had been punched in the face with brass knuckles. His throat constricted. He staggered, grabbed the table, then backed up and sat down on the desk chair.

He regarded the red-bearded stranger. Was he that hammered that he was hallucinating? No way. It wasn't as if he was drinking liquid heroin. But how was it that he knew about a girl being buried, yet he failed to see her climb out of the grave?

A *thud* made Coren's head snap left. The mutilated fat girl swung her carotids and slammed her head like a mace against the smeared glass. The sound was sickening – slapping flesh and crunching bone.

Coren looked to Jay and gestured over his shoulder. "You don't see that?"

Jay shook his head. Their disjointed conversation had him agitated. "See what? Your crappy lawn?"

Coren stood and seized Jay by his jacket sleeve. He tugged him as he strode into the living room.

"Hey!" Jay wrenched back, but Coren had his nails buried into the leather. "What the hell's your problem?"

"Follow me. Do you want to hold hands?"

Jay relented and trailed after Coren down the hall. He was convinced the guy was slamming more than gin. But boy was the whole experience going to make a killer story!

Coren stopped and outstretched his arm against the wall. Jay cursed as he was nearly clotheslined. Coren reached into the wall and yanked. The door opened and Jay's jaw dropped.

*****

The flatbed of Hank's two-tone pickup acquired a third hue as Barter's bodily fluids leaked like motor oil. It was hard to believe that the corpse had once been a man who had shot at him an hour ago. Now the detective was nothing more than scorched rags and melted flesh. His skin had dripped off and left a puddle on the tailgate when Hank had heaved him in.

Hank yanked a handkerchief from his back pocket, sopped up the gooey mess on the tailgate, and then tucked the rag beneath one of the many bags of apples. He slammed the door and hopped into the cab.

*The nerve of that stink hole leaving me the dirty work. Like I got nothing better to do than bury a homicide detective.*

At first he considered bringing Barter to the old Hodge place, then remembered that someone had moved in last week. He racked his brain for a good minute before settling on his barn. He figured it was the most inconspicuous place. He could remove some floorboards in one of the stalls and dig a grave there. Then when all was said and done he could cover it with hay bales.

He frowned at the thought. He knew that once he disposed of the body he would have to find a storage space for his torture collection. It would be a dead giveaway if a cop ever stumbled on it.

He turned the ignition and sighed. He knew the day would come when he would have to pack up his toys. He wondered, though, if he might have to use them one more time before the storm passed.

*****

Pritchard killed Sinatra's croon and answered the call on speakerphone.

"Frank?"

"This is Paul Pritchard. Who's this?"

"Ah, Sheriff. Robert Dalton, Chicago Police Chief. How's Onward holding up?"

"Like the Tower of Pisa."

Dalton chuckled. "Does that mean Detective Barter's giving you a hard time? I'm sure he appreciates your secretarial experience."

Pritchard fumed, but maintained his cool. He knew that if he blew his top the FBI would be flooding the streets. He was surprised they hadn't been involved on day one. He guessed it was due to the nation being on Orange Alert, and kidnappings fell short of terrorist threats.

"Actually, Barter's got me chauffeurin' him round town. He's shoppin' in the Texaco right now."

"Have him call me when he gets back. So, what's the word? Any new leads?"

"Shouldn't ya ask yer man that question? He's the detective."

"All of my officers do their fair share of investigating, Sheriff. Maybe you should, too, instead of taking phone calls. You know the townspeople better than anyone else does. You must have a few names in my mind."

"I've got one or two. It's all circumstantial though."

"Circumstantial or not, those suspects need to be interrogated. Three babies are missing in *your* town. Right now, you're just as high on our suspect list."

"Those babies ain't whinin' in my backseat! They're probably miles from here, but I'll be goddamned if I don't nail my man!"

"You tell Barter to call me."

Pritchard ended the conversation. He pocketed the cellphone as he drove the LeSabre down the train tracks. He was pleased the Chicago P.D. had their hands full. The last thing he needed was a stakeout on his every move.

Dalton made a valid point though. It was time to step up his interrogation. The Barter incident had sidetracked him. Coren Raines had been neglected. He didn't care if the newbie was innocent; he was going down for the kidnappings. He might even dig up a few corpses to slap him with murder charges. No, that was crossing the line. FBI and DNA would get involved, two acronyms he didn't want to mess with. He would play it safe and force a confession out of him first.

Pritchard parked the LeSabre between two boxcars. He knew the search party was done snooping around the train tracks, so it was the best spot that he could think of to stash the car. He wasn't keen on driving it any farther either, for fear of being seen by reporters and arousing suspicion. He left the keys in the ignition, slammed down all of the locks, and then stepped out.

*Damn Buick oughta go up in flames like Barter.* He shut the driver's side door and headed toward the woods. *Figure that one out, Dalton.*

S.D. Hintz

# CHAPTER FIFTEEN

Jay gaped as he stuck his head through the opening. A citric pungency hit him like a tidal wave. He stepped back and blinked. It stank as if someone had doused the room with apple cider.

He grimaced as Coren barged past him. "A panic room? What have you been doing in here?"

"Me? Look at them!" Coren pointed at the wall to Jay's immediate left, spun, and then gestured toward the window. "*Look at them!*"

Jay stepped into the room and shook his head. He dropped his crossed arms, flexed his palms. The farther the eccentric guy led him into his world, the more he wished he had his camcorder. He had more stories than the Bible brewing in his head for WNDY. He still could not believe that he stood in a panic room.

"What do you mean *them*?" Jay scanned his steel surroundings. There were rotten remnants of apples splattered on the floor, most covered in fruit flies. Piles of cardboard boxes littered the corners. "The walls? The mess you haven't cleaned up in days? I don't see a *phone* anywhere."

"Forget the phone!" Coren kicked the wall beneath the window. The twin girls were unresponsive. The one with twisted legs and barbed wire scars twitched on her back to the left of the doorway; the stumpy one inched across the room on Coren's right, her tongue lashing out as if she intended on snatching up some fruit flies. *"See this? It's a panic room! See them? They're dead! And I've been hiding them in here so Pritchard doesn't find them!"*

"Listen, I don't have time for this. I need a phone. *A phone.* And you need to sober up, buddy."

Jay turned to leave. Coren lunged and seized him by his sleeve. He yanked him around, and then shoved him down. Jay landed in a pile of boxes.

"Hey!" Jay glanced right and left. He considered heaving a box. "What is your problem?"

Coren gestured with both hands, resembling a frustrated traffic cop. "Look at them! Are you blind? Or am I the only one that can see them? There's no way I'm that crazy!"

"You're *that* crazy! There's no one else in here! So what are you pointing at?"

Coren froze as a cold dread drenched his bones. The redhead's quavering words burrowed in his head like a tumor. He shook his head. That was impossible. The dead girls were right there before his eyes. He had even dragged them out of their wells. The guy was putting him on. He had to be. Or had he drank one too many tumblers of gin, which in turn gave him disturbing hallucinations?

*It's not the gin! And I'm not hallucinating! I picked them up with my hands! I fed them apples and they swallowed them whole!*

"I'm pointing at the dead twin blonds." Coren gulped. He knew he sounded like a madman. Was this what happened to people that spent day in and day out on the Internet? He was beginning to wonder if it was all those flash banners he clicked on. Maybe they had triggered a subtle brain seizure. He was going crazy. "I pulled them out of my backyard. Now there's another one on the deck. It's probably another sister. Ah, Jesus, they're triplets!"

"What did you say?" Jay kicked the boxes at his feet and stood. "What did you just say?"

"The fat blond bimbo that chased you! She's their sister!" Coren pointed again while Jay tugged hard at his beard. "I knew it! The whole family's coming for dinner!"

"Christ, would you calm down?"

Coren balled his fists. He wanted to knock out Opie's teeth and make him choke on the molars. *Calm down?* There were kid zombies sprouting out of his yard like dandelions. Triplets at that.

Realization struck him cold and he paled. The Tribune headline glowed like a neon sign in his mind's eye.

**Six-month-old triplets kidnapped, bloodied**

Triplets had been kidnapped, now triplets sought him out. But the abducted children had been six-months-old, not teenagers. How did that make sense?

"Triplets. Blond triplets."

Jay began to piece the puzzle. "Wait a minute. What do you know about the triplets?"

Coren shook his head, dumbfounded. "They were twins, now they're triplets. But they're teenagers." He looked to Jay for an answer, glassy-eyed. "The dead girls in my house are triplets."

It was Jay's turn to lose skin color. He felt as if it drained straight to the floor. He swallowed hard. "Where are they?"

Coren snapped out of his trance. "They're dead. And you can't see them."

"Show me where they are. Show me, dammit!"

"They're dead! I can see them and you can't! How many people are in this room?"

"Counting your hallucinations?"

"You can't see them!"

"Four."

"You counted yourself three times!"

Coren stormed to the sliding door, flung it open, and then slammed it behind him. Jay stood rooted to the box pile and collected his thoughts. Despite the cider haze and burning orifices, he soon grasped wisps of clarity. For choosing a random residence with a headcase, the oddities seemed to parallel. He was convinced the disappearance of the Blondies fifteen years ago had something to do with the recent kidnappings. Now here he was in a stranger's presence that admitted to having dead triplets in his house. And to think that he had asked him where they were, as if the madman would tell him.

*But they're teenagers.*

The guy's comment rang in Jay's ears. Did that mean he wasn't hiding the babies in his house? Was it possible he had gone on a kidnapping spree and snatched up another set of triplets?

He needed to involve the cops. But who could he trust? Pritchard? Barter? Neither gave him the warm fuzzy feeling. He wished more than ever that he was covering yet another news story. But it was more than that. He felt as if the events were unfolding around him.

"Get out of here!" The shouts broke Jay's concentration. He crossed the panic room and opened the door.

\*\*\*\*\*

*As Francine stepped off the school grounds, the previous day's goings-on blinded her like winter sunrise. She saw herself sitting naked on the ditch embankment, vulnerable, trembling, asking herself why the Blondies would do such a thing to her. It was beyond humiliation. They had dumped her in a ditch and left her for dead. She knew that next time they would bury her. Their hatred for her had multiplied tenfold like a plague.*

*A halo of ache surrounded her head. Her mother had given her three Tylenol that morning and warned her that if she visited the nurse's office she would be grounded for a month. Her father had slapped her for being weak after she explained what had happened. He then threatened her with a lashing if she told anyone that the sheriff's daughters had harmed her.*

*She hated her father. She hated her mother even more for not standing up for her. They were both terrified of Sheriff Pritchard. Ever since the time her father rear-ended his cop car while driving drunk, they were deaf to her pleas of bullying. She tried her hardest to swallow the sobs and bury the Blondies in her subconscious, reminding herself over and over that she needed to be strong. Strong like her father, not weak like her mother.*

*She gazed at Railroad Street. It would be a long two and a half blocks. She hoped the Blondies would follow her. She had glimpsed them lurking near the entrance, probably having skipped their last class. She pretended not to see them as she passed the two school buses and left the grounds.*

*She glanced down East Walnut Street when she reached the corner. She spotted her house in the distance. She had the overwhelming urge to sprint there and lock the door behind her. She didn't fancy getting the shit beat out of her twice in two days.*

*She looked over her shoulder. The Blondies walked side by side a block back. Henna pulled a wrench out of her pocket. As if on cue, Loren and Sylvia withdrew screwdrivers.*

*Francine broke into a sweat. For a moment, dizziness clouded her. She bit her lip, blinked her eyes hard, and focused on the sidewalk. She bottled her fear like a firefly. It was pointless to worry. She had been through this before, the difference being that she was the cat and they were the mice. On that thought, she found strength and walked faster.*

*Henna slapped the wrench in her hand. "You might wanna start runnin', Smeller! I'm gonna kill ya this time!"*

*Francine was nearing Main Street. Her plan was to lead the Blondies through town and down the alley by Kate's Bakery. She had a good distance left to travel.*

*Loren sneered as her sisters chuckled. "Hope you're ready to get stabbed!"*

*Francine turned the corner onto Main Street and paused as she was hit with a brainstorm. She slipped off her backpack, unzipped it, and then whipped it at the Blondies.*

*"You can have my backpack, you pigs!"*

*Francine dashed toward downtown as her schoolbooks pummeled the triplets. Her Trapper Keeper knocked Henna's wrench into the street. Her lunchbox slammed into the side of Sylvia's head while her algebra homework landed at Loren's feet.*

*Unharmed, Loren pursued her as her sisters staggered and regained themselves.*

*"You're dead, Smeller!"*

\*\*\*\*\*

Hank unlocked and opened the barn doors. He then hopped into the cab and backed up the truck. Once the flatbed was inside, he killed the engine, and then dropped the tailgate.

"'*I'd hate to have to charge ya with manslaughter.*' You best find the evidence first, piggy."

He tossed aside a few bags of apples at the end of the flatbed and uncovered Barter's bloodstained loafer. He reached into the pile, seized his ankle. He grimaced at the cold and slimy feel of it.

He proceeded to tug the body forward until it was exposed and slid off the tailgate like a sack of flour. It landed on the dirt floor with a crunching thud, as if more than the skin had been melted away. Blood and brownish-yellow bodily fluids seeped around Hank's boots.

"Ah, Christ's Disciples!"

He turned his back on the mess and dragged his boots across the barn, intending to wipe them clean on a dirt floor. The cloud of dust trailed him to the last stall on the left. He stared at the splintered rack as reminiscence curled his lip. The residents a mile away on Sangralea had mentioned the next day that they had never heard his hogs squeal so much. His reply was that he had scared them with his new John Deere. In truth, unbeknownst to the townspeople, he did not own any farm animals.

He grinned at the ironic situation. Here he was about to bury the detective on the Trammell case beneath bloodstained evidence that was more damning than Ed Gein's homemade furniture. He was glad the FBI was far from Onward. He would be jailed for sure.

Yet he was reluctant to part with his collection. They were chock full of memories dating back centuries. How many people had shed blood on the leather straps? How many screams had been forced from the cranks? How many dying breaths had fogged the steel frameworks? Vengeance was carved into the wood grain like lovers' initials.

"What's going on here, Hank?"

Hank whirled to see Burl Nelson squinting between the right barn door and left headlight of the pickup.

The old man twisted his beard, and then straightened his glasses. "The last time I saw your truck in the barn you had blood on your hands."

Hank glanced down at Barter's body, and then met his friend's gaze. He turned his head and spit. The cop's corpse was a yard out of Burl's periphery. He hoped the geezer smelled apples, as death hung in the air like London fog.

*****

Pritchard emerged from the pine trees and stamped out his Marlboro. He was glad the rain clouds had dissipated. It was a long walk from boxcar alley to the Texaco. He was exhausted, huffing and puffing, out of gas and in need of a refill. He seldom walked anywhere. Though Onward was smaller than most towns, if he couldn't drive there, it wasn't worth his time. In fact, he failed to recall an instance in which he abandoned his cop car and traveled on foot. What was the world coming to?

He approached the rear of the gas station. The back door was shut tight. He rounded the concrete building, removed his Stetson, and wiped the sweat from his brow.

*"Sheriff? What in Judas happened here?"*

Pritchard paused at the corner of the storefront. He slapped on his hat and regarded Deputy Marten. He was a wisp of a man; he was tall as a basketball center, skinny as a Hollywood actress. His uniform was in disarray. His shirt was bunched and unbuttoned while his khakis were stained with coffee dribbles. He was his right-hand man - besides his only other officer Ernie Edsel - and nagged worse than a housewife. Now here the nosy pest was with his hands on his hips gazing at the disaster area.

"How the hell should I know?" Pritchard thumbed his belt buckle as he approached Marten's squad car, which was parked beside his own. "Ya think I've been sittin' here buyin' Slurpees all day?"

Marten shifted and backed into the fly-splattered grill of his Ford. "No, sir. I just thought that maybe you'd…What happened to your hand? Jesus, sir! We need to get you to the doc!"

"It's a paper cut, Marten. Must've hit an artery." He motioned with his bloodstained stump. "Now I'm gonna be goin' on inside, if ya care to have my back. Christ Almighty. Where is Edsel? How is it we have only one officer posted?"

"Well, the crowd's pretty much split. Most of 'em ran off to that bomb scare on the el. Heard there were two more threats at Soldier Field and the Sears Tower. Ernie and I laid some spikes and strung up the yellow tape."

"Ya kiddin' me? What if we get ourselves another redhead who thinks he's Evel Kenevel? If anymore of that chaos goes down, both y'all will be pullin' spikes outta yer face."

Pritchard turned his back, drew his Magnum, and kicked in the front doors. They snapped off the hinges and crashed. Marten drew his service revolver and followed his boss into the store.

"What do you think happened here, Sheriff?"

"Sounds like a helluva question for Adler, seein' how he should be workin' the register." Pritchard waved his pistol. "Scope out the back room. Make sure our suspect ain't hidin' in the john."

"Should I radio Ernie?"

"Why? Ya need him to hold yer woody? Get yer ass back there!"

Pritchard was grateful Marten was dumber than Barney Fife. The guy had walked across smeared bloodstains and passed a scorched counter without so much as a turn of his head. Then again, maybe he had noticed, but wasn't about to piss off his boss with stupid questions. After all, small town cop qualifications amounted to gun licenses and Good Enough Diplomas. That was how Pritchard preferred his officers, obedient and submissive. If one of them ever became smarter, they would think that they could do a better job as sheriff. Over his burning dead body.

"Hey, Sheriff! I think we got something here!"

279

Pritchard raised his Magnum. *What the hell did that pig farmer leave behind? He sure didn't mop worth a damn.*

Marten had his back turned, crouched near the pantry door. He lifted Barter's blue C.P.D. cap with the barrel of his pistol. The right side of the brim was shot off. The underside was crimson.

"Sheriff, this belongs to that Barter fellow. It's bloodier than a damn tam -"

Pritchard's Magnum cut off Marten. The point-blank blast knocked his brains into Barter's cap. His body dropped and drained red.

Pritchard holstered his gun, withdrew a Marlboro, and then sparked it. He savored the nicotine rush as it slowed his adrenaline. "Looks like Edsel earned a promotion."

He stared at the skeletal, bleeding body as the implications of his crime set in. He had reacted defensively, as Marten – regardless of his stupidity – would have figured out that something bad had happened to Barter, which in turn could have led to an FBI tip. He realized now that he had another mess to clean, and another squad car to conceal.

He smoked the cigarette down to the butt while reflecting on his misdeeds. He then flicked the smoldering remains into the pool of blood.

He snatched the walkie-talkie off his belt. "Edsel!"

"Sheriff?"

"Any sign of Adler? The store's vacant and I need a word with him."

"No sign, but he never goes farther than his farm. You want me to make a house call?"

"No. Stay posted. I'll pay him a visit."

Pritchard reattached his walkie-talkie, and then removed his badge. He swapped it out with a shiny replacement.

"Onward and upward."

S.D. Hintz

# CHAPTER SIXTEEN

Jay hurried down the hall. He crossed the living room and paused at the edge of the linoleum. The crazy guy braced himself, tugged hard on the sliding glass door, as if fighting to keep something out.

"Hey, buddy!" Jay was sick of the guy's antics. He wanted to walk out the front door, but he knew he had to calm him down. He was certain the maniac was involved in the kidnappings. He was too irascible not to be. "Whatever the hell your name is!"

"Coren! Prop the 2x4! Now, Opie!"

Jay shook his head as he entered the kitchen. If it calmed the guy down from boiling to simmering, then maybe he would be able to question him further.

"The name's Jay. Not Opie." He crouched down, picked up the lacquered 2x4. "If I do this, are you going to calm down and tell me what's going on?"

"*Yes!*"

Coren's fingers were slipping. His face was flushed. He gritted his teeth. His eyes were glued to the glass. While Jay saw an unkempt backyard, he saw a dead obese girl struggling to get the best of him. She had wrenched her hands out of the barbed wire, skinning them to the bone, and then had shifted all her weight to the tug-of-war. Her upside-down head gasped and coughed up greenish-black swamp water, which dribbled down the glass. Coren was uncertain why he refused to let this sister into the house, but he had a bad feeling about her. After all, she had emerged from the grave on her own, without his help.

Jay dropped the 2x4 into the gap between the wall and the door. "There. Are you happy?"

Coren released the handle. No sooner had he done so the 2x4 snapped in half and exploded into splinters as the door slammed it against the wall. Jay staggered back and shielded his eyes. Coren was thrown to the floor. A blast of hot air screamed through the kitchen, a hint of rotten apples permeating within. The dining room table and chairs overturned. The cupboard doors clapped open and shut.

Coren watched agape as the third sister barreled into the house like a bull, shrieking her decapitated head off. It was as if a hellish hurricane propelled her forth. He watched her blackened feet slap on the linoleum. Her skinless hand clutched the living room wall. She rounded the corner, her screams echoing down the hall. He knew she was searching for her sisters.

Jay dropped his hands from his ears and peeled his trembling body off the wall. *"What was that?"*

"If I told you -"

"I wouldn't believe you. You're damn right! So start explaining!"

A *bang* resounded from the other end of the house, which was followed by cries that were cut short by a second *bang*. Coren knew by the sound that it was the panic room door. The fat zombie was dying to be with her sisters.

Coren brushed the splinters off his pants and stood. "You should've listened when I told you the first time."

"Well, I'm listening now."

"There are dead triplets in my panic room! If you can't see them, then I don't know, this place must be haunted! But they're back there, doing God knows what!" Coren crossed the kitchen, slammed the deck door, and then opened the refrigerator. "Don't tell me you didn't feel the last one come through here. There's no way I've got the strength to crush a 2x4."

Jay shut his eyes for a few seconds. He had indeed felt the hot rush of air. He had even smelled apples again. And Coren had a point. He had never seen a deck door reduce a 2x4 to splinters on its own. He opened his eyes, and then narrowed them as Coren removed a red mesh bag of Fujis.

"What is it with the apples?"

Coren shook his head and shut the refrigerator. "I don't know, but they eat them."

"I thought you said they were ghosts."

"They are, but they're not. I dragged two of them out of the wells in the backyard." Coren stepped into the living room. "I don't know what they are."

A floodlight shined in Jay's head. "You have the Trammell triplets somewhere in that panic room and you're trying to hide the smell with the apples. Aren't you? *Aren't you?*"

Coren whirled. "I told you they're teenagers! How would a baby throw open a door?"

Coren and Jay stared at one another for a good thirty seconds. Their wheels were spinning on the same track. Jay was lost in thought on the Pritchard triplets. They were blond, they were teenagers, and they had mysteriously disappeared. But what would they be doing in Coren's house? If they were in fact ghosts – ones that he failed to see, mind you – was it possible that they had died on the property?

Jay killed the silence. "Who owned this house before you?"

Coren threw up his arms. "What does that matter? I own it now and I have to deal with this. You think I'm going to call the previous owner and tell him he forgot to take his ghosts with him?"

"No. Whoever owned the place killed those three girls you're seeing and buried them in your yard."

"What are you? A detective?"

"A reporter. I work for WND -"

"Y. Jay Donovan. I thought you looked familiar." Coren shook his head. He tossed the bag of apples. "Catch!"

"If we're going to the panic room, I told you I can't see them."

"But you can feel them. I'll prove to you they're here."

Jay sighed, cradled the bag of Fujis, and followed Coren through the living room. Thanks to the panic room, the house was dead silent. Jay had the urge to tiptoe, but fought it, reminding himself that if there were indeed ghosts they were probably holding their hands.

Coren stopped at the end of the hall, grasped the slit in the wall, and yanked hard. It refused to budge. He gave it two more tugs for good measure, which yielded the same result.

Jay slung the bag of apples over his shoulder. "Any chance you locked it from the inside?"

"Uh-uh. The fat chick wants to play tug-of-war again."

*****

"What brings you out to the farm, Burl?"

"You passed me back there on East Walnut. You're usually hauling apples to the store, not to your barn. So I guess you could say it was a bit of a red flag."

"Is it just you here?"

"Yeah, it's just me! Why? What did you do, Hank?"

"It wasn't nothing I did. It was Pritchard."

Burl rounded the grill of the pickup. He froze as Barter's remains came into full view. His jaw dropped. He turned his head and vomited into a stall.

Hank approached the charred body. "Now don't be jumping to any conclusions."

"What am I supposed to think?" Burl faced Hank as chunks of vomit dribbled down his beard. "Whose body is that?"

"Well…Did you hear about that Homicide detective in town?"

"Oh Christ no. Tell me you didn't. It was only all over the Tribune!"

"I didn't do this!" Hank kicked Barter's midsection. Blood squirted out of his bone-white mouth like some sick condiment dispenser. "Pritchard did!"

"Then what's the body doing here?"

"He's making me hide it."

"*In the barn?*" Burl rubbed his scarred chin and paced the short distance between the tailgate and Barter's corpse. "Not again, Hank! *Not again!* Why don't you hang a big "X" from the hayloft while you're at it?"

"Screw you! This would be the last place anybody would look."

"Wake up, you stupid idiot! It's a torture museum! I told you to get rid of this junk years ago! It's a crime lab's wet dream!"

"I ain't getting rid of 'em." Hank turned his back and walked over to the rack. "I need a reminder of what I've done. I don't bury my guilt like you do, Burl."

"No, you just bury detectives. We shouldn't be revisiting the past, Hank! Once the P.D. finds out Barter's missing, those bomb scares will be on the backburner."

"Bomb scares?"

"Don't you own a TV?" Burl stopped pacing. The stench of death blended with the sweet cider. "Oh, that's right, you've been acting out your own drama. Why do you think they forgot about the kidnappings? Something more important came up, that's why."

"They've got no reason to search my barn." As Hank uttered those words, the Texaco glared in his mind's eye. There was no sweeping that wreckage beneath a rug. That mess alone would lead a SWAT team to his doorstep. "Besides which, I don't have a choice. Pritchard said he'd pin the murder on me."

"I've got no part in this, Hank, nor do I want the helm in your boat. My hands are clean and they're going to stay that way."

Hank whirled and dug his right spur into the leg of the rack. "Your hands are stained, Burl! You can't wash 'em of the past!"

"My lips are zipped and I'm out of here." Burl shook his head, twisted his beard, and headed toward the doors. "And don't think you're getting anymore apples from me!"

"Don't leave me, you murderer!"

*****

*Francine ran past Kate's Bakery without so much as a glance at the window of pastries. She rounded the storefront and followed the alleyway. Unlike in a big city, it was a clean, narrow passage with floodlights an inch below the roofline. The walls were devoid of dumpsters and cardboard houses. Instead, there were steel side doors on the left and right and a seven-foot tall cedar privacy fence marking the dead end.*

You can do this. *A scrape of pebbles snatched Francine's attention. Loren slipped around the corner, almost losing her balance.* Just pretend it's the monkey bars and use the posts for footholds.

*"Smeller!" Loren raised the screwdriver and hurled it like a throwing knife. The flathead stabbed the fence a hair from Francine's arm. "You're dead!"*

*Francine ignored Loren. She lifted her leg and jammed her shoe between the splintered slat. The second 2x4 was a foot higher. She scaled it like a ladder. She had one more post to climb to reach the top. She pulled her shoe out of the slat and raised it to the next level.*

*"I got ya!"*

*Loren seized Francine's ankle with her left hand and wrenched the screwdriver out of the fence with her right. Francine had her right foot braced on the topmost 2x4 and struggled to pull her left from Loren's grasp. She kicked down, and then yanked up her leg. Her ankle broke free. As she raised it to the top of the fence Loren jumped and jabbed the screwdriver into her calf.*

*Francine cried out. She heard whoops and hollers, then spotted the sisters barreling down the alley with weapons in hand. She clenched her teeth against the pain as tears streamed down her cheeks. She had to get over the fence. She had to.*

*The fence rattled. Francine looked down. Loren was trying to shake her off. Instead, the blood from Francine's wound trickled and splattered on her face. Loren let go, disgusted.*

*Francine straddled the top of the fence and clambered to the other side, trembling on the opposite 2x4. She grabbed the screwdriver and yanked it from her calf, crying out as blood squirted and dripped off her shoe.*

*Henna, red-faced and eyes bulging, shouldered the fence like a linebacker. It lurched back as if on the verge of collapsing. "Yer dead, Smeller! I'm gonna kill ya!"*

293

*Francine stepped down to the next 2x4. Henna leaped and grabbed the top of the fence. Without a second thought, Francine jabbed the screwdriver into her knuckles. Henna hollered and tried to retract her hand, but it was pinned to the slat by the flathead.*

*Francine stepped down, missing the last 2x4. She fell back and gasped when her fall was cushioned. She looked up into the worried faces of Burl Nelson and Hank Adler. Biting their tongues, they hauled her towards the orchard.*

*****

Pritchard regarded Marten's squad car. He hadn't anticipated killing one of his own. The plus side was that he would have no problem pinning the crime on Hank. After all, it was his store. His shotgun casings littered the aisles. And wherever Barter's body was buried, it would be covered with the farmer's fingerprints.

Pritchard grinned. A house call seemed unnecessary. It was wiser to let Hank think that only one officer's blood was on his hands. In that case, maybe it was best to leave the squad car parked before the storefront. He was uncertain if it would raise suspicion. Though the Texaco was in ruins, the eyewitness news traffic had died altogether thanks to terrorism in Chicago. His mind was made up. He was going to slash the tires and leave Marten's body to rot.

He reached into his pant pocket, withdrew a Swiss army knife. It was one of the few mementos left behind by his daughter Sylvia. It always sparked the same memory of her carving Henna's name into her forearm. It still filled him with pride knowing how much his children had loved one another.

He slashed the tires one by one. He stepped back, pocketed the knife, and regarded his handiwork as he sparked the last Marlboro in his pack.

S.D. Hintz

# CHAPTER SEVENTEEN

Coren released the handle, stared at the door.

Jay's shoulder ached from the bag of apples. "Maybe you should kick it down."

"And what if Pritchard makes another house call?"

"Then he's going to see what I've been seeing. *Nothing!* You've got *nothing* hidden in that panic room!"

"Give me that!" Coren snatched the bag from Jay, and then kicked the door with his right foot. It reverberated, but stood tall.

"Stand back. Let me try."

While on location Jay had seen numerous police officers gain entry into locked doors. Since his left shoulder was sore, he planned on slamming his right near the handle. Coren stepped aside as Jay backed into the hallway wall. He then took his five-step running start.

The door opened. Jay ran inside and his shoulder connected with a cold, invisible wall that knocked him to the hardwood floor. The scent of cider flooded his nostrils.

Coren hesitated at the doorway, his face a cross between surprise and disgust. He had watched Jay rush into the room and collide smack-dab with the fat zombie. His shoulder crushed her upside-down face, which dangled between her breasts. It was probably better the reporter didn't know what hit him.

Coren stepped into the room, glimpsing Well Girl #1 doing a handstand against the wall with her twisted, black-and-blue feet braced in the door handle. He reached down, grabbed Jay beneath the arms, and lifted him to his feet.

Jay was pale. He ran his palm over his face as he realized it was coated with a transparent slime. "What the hell?"

The door slammed. Coren spun and saw that Well Girl #1 blocked it. Her eyes rolled back in her head, on which she still stood, as her entwined legs swayed like a metronome.

Coren nibbled his thumbnail. "You just ran into the fat chick. Crushed her face like a pumpkin. Her sister's guarding the door. Oh crap, here comes the other one."

Well Girl #2 crawled from the box pile while slapping her stumps on the floor. She grabbed her fat sister's blistered ankles and pulled herself forward.

Jay stepped back. "*Who's* coming?"

Coren was at his wits' end. He had to do something fast. The bag of apples slipped from his shoulder, reminding him why he had brought Jay to the room in the first place. He was intent on proving a point.

He opened the bag and dumped it across the floor. "Watch the apples, man."

The fruits rolled across the floor; a good twenty to thirty bounced off the sisters. Coren braced himself while Jay hoped the guy wasn't out of his mind, seeing how he was pouring apples into an empty room.

The triplets froze. Their sockets squeezed with a squelch. Coren felt like a top, spinning on his heel to see that the sisters were in unison. He wished once again that Jay saw their reactions.

Jay turned toward the door. "Listen. I don't see anything, and your whole obsession with apples -"

Coren grabbed Jay's jacket sleeve. "Did you or did you not just run into an invisible wall?"

"You probably have Plexiglas dividing half the room."

Jay took another step. As Coren released his grip, the sisters unleashed their ear-piercing screams. It was as if the trio had spotted the apples at the same time. Coren clutched his ears, the soundproof walls compressing the shrieks to a deafening level. He glanced at Jay and was surprised to see him collapse on his knees with his head buried in his forearms.

Coren was beside himself. *He can hear them! He can really hear them!*

Jay's face was screwed up, looking as if he was about to cry.

The screams faded. Jay peered between his forearms. His eyes widened and he yelled. He scooted back, but then froze and scrambled toward the right wall when he glanced over his shoulder.

"*Jesus, Mary, and Joseph! What the hell? Make them go away!*"

Coren dropped his hands from his ears and shook his head. He smiled, glad his visitor had finally seen the light. "Wish I could. Now you know what I've been seeing."

Jay's back slammed against the wall. "*Okay, okay! I don't want to see it anymore! I don't want to see it!*"

His heart rattled his ribs. He was in a room with three mutilated dead girls that had appeared out of nowhere. A curly blond with mangled legs doing a headstand blocked the door he wanted to run through. Another blond with straggly hair crawled toward him on bloody stumps. And the "fat chick" Coren had referred to stood naked in the sea of oranges, swinging her bleeding head on blackened arteries as her caved-in face twitched between her flabby breasts. Trembles shook Jay from head to toe. They were indeed teenaged triplets.

Coren had a crazy grin on his face and pointed like he had discovered gold. "Look at them! I told you! They're sisters!"

At that moment, the word "sisters" sank deep into Jay's subconscious. He saw the photograph of the Blondies going up in flames. The sisters. The seventeen-year-old sisters! The ones that had disappeared over a decade ago only to appear in a panic room!

He glanced at the gaping ghosts – or were they resurrected corpses? He put the names to their maimed faces. The one doing the headstand was Loren; her curly hair was unmistakable. The rawboned one missing half of her legs was Sylvia. And without a doubt the obese sister was Henna. It was as if the three of them hopped out of the photograph in Halloween makeup.

Jay steeled his nerves and spoke through clenched teeth.

"The Blondies. You have Pritchard's daughters in your panic room."

\*\*\*\*\*

Hank dislodged his spur from the rack and pursued Burl. He couldn't let the man wash his hands as if he hadn't seen a thing. He was a liability. With Onward smeared across newspaper headlines, the temptation to snitch was overwhelming.

"Get back here, Burl! Don't you walk out on me!"

Hank stepped over Barter's corpse and brushed past the pickup. He snatched a hoe from the barn wall as he charged outside. Burl turned and pointed a finger.

His words caught like a death rattle. His eyes widened to the size of his bifocal lenses. Hank was huffing toward him, red-faced and scowling, clutching the hoe over his shoulder in a stabbing position.

Burl turned and ran for his life. He knew the look on Hank's mug all too well. The man was out for blood. He wore the same expression fifteen years ago on that sweltering night inside the barn.

Hank cocked back his killing arm. "You ain't squealing on me, pig!"

Burl stumbled for the field and abandoned his truck. He had a fleeting thought of burning rubber off Hank's property, but then remembered that the door locks were busted and he would have been caught behind the wheel before he could punch the gas. He glanced

back as the bean plants scraped against his hands. There was maybe

ten yards between them. His arthritis burned in his knees. He would

be unable to lead the race for long.

Hank was determined to quiet Burl. The man had stood by

his side once, had even promised friendship, and now he had turned

his back on him. He was running scared hell-bent on babbling to the

first cop he encountered.

"You lied to me, Burl!" Hank hurled the hoe.

The flat blade arced like a javelin. It landed a yard ahead of

Burl. He reached down, grabbed the handle, and swung around. The

blade sliced open Hank's shoulder a hair below his gunshot wound.

He yelled, and then tackled Burl to the ground. The hoe flew off to

the side and they rolled across bean plants as they kicked and

punched one another.

Burl raised his forearms before his face. "Get off me!"

Hank put his fist through the gap in Burl's block and caught

him in the chin. Burl hollered, having bit his tongue, and blood

gushed from his mouth. Hank clamped his hands on Burl's throat.

Burl flailed and rolled, but Hank refused to let go.

"You killed those girls, Burl! You raped 'em and you tortured 'em! And you locked me out of the barn while you did it!"

Burl gasped for air and slapped at Hank's wrists, but his bones throbbed and weakened his defense. He wormed back, trying to crane his neck out of the chokehold. He looked up and saw the ashen sky through the barbed wire fence. At that moment, he knew he had to fight until it pained him to death. He had lived too many years to go out like a light.

He snapped his neck forward and head-butted Hank in the nose. A grin cracked his bloody lips as his old friend howled and lost his grip.

*****

Pritchard pulled away from the tainted Texaco and headed into town. He had told Edsel that he was going to drop in on Hank, but he had a different agenda.

Barter's words haunted him. *If no one's left town, then how many people have you questioned?*

He had interrogated Coren Raines, and that about summed it up. Truth be told, he wanted the innocent man to take the fall so he didn't have to deal with this stress anymore. All the case did was dredge up memories of his daughters.

He eyed his cigarette, and then flicked it to the roadside. That was his last drag of nicotine. Nothing would calm him down now. Coren Raines was on the verge of feeling the wrath of Hurricane Pritchard.

As he squealed the Crown Victoria's tires onto East Walnut Street, movement near the right ditch caught his eye. He tipped his sunglasses. He slowed his roll and peered through the passenger's side window as he passed by.

At first, he thought he was looking at two dogs playing in Hank's field. Then he realized it was Hank straddling Burl Nelson. The bearded old man head-butted the wild-eyed farmer.

"Ya kiddin' me?"

Pritchard's brain fired off split-second speculations. What were the friends fighting over? And why wasn't Hank off burying Barter? Had Burl happened upon Hank's dirty work?

Whatever the reason, Hank had the same look in his eyes as when he had torched the detective. He watched him in one swift move grab the barbed wire fence, wrap it around Burl's throat, and choke him. The barbed wire snapped in Hank's bloody hands and Burl's head rolled into the ditch.

"Jesus Christ!"

Pritchard turned left on Oak Street. He released the steering wheel and pushed up his sunglasses with his only index finger. He wasn't about to deal with all that. Hank had better make sure he had the mess cleaned up by the time he was done torturing a confession out of Raines. The farmer had two bodies to bury by the hour's end. Hank was so red-handed he would be facing prison time.

He thought about Burl. The old man had been one of the more trustworthy residents. Now he died at the hands of his best friend.

*Guess it's the last season for apples.*

307

*****

Francine stared out the third-story rose window as she puffed like a smokestack. The two men that had stood up for her fifteen years ago wrestled in the field. She choked back her tears as Hank decapitated Burl. She dropped her cigarette, ground it into the hardwood floor, and turned her back on Onward.

# CHAPTER EIGHTEEN

*Hank clamped his hand over Francine's mouth. He sat her down near the porch steps as she clutched her bleeding calf. He crouched to eye level.*

*"Keep your mouth shut, understand?"*

*Francine nodded. Hank and Burl ran into the orchard. She struggled to compose herself, stiffening her body against the trembles. She was certain the Blondies were going to kill her. She was proud of herself for evading them. As far as she could recall, it was a first.*

*Hank and Burl met at the wobbling fence and exchanged lascivious looks. Blood dripped down the slats. Henna yanked the screwdriver out of her hand, hollering, and then proceeded to clamber over. She plummeted with a thud. Her scowl faded to a cross between surprise and confusion.*

*Hank revealed a softball-sized apple. Henna gaped and he slammed it into her mouth before she could unleash a warcry. Burl punched her in the gut, causing her to drop the screwdriver, and then pulled out a dark bottle.*

*Hank nodded and tossed him the handkerchief. Burl doused and shoved it in Henna's face. The clear liquid dripped down her oversized T-shirt and she collapsed within seconds. Hank and Burl let her body crumple on the ground, surprised she had gone down easy.*

*"I still want to know where you got chloroform," Burl muttered.*

*Hank grinned. "It's halothane. Why do you think I ain't got any animals?"*

*Two blond heads poked above the top of the fence. Sylvia's screwdriver was intertwined in her split ends. Loren was unarmed with her Pirates cap askew. The sisters glared over the slats, searching for their prey like starving wolves. Their eyes narrowed as if on the same wavelength.*

*Hank jumped and seized Loren's wrists. She flipped head over heels and landed on her back, groaning in tears. Sylvia hopped down and lunged at Hank with the screwdriver. The farmer tripped on Henna's unconscious body and fell out of harm's way.*

*"Over here!"*

*Sylvia had no sooner spun when Burl splashed her face with halothane. She screamed as it burned her eyes. Burl punched her in the mouth. She hit the ground out cold beside her sisters.*

*Loren moaned, rolled onto her stomach. She rose to all fours and crawled toward Henna. Burl ran at her with the halothane and hurled the bottle. It smashed on the side of her face. She collapsed face down at Henna's feet, her left cheek bleeding through black shards.*

*"Nice one, Burl." Hank stood, snatched his handkerchief from Burl's hand, and then smothered Sylvia's face in it. "That ought to keep her under."*

*Burl headed toward the orchard. "I'll get the wheelbarrow."*

*Hank regarded their handy work. It was a Kodak moment in any album. The Blondies had received a dose of their own poison. The townspeople would pay to see the triplets incapacitated. He felt like a regular hero.*

*He turned to Henna, kicked her in the ribs with his cowboy boot. Her body jiggled and her parted lips driveled, but she failed to stir. He raised his boot, dug his right spur into her stomach, and rolled it across. He grinned as a trail of blood soaked through her T-*

*shirt. The bold, glittered phrase "Eat me!" brightened as if lit by*

*neon.*

\*\*\*\*\*

Coren furrowed his brow. "Pritchard's daughters? What are you talking about? That psychopath has children?"

"They disappeared fifteen years ago, just like the Trammell triplets."

The Tribune headline haunted Coren. Then he realized how he must have sounded when he was ranting and raving about pulling triplets out of his backyard. He paled.

"Jay, listen to me. I don't know how -"

Coren's words were sliced short as the Blondies screamed bloody murder. He clapped his hands on his ears, as did Jay, but to no avail. The shrieks pierced their eardrums like drill bits. Both men yelled and collapsed to their knees. Jay buried his head in his arms.

The shrieks died. A teeth-gritting screech filled the silence. Coren and Jay looked up, confused by the metallic grinding.

Their eyes glued to the walls. The steel plates peeled and rolled down to the floor on their own accord. Beyond the soundproofing should have been Sheetrock or insulation. Instead tomato red muscles and stringy tendons pulsed and bled. Jay vomited. Coren's butt was frozen to the floor. He was awestruck, his head snapping to see each wall wrench down, the fleshy fluid squirting and trickling into the room.

Jay panicked and shook his head. "This isn't real! The Blondies aren't there, these walls aren't -"

Coren stood and pointed. "You think the walls are ghosts, too? I'm telling you! I carried these girls into the -"

The throbbing muscles in the walls popped like spit bubbles, spraying blood from all four corners. Coren hopped back as a mottled wad splashed his shoes.

Jay was at the breaking point. He glanced at Coren. He looked as if he had adapted to the madness and had no intention of fleeing.

Jay rushed the door.

Loren fell from her headstand onto her knees and bawled. Tears streamed down her scars. "*Oohh! Oohh!*"

Jay was taken aback. Moments ago the ghost had seemed horrifying, now she was a mere child pleading for open arms. She reached her hands out. Jay was entranced. She reminded him of his own daughters when they were young, crying to be picked up and held. He knelt.

Blood seeped from the barb wounds that stretched from Loren's mouth around the back of her head. *"Oohh! Oohh!"*

Jay extended his embrace. Henna unleashed a bellow that flattened the piles of boxes and crushed their contents. The boom box exploded and the window cracked. Jay whirled and ducked off to the side while Coren shielded his head with his forearms.

Henna's cry sank into the core of the walls and the muscles quivered, spurting greenish-red pus. She clutched her carotids and raised her head shoulder level. The rotted skin peeled off her face, then plopped on the floor. The rest of her flesh followed suit. It curled back like age-old wallpaper from her bludgeoned neck, dropping in clumps to the floor.

Jay lost his gorge. He turned his head, refusing to watch the freak show another second, only to lay his eyes on Loren. The curly-haired sister clawed at her face and raked her arms. Her flesh and clothes peeled as one.

*"Coren, make it stop!"*

Coren broke his gaze. He saw Jay backpedaling toward him as Loren crept forth. He looked to Henna. She was skinned to the bone, a mass of muscle. Sylvia had shed her skin and rags as Loren had and pulled herself up on her stumps at Henna's side.

Coren clenched his fists. His only thought was to fight his way out of the room. Being holed up like mental patients would drive them crazy before long. He regretted having tossed the bag of apples, though it proved his point. Jay was a firm believer.

Coren charged Henna. He threw a punch and she blocked it with her head, which ruptured like a dropped watermelon.

A buzz of chainsaws resounded from the walls, the floor, and the ceiling.

Coren turned on his heels, confused and thrown for a loop, as he staggered back toward Jay. His eyes rested on the triplets. Sylvia and Loren embraced Henna. Their bleeding bodies molded into Henna's flesh like Playdoh. Their limbs liquefied into her muscle. Their faces faded in silent screams. In a matter of a minute, the triplets had become one, leaving behind piles of reddish-blond hair and blackened teeth.

Coren clutched Jay's arm and stepped backwards. Jay's jaw had long since dropped to his gut. He knew that what he saw he would be unable to recount. He would sound like a raving lunatic rather than a reporter. His mind was blown and he was trembling as if he was hypothermic.

Henna's bleeding flesh rippled from head to toe. Her headless body cracked down the middle. The gash poured maggots as the torso and limbs fell apart like a hatched egg.

Jay vomited on the door. Coren reached back for the handle, wide-eyed and agape. He froze.

A short, stocky teenaged girl with straight hair smiled in the mess of shed flesh. She clutched her denim skirt in one hand and the strap of her backpack in the other.

Coren seized Jay by the arm and spun him. "*Look.*"

Jay wished that he had been blind the moment Coren had dumped the apples. He blinked his watery eyes.

The girl giggled. She then skipped around the pile of carnage.

Jay gasped. "*Who the hell is that?*"

"Guess the fat chick was pregnant." Coren shrugged his shoulders when Jay shot him a this-is-no-time-to-be-joking glance. "How should I know?"

"She's not like the Blondies."

"I see that. And we don't need quadruplets."

"Not that. She's unharmed."

Coren looked closer. Jay was right. The girl, though blood-soaked, was clean of cuts, bruises, and amputations. He nudged the handle. To his surprise, the door opened. The girl giggled and dashed past them.

Coren stuck his head out of the room. The hallway was deserted. A trail of bloody footprints ended at the living room. Shrill laughter echoed, and then died to a welcoming silence.

*****

The CB radio crackled.

"Sheriff?"

Pritchard cursed, pulled over the Crown Victoria, and slammed it into "Park." Life with one hand was irritating him. He snatched the CB.

"This better be important, Edsel."

"I got a gray two-door Cougar approaching. Looks like Ms. Heller."

"Hold her there. I'm on my way."

*****

Vance Trammell led the search party into the wetlands a block from Oak Street. It was the last place in town they had yet to scour. Sam Emory, eyes on his galoshes, had suggested the swamp, muttering that he had once heard of a man burying bodies beneath algae. Vance sighed and trudged through the brush with the team of fifteen spread out behind him.

Wendell Wurtz matched Vance's stride and pulled down his poncho hood. He peered at his friend in concern behind rain-spattered lenses. "What happens if we come up empty here, Vance?"

"Then we cross the county line and keep searching."

"Don't you think that's been done already? They had a chopper out on day one."

"They were up *there*, we're down *here*."

Vance walked faster, hoping Wendell would fall back with the rest of the gang. Instead, the pharmacist kept pace. Vance was on the verge of screaming at everyone to go home and leave him alone. He would find his daughters by himself.

Wendell grabbed Vance's shoulder and stopped him. "Vance! Would you listen to me? After this you need to take a breather. If you drive yourself into the ground, who's going to find your girls?"

"You are, Wen." Vance brushed the hand off his shoulder. "You are."

Vance walked off into the woods. Wendell fell in line with the search party, shaking his head.

After a five-minute trek they entered the wetlands. The brush faded to marsh and the elm trees dwindled, giving way to withered willows. The swamp came into view. Vance held up his hand, turned to the townies.

"We search around this swamp and then we disband. We'll call it a day." Vance's voice cracked and he cleared his throat. "Everyone can go home to their families. Sound like a plan?"

The team nodded. Vance turned and headed toward the swamp. The pungent flora stung his eyes, urging his welled up tears to fall. He refused to quit looking until he found Stephie, Ellie, and Amanda. He refused to return home empty-handed and see Teresa's disappointed face. That would cripple him for sure.

His gaze darted from branch to boulder, bush to puddle, starving for a scrap of evidence.

Then something caught his eye in the dirt. His stomach fluttered. He crouched for a closer look.

Sam approached from behind. "You got something, Vance?"

"Footprints."

"Could be from Pritchard or that big city cop."

"Could be a lot of things." Vance stood and noticed that the trail snaked toward the swamp. "Could be we follow them and see where they lead."

Vance walked along the prints. Despite the morning's rainfall, he could tell that they were fresh. Someone in tennis shoes had ventured to the deepest parts of the wetlands. And there was only one set of prints.

Vance followed the trail with Sam at his heels. He stopped at the swamp's muddy shore. The footprints led to a hole from which red cloth fluttered in the breeze. Vance thought he would collapse and pass out. Dread gnawed at him. What if it was his girls? What if he found them…dead…and buried?

Sam paused beside Vance. "Aw crap. What the hell is that?"

Vance was deadpan as the tears brimmed. "Go look for me, will you, Sam?"

Sam's galoshes squelched on the shore. Once he was within a yard of the cloth he craned his neck over the hole. A skull alive with snakes was up to its sockets in swamp water.

Vance clenched his fists and trembled. "Well, Sam, is it them?"

"It's someone. Someone other than your daughters."

Vance seemed to snap out of his trance. He willed his legs to move and joined Sam at the hole. Sam was right. It was someone else; someone's head wrapped in a T-shirt with the phrase "Eat me!" in stained letters. Relief washed over him. He gazed at the large skull and empty sockets. His brows knitted.

Sam read Vance's facial expression. "You know who that is?"

"I know that shirt. It's Henna Pritchard's. She used to wear it all the time. Paul's gonna fly off the handle when he finds out."

"Maybe we shouldn't tell him then."

Vance glared at Sam and stood in his face. "If this was my own daughter and someone found her, then failed to tell me and I found out…"

Sam gulped and nodded. Vance eyed the ground. He spotted a broken piece of driftwood with a clump of mud on the end. The trail of footprints led to it, circled the hole, and disappeared in the opposite direction. He had a feeling that they led to the killer's backyard. And maybe that same killer had kidnapped his daughters.

"Go get Paul. Now!"

Sam uprooted his galoshes and ran back to the huddled search party. Vance stole a last glance at Henna's decapitated head and knew he had no time to waste. He traced the footprints east toward Inventory Street. With each stride it sickened him to think that he walked in the killer's footsteps.

# CHAPTER NINETEEN

Hank released the barbed wire and scaled the fence, indifferent to the pain. He then scrambled down the ditch after Burl's rolling head. He found it resting in a puddle. He grabbed it by its blood-streaked strands, and then ran up the hillside. Once he crossed the property line, he caught his breath and cursed his friend.

"What the hell were you thinking? You got to be brain dead to think you're gonna pin all this on me. This is all for the man. You think I bury people in my barn every day?"

Hank looked across the field. He had no choice but to drag Burl's body. The problem was that it would take two hands to complete the task. He regarded the dripping head.

"Sorry, Burl."

He cocked his arm back and hurled the head as hard as he could. It flew over the field in a spray of red and bounced on the gravel drive. He reached down, seized the body by its wrists, grimacing as the severed neck spurted blood. He then tugged it with what little strength remained in his exhausted body. His wounded

325

shoulder throbbed, but he gritted his teeth and forged toward the barn.

"I told you not to walk out on me. But you had to be stubborn. Now I got to dump you with the rest of 'em."

*****

*Hank and Burl scrambled to haul the Blondies onto the flatbed and bury them with crates of apples. They were relieved that the area was deserted, but had to act fast nonetheless. While they did that, Francine was given the task of scrubbing the blood off the fence with a handkerchief. When all signs of foul play were cleared, the three accomplices climbed into the pickup, Francine sitting between Burl and Hank.*

*Hank made Francine slouch in the seat so as not to draw curious looks. They wouldn't raise suspicion if he and Burl were seen driving through town, as they conducted business on a daily basis. They cruised down Main Street, then right on Sangralea without so much as a glance from passers-by.*

*Francine's heart was hammering. She was relieved when they pulled up Mr. Adler's driveway. The entire time she had worried that Sheriff Pritchard would stop them and throw them all in jail. At that thought, she realized how criminal their vengeance had become.*

*After filtering out of the truck, one by one Hank and Burl lugged the Blondies into a wheelbarrow and transported them to the barn while Francine fought her conscience. It took them both to push*

*Henna, which felt more like shoving a stalled Volkswagen uphill. They dumped the triplets in a pile. Hank ran to the double doors, waved Francine inside, and then sealed the barn tight with a 2x4 and rope.*

*Burl stared wide-eyed at their surroundings. "What is all this, Hank?"*

*"This here's my collection. I plan on finally putting it to some use."*

*"No. No. The hell you are. You said we were going to slap them around a bit. Scare them off from the bullying."*

*"Well, we are. And then you two are gonna watch me torture them. I'm gonna make sure they don't ever mess with us again."*

*"That's going too far, Hank."*

*"Too far? They stripped Franny here and dumped her in a ditch. They just chased her with screwdrivers down the alley. If you ask me, that ain't far enough."*

*"This isn't the Middle Ages!"*

*"Why don't you ask Franny what we should do then? She's been bullied the most."*

*Hank and Burl looked to Francine, who lingered by the doors with her arms crossed, focused on the dirt floor. She shuffled her feet as recollections prodded her. She saw the razor blade slash her mouth and the baseball bat strike her temple. She saw herself disrobed and punched in the stomach. She bit back the tears, looked up.*

*"They deserve whatever they get."*

*Hank grinned. "There you have it. Now what do you say we have some fun?"*

*Burl shook his head. His arthritis flared in his arms from all of the heavy lifting. He wanted nothing more than to go home to his rocking chair and pop four Celebrex. "I don't want any part of this, Hank. I was satisfied when we knocked them out cold. Why don't we just dump them in a ditch outside of town or something?"*

*"No. We're here now. No sense in complicating things."*

*"Well, then, I guess you're on your own."*

*Burl turned, but Francine's distraught face stopped him from marching toward the doors. She nibbled her bottom lip, and then sighed.*

*She stepped aside to let him pass. "They hurt me, Mr. Nelson. And they'll hurt me again."*

*Burl's face flushed and he gritted his teeth. It was obvious he was on the verge of blowing his top. He faced Hank. "Let's get this over with already. I got a seed run to make by sundown."*

*Hank grinned and undid the straps on the rack.*

\*\*\*\*\*

Coren joined Jay in the hallway, rubbing his watery eyes. It was a relief to escape their prison. "It means something. You know that right?"

Jay nodded. "What was all that? They were all here, now they're gone. I touched one of them."

"I hauled every one of them into the house. I'm telling you, sometimes they're ghosts, sometimes they're…zombies."

"But what does it mean? Who was that little girl?" Jay seized his hair. It was either that or slapping himself in the forehead. "Francine Heller!"

"Who?"

"Francine Heller! She used to get bullied by the Blondies all the time!"

Coren shut the sliding door, headed into the living room. His houseguest followed at his heels. They paused near the kitchen and glanced from wall to wall, searching for the runaway.

Coren pointed at the deck door. "So who buried them in my backyard?"

Jay threw his arms up and fired off the same question he had asked a half-hour earlier. "Who owned this house before you?"

Coren shook his head. "It's weird. I Googled the county records the other day and it said a Ray Hodge owned it. But then a month before I bought the house it had been signed over to an Edwold Gentry. I'm thinking Hodge was in some kind of financial trouble."

"Yeah right. The Blondies are buried in your backyard, but you think Hodge signed over his house and skipped town?"

"He could've died. They don't have to release that information."

"Unless he was killed without a trace. I've reported on my fair share of cold cases."

"If Hodge was killed he'd be knocking at my back door."

A hollow tap spun Coren and Jay's heads.

Someone rapped on the sliding glass.

*****

Vance clambered over the worm fence and staggered as if an alien hit him with a freeze ray. His limbs weakened. His bloodshot eyes perked.

He stood on the perimeter of Ray Hodge's backyard. He knew it was now owned by the newbie Coren Raines, but he could not help but think it was still Ray's. He had helped the old man build the cedar deck. It was then that he had learned of Hodge's odd predicament while toasting Old Milwaukee.

The retired postman, being a close friend of Vance's, had conceded that Hank Adler and Burl Nelson were pressuring him to sell his property. He said the men wanted to form a co-op and turn his rambler into a farmer's market. Burl had boasted about apple and pear trees while Hank had suggested striped kiosks full of fresh vegetables. They had offered to pay off Ray with a lump sum if he signed over his homestead. At the time, the old man had feigned interest. But two weeks later, to Vance's shock, he had packed up and shipped out without so much as a wave goodbye. Even now he thought it peculiar. The state of the backyard only stirred his latent suspicions.

He approached the hole near the rusted scrap metal. A pile of dirt and a discarded shovel remained as evidence. He peered over the eroded lip. He turned his head and vomited in the grass. He clutched his knees, and then shook his head as he fought to keep his gorge down.

He knew it was the decomposed skeleton of Sylvia Pritchard staring back at him. If the other one had been Henna, then this was surely her sister. Though riddled with worm holes, there was no mistaking the rawboned jawline and broad forehead. Her frail body had been crammed into the pit; her arms and severed legs pointed at the overcast sky.

Vance wiped his mouth on his coat sleeve. "Lord give me strength."

He faced the pit and took a second look. Chunks of brick protruded through the dirt on all sides. It appeared to have once been a well that had dried up and was then filled in.

His head spun. Who would have killed Paul's girls and then buried them? Certainly not Ray Hodge, though the more he considered that notion, the more plausible it seemed. If his memory served him right, Ray had disappeared around the same time the Blondies had, if not a week earlier.

But another insistent question prodded Vance. Who had dug up the girls and left the evidence in plain sight?

His bleary gaze settled on the well with the lopsided roof halfway across the weedy yard. He could tell from his standpoint that the stone walls had been hammered on. He walked toward it, glancing at the dark house. Either Coren Raines had taken a road trip or he was spying from a rear window. Vance did not care either way. He would catch up to him in due time.

He stepped up to the well. His gut retracted, but he forced the sickness back down. The walls had been pried apart. Poking from the dirt was a jaundice skeleton. The jaw was gagged with barbed wire and twisted legs dangled into the dank darkness. Vance knew it had to be Loren Pritchard. It was the only theory that made sense. And Coren Raines was the one playing gravedigger.

He looked to the deck. He clenched his trembling fists. Inside that house were his girls. He was certain. He owed it to Teresa, himself, and Ray Hodge to beat the living daylights out of Raines.

Fragments of a brief conversation with Paul Pritchard danced in his skull as he marched toward the steps.

*"I've got a suspect. Lives at Ray Hodge's old place. He's hidin' somethin', guaranteed."*

Vance felt like a semi careening off a cliff. Nothing was going to stop him until he hit rock bottom and exploded. It was time to look his daughters' killer in the eyes.

*****

Pritchard turned off Sangralea onto Main Street. He spotted the narrow taillights of Francine Heller's Cougar a mile ahead. The loony was probably heading to the cities to replenish her supply of cheap vodka. He chuckled at the thought of her being weak-willed courtesy of his daughters, drowning in her sorrows as her liver shriveled up. Why else would she leave town? She was so hermitic she wouldn't step out of her house if it was on fire.

The CB crackled.

"Sheriff?"

"Goddamn it all to hell!"

He had a mile to drive to the county line. There was no way he was pulling over to answer Edsel's call.

"Sheriff? Do you copy?"

Pritchard let go of the steering wheel and punched the radio. The face cracked. He clocked it again. It shattered and dangled on its mount.

"Shut up!"

He grabbed the wheel before he veered off the road. With every throb of his bleeding stump he wanted to inflict pain with his good hand. And the idea of being a gimp riled him even more.

Simple actions such as urinating were a challenge. He was glad he could still handle his Magnum. He had a sudden urge to unload it on the first moving target that crossed his path.

He chirped the siren once to announce his arrival. Edsel paced, then sighed and belted his CB when he spotted his boss. Pritchard noticed that Francine Heller watched him in her rearview mirror as he stopped a car length behind her.

He opened the glove box. The Ziploc with the bloodstained knife and juice carton popped out, falling on the floor, along with a handful of shiny badges. He arched his brow. He saw his chance to get in Heller's head. It would be like old times, except he would be bullying her instead of his daughters.

He picked up the baggie and set it on the passenger's seat. He then grabbed the tape recorder. He regretted not having used it on Coren Raines, but now he realized it had been waiting for a greater purpose. He would get a loose confession out of Heller and plant the knife in her trunk. She probably wouldn't go down without a fight. He had heard she was quite feisty.

He bit back a grin as he stepped out of the car. Nobody left his town when there was a grieving family to support. Especially not Heller.

S.D. Hintz

# CHAPTER TWENTY

*"Let's put the skinny one on the rack." Hank grabbed Sylvia's wrists. "Ain't this gonna be a sight when they wake up?"*

*Burl shook his head, hesitated, and then crouched and clutched Sylvia's ankles. He and Hank carried her across the barn and dropped her on the rack. She stirred, murmured. Hank raised her arms and slapped the leather straps on her wrists.*

*Burl buried his face in his hands. He looked up, still shaking his head. "This is barbaric, Hank."*

*The farmer's stringy hair clung to his sweaty forehead. He secured Sylvia's ankles and grabbed the giant crank. He extended the rollers one notch. They creaked from centuries of disuse. Sylvia's eyes fluttered. Hank removed his handkerchief and blew his nose. He then shoved it in her mouth as she came to.*

*Sylvia's gaze focused on Hank and Burl. Her blue eyes bulged and she struggled to break free. The handkerchief muffled her screams to mouse squeaks.*

*Hank chuckled. "This is what happens to bullies, little missy. And this ain't even the tip of the pitchfork."*

*Burl turned his back on the rack. He looked to Francine. He had expected to see her wringing her hands or hiding her face. Instead she beamed near the first stall.*

*Burl stormed at her and jabbed an accusatory finger. "You think this is fun and games? You think she deserves to be tortured?"*

*Francine nodded.*

*Hank grabbed Burl's shoulder and spun him. "Let her join in the fun if she wants to. This ain't show and tell."*

*Burl knocked his hand away. Hank responded with a right jab, smashing his knuckles against Burl's cheekbone. Burl lost his footing, fell, and cracked the back of his head on a stall post.*

*Hank spat and kicked his friend's shoes. "Damn that old-timer's a hardhead. Guess it's just you and me, Franny."*

*Francine shrugged.*

*A moan turned their heads. They looked at the bloody sisters sprawled on the dirt. Henna rolled over and blinked. She spotted Sylvia wriggling on the rack and sprang up.*

*Hank nodded at Francine. "Now's your chance to whoop her."*

*Francine's smile widened. She glanced around the stall*

*behind her. She grabbed a spade off the wall, whirled, and swung it*

*like a tennis racket. The back of the blade cracked Henna a hair*

*above her right ear. She collapsed to the dirt as a small gash bled*

*down her neck.*

*Hank grinned. "Atta girl. I think you and I are gonna get*

*along just peachy."*

*Francine giggled. The adrenaline rushed through her veins.*

*She felt as if she was on top of the world after inflicting pain on one*

*of the girls that had made her life hell for as long as she could*

*remember. She wanted to continue beating Henna, but she knew she*

*had to restrain herself. Mr. Adler had bigger and better plans. It was*

*the first time she had seen the old farmer smile, so it was obvious the*

*fun had yet to begin. She hung the spade back on the wall.*

*Hank picked up Loren and heaved her onto his shoulder. Her*

*face was freckled with black shards and dried blood. Her bangs*

*were strawberry blond and matted to her forehead. She coughed,*

*drooling onto Hank's back. He carried her to the third stall on the*

*opposite side of the barn. He slammed her down on a splintered electric chair. The wires and power had long since been removed, but the worn leather straps remained.*

*Loren cried out. Hank slapped her, and then bound her wrists and ankles. He unbuttoned his plaid and removed it. Before she could scream he tied it around her mouth and the back of the chair.*

*He fingered the shoulder straps of his wife beater, spat, and then looked over his shoulder. "How do you reckon we ought to punish her, Franny?"*

*Francine had wandered to an adjacent stall. There was a workbench scattered with medieval tools. All were unfamiliar to her. One looked like a pair of tongs used for corn on the cob or dumplings. Another had an ornate pear with leaves on the end of a silver handle. She picked it up, eyed the intricate carvings. She wondered what it was used for. Coring fruit maybe?*

*"What's this one do?"*

*Hank chuckled and crossed the barn. "That one's called the Pear of Anguish. It's perfect for smart mouths, like that one in the chair. The leaves open up like a flower. You'll have to see the rest for yourself."*

*"I like it. It's pretty."*

*"Since you think so, maybe you want to try it out on her."*

*Francine looked at Loren. She thrashed and shook her head as if an electric current flowed through the chair.*

*Francine brushed past Hank and approached Loren. "Remember that time you locked me in my locker? You poked me with X-acto knives." She paused and pointed at her bloodstained calf. "You did this to me on the fence."*

*Loren froze as the recollections hit home. With her Pirates cap gone, her face possessed a raw innocence. Her brow raised into the deep lines that creased her gashed forehead. Francine waved the pear before her face and pulled the handle. The spoon-shaped leaves sprang open like a reverse bear trap. Loren bucked and squirmed as if she was having an epileptic seizure.*

*Hank placed a gentle hand on Francine's shoulder. "Hold on. It'll be mighty difficult with the shirt in her mouth."*

*He crossed the barn, kicking Henna in her head for good measure, and crouched in the corner of a stall. He returned with faded leather gloves on his hands, a wire cutter, and a ball of barbed wire. He set the fence material on the floor and snipped off a strip.*

345

*He then walked over to Loren with the strand of wire in hand. Both sisters writhed and choked on their shrieks.*

*Hank shook the barbed wire. "This'll keep her mouth open. But you make sure you gag her with the shirt when she starts screaming. Understand?"*

*Francine nodded as Hank rounded the chair, yanked the plaid from Loren's mouth, and then wrapped the wire around wood and flesh. Loren shrieked. Hank slammed his elbow on the top of her skull. Her eyes became waterfalls as the barbs dug into her lips and the wire was fastened behind the chair.*

*Loren's tongue struggled to enunciate. "Oohh! Oohh!"*

*"Franny, shut her up! I'm gonna wire this one. She ain't feeling her sister's pain. Are you?"*

*He cut off another barbed strand. Sylvia was still, aware that any movement strained her muscles. Hank could tell that it would only take a couple of cranks to pop her joints. He approached the rack, removed the handkerchief, and bound her mouth. Sylvia screamed louder than her sister had.*

*Hank tied the wire, then reached over the rack and gouged her eyes. "Shut up! Shut up, damn you!"*

*Sylvia's blues pooled red and bled down her cheeks. Hank stifled her screams with the handkerchief as he eyed his handiwork. He had crushed her eyeballs and rendered her blind. That was payback for the time she egged his pickup.*

*Francine inched the pear toward Loren's mouth. The Blondie trembled and cried. Francine smiled. She snapped the sharp leaves open and shut. Loren whined, reluctant to scream, though knew it was inevitable.*

*A guttural moan that elevated to a yell broke Hank and Francine's concentration. They jerked in unison and snapped their heads back.*

*Henna charged at Francine, her T-shirt speckled with blood from the dripping gash above her ear. She plowed over her target and pinned her on the ground. She punched Francine in the eye, and then cocked back for another jab.*

*"Henna!"*

*The Blondie froze, looked back. Burl staggered forth with the spade in hand. He raised it like a sledgehammer.*

*"Get off her!"*

*Francine dug her fingers into Henna's injured hand, stabbing the hole the screwdriver had made. The Blondie cried out and swatted her aside. Francine remained on the ground, stunned from the blow.*

*Burl charged and swung the spade. Henna stood and blocked it with her forearm. She then grabbed the handle and wrenched it from his grip.*

*"I'm gonna kill ya, old man!"*

*Burl ducked, the blade missing his scalp by inches. Henna followed through with a pendulum swing and uppercut him with the flat side. He caught air and landed on his back, knocked unconscious once again.*

*Henna half-turned, but glimpsed her attacker too late. Hank crashed into her with his wire cutters in hand. The spade was lost in the collision as they toppled into a nearby stall.*

*Hank slammed her into an antique meat block. The top was three feet thick and bloodstained from hundreds of butcherings.*

*Hank bent her back over the block. "You want to bully someone? I'm right here, pig!" He braced his arm against her throat* and stabbed her shoulder with the wire cutter. She growled through gritted teeth. "C'mon, bully me!"

Francine sat up, massaged her jaw. Her gaze roved the barn. Loren and Sylvia twisted and twitched with fixed grimaces. Mr. Adler shoved Henna onto the butcher block and worked her like a piece of meat. She could tell he had lost it, as his face was blood red and his eyes crazed as a rabid dog's.

Hank snipped Henna's chin. "You like that? Burl didn't like it either!" He punched her temple with his free fist. Her eyes glazed. "Now it's payback!"

Hank used the wire cutter like scissors and halved Henna's T-shirt. He punched her in the nose and tore off her jeans. He then dropped his overalls and mounted her on the meat block.

Francine attempted to stand, but her rear end was frozen to the ground. She knew that what Mr. Adler was doing was terribly wrong, yet at the same time she knew Henna deserved it.

Henna flailed, but to no avail. Hank snipped the wire cutters across her throat, grazing her carotid arteries. She gurgled as blood poured in rivulets down her chest. Hank cut the skin like it was paper, tossed the tool aside, and then shoved her chin back.

*Francine clamped her hands on her ears at the mingling of moans and death rattles. Henna's head fell off her shoulders and dangled by the carotids as a tremble coursed through Mr. Adler's body. Blood spurted and gushed like a kinked garden hose.*

*Francine's sanity snapped. She realized, as Mr. Adler led by example, that the barn was the Blondies' torture chamber. She would not see the light of day until the bullies were dead. Nobody could see them. Hopefully nobody could hear them. Nobody would know what occurred beyond closed doors.*

*Francine yelled as her pent up ire bubbled over. She charged Sylvia, clutched the massive lever, and cranked it with all her might.*

\*\*\*\*\*

"Do you think Francine Heller wants back in?"

Jay stepped into the living room. "I've had enough surprises for one day."

Coren peered through the glass. "Well, it sure isn't Pritchard."

"Who is it?"

"I don't know. Could be a neighbor."

Coren opened the door. Vance stepped into view and said hello with a right jab. Blood sprayed from Coren's nose as he staggered against the kitchen table. Vance crossed the threshold and dropped a hammer fist. Coren rolled onto the floor, the attack missing his head by inches.

Jay raised his hands in surrender. "What the hell's going on here?"

Vance's leer leeched onto Jay. He advanced over Coren, cocked his fist back, and then paused. His arm dropped to his side and he blinked.

"Jay Donovan? What's going on?"

Jay shrugged and lowered his hands. "That's what I'd like to know."

"Are you Coren Raines?"

The homeowner in question stood to his feet and pinched his nostrils. His voice was nasal when he spoke. "I'll go get him. I think he's in the john."

"The hell with that!"

Coren backed against the wall. "Listen, whoever you are, you're breaking and entering, trespassing, and -"

Vance punched Coren in the jaw with a left jab. Coren crumpled to the floor.

Jay stepped in front of Vance. "Enough! I've got TV cameras set up in every room of this house!"

Vance backed off and rubbed his knuckles. "Good, because this guy has my daughters!"

Coren glared at him. "You're crazy."

"I'm not the one with three open graves in my backyard! And I know for a fact that those bodies are Pritchard's girls!"

Jay waved his hand before Vance's face. "Who disappeared fifteen years ago. He didn't even live here then."

Coren stood, swayed, and then regained his balance. "Vance Trammell? Coren Raines. Nice to meet you."

Vance knocked away Coren's outstretched hand and cocked his arm.

Jay stood his ground. "Vance! I know you're hell-bent on finding your daughters, but they're not here! I already looked!"

Vance pointed in Jay's face. "You expect me to believe that? There's triplets buried out there. It seems pretty obvious that he's guilty."

"*They've been buried out there for fifteen years.*"

"Then why is he digging them up?"

Coren glanced around the room for a means of self-defense. "Hey, they dug themselves out!"

Vance rushed. "*You liar!*"

Jay held him back. "Vance! Listen to me! I've already interrogated him! And believe you and me, he didn't dig up Pritchard's daughters!"

"Malarkey! Pritchard told me he's hiding something!"

"Is that right? Well, who lived here before him that's so saintly?"

"Ray Hodge, that's who! A friend of mine!"

Coren stepped forward. "Then who is Edwold Gentry?"

"How should I know?"

"Because Hodge signed his title over to him."

Vance blinked. His reminiscence from a mere ten minutes ago returned full force. He stepped back and Jay released him. "How do you know that?"

"Google."

"Google." Vance shook his head and grabbed a chair. "Mind if I sit down?"

"Be my guest. You just punched me in the face." Coren joined Jay's side. "What do you know?"

"I know something's not right here." Vance buried his face in his hands, grumbled, and then looked up. "Ray told me once that Hank Adler and Burl Nelson were pressuring him to sell the house. Now I learn that he signed over the title. It makes perfect sense. Edwold Gentry was probably an alias so they could sweep it under the rug. But why? They never did anything with the property."

"Sure they did. They turned it into a cemetery."

The three men exchanged glances as the pieces of the puzzle glued together.

Vance trembled and his face contorted. He was on the verge of breaking down. His voice was hoarse. "They took my girls. Hank and Burl took my girls." He shook his head. "Why?"

Jay scratched his beard. "Because they're triplets. They didn't want three more bullies in this town."

S.D. Hintz

# CHAPTER TWENTY-ONE

*Sylvia's legs tore at the knees with a pop and squelch, spraying blood on Francine. She cried out, her face crimson and twisted. She writhed as she dangled on the rack, teetering on unconsciousness.*

*Francine released the crank. She stared, dumbfounded by the surreal image. Sylvia's legs twitched in place, secured by the straps, spurting like fountains. Loren's relentless screams snapped Francine back to reality.*

*"Oohh! Oohh!"*

*Francine raised her hand as she approached Loren. She still clutched the pear. Loren jerked from side to side and strained her neck like a bobblehead. Francine taunted her, opening and shutting the razor-sharp leaves as she inched them toward her face.*

*Francine glanced out of the corner of her eye. Mr. Adler pulled up his overalls and kicked aside Henna's decapitated body. He was drenched in blood. He wiped the sweat off his forehead.*

*Loren's sobs reinforced Francine's focus. She cocked back the pear in a punching stance.*

*Hank laughed and nodded. "Jam it in there real hard."*

*Francine followed orders. She charged Loren and jabbed the pear. Loren clamped her mouth shut seconds before impact. The metal tip shattered her incisors. Her cries were cut short as Francine squeezed the handle. The leaves sprang open. Francine yanked the pear from her mouth and stepped back. Teeth poured from Loren's bleeding mouth, as did a severed tongue, and plopped on the dirt.*

*Francine grinned as Loren choked on blood and canines. Her face paled and turned purplish-blue, at which point her body went limp.*

*Hank barged in front of Francine and crouched. He undid the chair straps and grabbed Loren's ankles. He then twisted her legs like a pretzel, breaking bones through skin. "There. Now she won't be going nowhere."*

*Francine's wide-eyed stare roved the stalls. All of the Blondies were still, either unconscious or dead. Sylvia dangled from the bloodstained rack, dismembered and agape. Loren was slouched forward, red drivel splattering her entangled feet. Henna's decapitated and defiled body seeped fluids in the dirt like a* slaughtered cow. Francine was beside herself. The bullies would never harass her again.

"Hank? What have you done?"

The accomplices turned in unison. Burl walked toward them with the shovel in hand. His chin was black-and-blue and the gash on his head trickled blood down the back of his neck.

He pointed the shovel. "What's the matter with you? You're a lunatic!"

Hank wiped his hands on his overalls. "I had help, seeing how you decided to nap."

"You killed them!"

"We didn't buy Hodge's property for a farmer's market, Burl. We needed burial grounds."

"For the sheriff's daughters?" Burl shook his head, then jabbed the blade into the dirt. "I had no part in this! I'm not even here! This is all your doing!" He gestured at Francine. "Yours, too! They bullied you! You're still alive, aren't you?"

Francine nodded. When she spoke, her voice was monotone, as if hypnotized. "If they were alive, they'd bully me."

"Oh waa waa, you baby!"

*Hank stepped into Burl's face. "Shut it, Burl! You act like they never bullied you! You were scared of 'em!"*

*The shovel trembled in Burl's fist, a mixture of ire and arthritis. "You lied to me, Hank! That farmer's market…That was my dream!"*

*"You can have your dream. You'll just have some bodies beneath it."*

*Burl's mind kept pace with his stomach, twisting and knotting. He wished he had avoided vengeance. He sure should have distrusted Hank. Now he had three bodies on his conscience in the presence of two murderers. He itched to crush Hank's skull with the shovel and knock some sense into Francine.*

*He closed his eyes, and then opened them. He yearned to sweep the mess under a rug. Pritchard's daughters had to be buried. Calling 9-1-1 would land him a death sentence. There was no hiding the fact that he was an accomplice.*

*"As soon as it's dark we haul them out! That's it! You hear me? Then you forget I was even here."*

*Hank sneered. "We'll bury them in Hodge's backyard, put that swamp to use. You best believe I got their plots picked out."*

*Burl turned his back, headed for the doors. "I'll get the truck."*

*Francine was entranced. The images played over and over in her head. Loren choking at her hands. Sylvia's limbs severed, twitching in their shackles. Mr. Adler with his pants down, forcing himself on Henna as he decapitated her. She held herself tight, and then rocked back and forth. She wondered if her parents were looking for her yet. Home seemed so distant; a dream forgotten seconds after waking.*

*The pear slipped from her fingers, clanked on the dirt. Her actions would yield consequences. Her father would beat her. Her mother would cry herself to sleep. Sheriff Pritchard might even lock her up.*

*She sat on a hay bale and stared into space. A grin teased her lips. The Blondies were gone, problem solved. That was all that mattered. Regardless of the repercussions, her life would be peaceful and worry-free. And she would live happily ever after.*

*The end.*

\*\*\*\*\*

"The barn! Of course!"

"Jay, what are you babbling about?"

"Adler's barn was a torture chamber! I was snooping around there the other night!"

"*What?* You just now remembered that? That whole time you were pointing fingers at me you knew that he was hiding a torture chamber? When did you plan on breaking the news?"

"It didn't click. I just thought it was a sick collection at the time. I'm a reporter, not a P.I."

Vance clutched his temples. "I'm going to kill him."

Jay ran into the living room and peered out the window. "Coren, does your truck run? We need to get to that barn."

"Both of you calm down. Are you sure we're not jumping to conclusions? Vance here was ready to kill me a second ago and Jay you weren't far off the same ledge."

Vance grabbed Coren's shirt collar and slammed him against the wall. "Jumping to conclusions? Pritchard's daughters are buried in your backyard, which used to be owned by Adler and Nelson, and Farmer Hank has a torture chamber in his barn! No one's jumping to conclusions!"

"Alright, alright! The keys are on the fridge!"

Vance released Coren, reached over the freezer, and found the keys. "Let's go. I'll drive."

Coren was at his heels. "Just to warn you, Pritchard's been staking out my house for the past day."

"Pritchard stakes out everybody's house. He's a small town sheriff. He'll fine you for breathing."

*****

Hank dropped Burl's decapitated body on Barter's burnt remains. He caught his breath as he scanned the barn. His mind was set. He would bury Barter beneath the rack and Burl a stall or two over, not far from where he slaughtered his first pig.

He chuckled and grabbed the shovel. He needed the graves dug by sunset. A light in the barn would yield unwanted attention. He crossed the dirt and proceeded to move the rack as sweet reminiscence made him drool like a rabid dog.

*****

With the tape recorder rolling and the baggie in his pocket, Pritchard slammed the driver's side door. He withdrew his Magnum, knowing that if the situation exploded he would be prepared.

"I tried calling you, Sheriff."

"I know, Edsel! I got one hand! One hand! Five fingers to drive, no fingers to flip ya off!"

"Sorry, sir." Edsel met Pritchard at the grill of his squad car and lowered his voice. "Ms. Heller has been ignoring me. Won't even roll down her window."

"Ya kiddin' me? Use yer club."

"Thought I'd wait for your lead."

"Stay here and cover me."

Pritchard approached the driver's side of the Cougar. He tapped the Magnum barrel on the window. Francine rolled it down, but stared straight ahead.

Pritchard grimaced. The inside of the car reeked of cheap cigarettes and brandy. Francine Heller looked like a recluse. Her hair was ratted and fuzzy as if insects had nested on her scalp. Her face was set in a gaping frown, baring her bumblebee teeth. Her stained T-shirt was torn from her shoulder to her navel, which provided a glimpse of her saggy breast. She raised a GPC to her mouth and inhaled for a good five seconds.

"Ms. Heller? Step out of the car please."

She sat there, blew smoke into the dirt-streaked windshield. "No."

Pritchard aimed the barrel. "Ya think I'm bluffin'? *Get outta the car!*"

Edsel had his firearm trained on the Cougar's windshield. He prayed that Ms. Heller would avoid stepping on the gas pedal, as the engine still idled.

Francine turned her head toward Pritchard's Magnum and licked the barrel.

The sheriff looked to Edsel, red-faced. "Blow out the tires."

Edsel knew better than to question Pritchard's orders. He opened fire and flattened the front tires.

Francine sat like a stone, unfazed. She looked daggers.

Pritchard jabbed her face with the barrel. She fell across the passenger's seat and opened the glove box. Pritchard reached inside and pistol-whipped her. He knocked her hand off the compartment, and then proceeded to beat her head and chest.

Edsel shattered the passenger's side window with his billy club. He holstered both of his weapons and slapped the handcuffs on Francine's flailing wrist. He locked the opposite restraint beneath the seat. She thrashed like a straitjacketed mental patient.

*"You pig! Your daughters were pigs, too! All of them! You knew they were bullying me!"*

Pritchard pressed the trunk button as he ducked out of the car. His eyes welled with tears. The Magnum trembled in his hand. Heller might as well have punched him in the gut. He wanted to blow her brains out. Maybe he could shoot her, and then turn the gun on Edsel.

His right-hand man rounded the front of the Cougar. "Paul? You okay?"

Pritchard looked away and bit back his scowl. Francine's rants burned his ears. "Search the back seat. I'll check the trunk. She's up to somethin'."

He rounded the rear bumper, looked in the trunk. There were two bulky garbage bags and a tire iron. He holstered his Magnum and unwound a twisty tie. Inside the bag were musty clothes. He pulled out some pants and shirts, convinced that there was paraphernalia hidden within. After tossing aside a skirt, his fingers clawed something cold. He removed it. He grinned at the half empty bottle of E&J. He made a mental note of the additional charge, and then set the brandy beside the tire iron.

Edsel joined him at the trunk. "We got a live one, Paul. Found some kind of a rusty fruit corer under the seat cushions."

"Confiscate it along with this open container. I got one more bag to go through."

Edsel left Pritchard to his search. The second garbage bag was full of socks and panties. Not one thing incriminating. He cursed under his breath. This psycho was getting nailed. There was no way she was going to slam his daughters to his face. He reached in his pocket and removed the baggie. With two fingers he managed to open it. As he attempted to inch the bloodstained knife out, it slipped through his fingers and clanged on the blacktop.

He crouched and looked beneath the undercarriage. The knife glinted below the muffler. He grabbed it, and then froze as a flutter caught his eye. He craned his neck beyond the bumper.

"What the -"

# CHAPTER TWENTY-TWO

*It was sunset when Burl parked the pickup a block from Francine's house. Hank sat in the passenger's seat and leered at their seventeen-year-old accomplice.*

*"You keep your mouth shut, you hear me? If any word of this comes back to me I'll be a bigger bully than the Blondies ever were. Understand?"*

*Francine nodded. Hank opened the door and slid out onto the sidewalk. As Francine followed suit he placed his hand on her shoulder.*

*"You were volunteering on the prom committee. That's what you tell your folks."*

*Francine walked away with her backpack held in front of her, concealing the blood splatters on her shirt. She hoped her parents were gone, having dinner out of town or seeing a movie, as they often did on a Friday night. The last thing she wanted was a confrontation. Though it had been hours since the torturing, her body surged with adrenaline. She knew she would lash out if her parents disciplined her. She was done being the victim.*

*Burl turned on Sangralea and headed for Inventory Street. His conscience burned as his suspicions of Hank boiled over.*

*"You've been planning this for weeks. Just like the barbed wire fence. You waited to put that up until the field was tall enough and you knew the high school track team wouldn't see it."*

*"Shut your mouth, Burl. This ain't no comparison."*

*"Bull! How did you even get Hodge to leave town so quick? Huh? Did you strap him up in the barn, too?"*

*"No, but that's where I buried him."*

*Burl slowed the truck to a crawl. He could have cared less that there were three bloody bodies beneath a mountain of apples in the flatbed. He glared at Hank as he approached the gravel drive.*

*"What did you do? What did you do to Ray?"*

*"Got him to sign the title over. Ain't that enough?"*

*"What did you do?"*

*"Cut off his head with sheep shears. Had to remove some knuckles just to get his Henry."*

*Burl slammed on the brakes. A cloud of dust engulfed the pickup. He turned and punched Hank in the jaw. Hank's face met the window and he bounced back with both hands around Burl's throat. He choked him against the dashboard.*

*"Listen to me, you idiot! We ain't got time for this! We got Paul's daughters in the flatbed!"*

*Burl kneed Hank in the gut and shoved him in his seat. "Paul? You're on a first name basis? What's going on, Hank?"*

*Hank gasped and turned to Burl, his scowl cast in shadows. "Back the truck up to the door. Ray's got a panic room. I'll hide 'em in there while I dig the graves. Thanks to you I'll be doing this all stinking night."*

*"Maybe you should call Paul over. Have a potluck."*

*Hank pulled a bloodstained screwdriver out of his pocket. "He made me do this! He wanted those girls gone! They were a liability! Now back the truck up or I'll bury you, too!"*

*Burl hesitated, then obliged. Hank scowled, hopped out of the cab, and dropped the tailgate. Burl stared at the dark drive, feeling dead inside from the flood of guilt.*

*The night was silent, save for the thuds of apples and corpses. It took Hank a half-hour to drag the Blondies out of the pickup and into the house. Once the farmer lugged the last Blondie out of sight, Burl floored the gas pedal and sped into the darkness with the headlights off.*

\*\*\*\*\*

Coren, Jay, and Vance climbed out of the Suburban. The weathered barn burned bright against the darkening sky. A slumped silhouette flitted past the windows. The double doors rattled in the wind, banging back into metal, as if farm machinery barricaded the other side.

Coren looked to his counterparts. "It's a little late to be milking, isn't it?"

Jay shook his head. "So what do we do if Adler's in there with your daughters?"

Vance's face was grave. "There's three of us. We beat him to death."

"We're unarmed. What if he has a gun?"

"There's *three* of us. We rush him. A full clip won't stop me from getting my girls back."

Jay nodded, realizing that he missed his own daughters. What if their plan backfired and he never saw his family again? At this point, Jeanette probably thought he had skipped town with another news bimbo. He really needed to call her.

"We can't go in there unarmed. That's crazy."

Coren raised his index finger. "Hold on. I might have some stuff in the back of my truck."

"Some stuff?"

"Yeah, some stuff. There's some boxes I forgot to unpack."

Vance stood his ground, his head jerking from the barn to the Suburban. "Hurry up. Or I'm going in there without you."

Coren returned holding three items. "Outdoor stuff." He handed them to Jay and Vance. Both raised them toward the waning light.

Vance's eyes narrowed to slits. "What the hell is this?"

"A wicket. Jay's got the mallet. I guess it's all horseshoes and no croquet out here."

Jay's nerves calmed and he took a practice swing. "What do you have?"

"A lawn orb. I figured it was better than a croquet ball."

Vance clutched the wicket and marched toward the barn. Coren and Jay trailed at his heels. The gravel crunched in the quiet darkness. Jay had the urge to tiptoe while Coren wished he walked with Seagram's.

Vance locked his sights. He would have stormed the barn with a cowbell around his neck and a revving chainsaw in hand. The consequences were meaningless to him. He refused to face Teresa without his girls.

They hesitated at the clanging doors. Vance curled his fingers on the handle, and then pulled with the gust. The door caught, scraped open. Vance held it tight as the wind shoved it toward him. Coren and Jay snuck inside and crouched beside the rear right tire of the pickup. Vance slipped behind them, lodging the door shut against the bumper. The howling wind and grunting drowned out their entry.

Coren inched forward, but Vance grabbed his shoulder and took the lead. He crept to the flattened tailgate, clutched the wicket, and peered past the bumper. He swayed, flabbergasted. Coren and Jay snuck beside him. The same shock, frigid as a winter lake, flooded their bodies.

Hank was hunched in the far stall. He shoved a charred mangled body and stepped back. The remains slid into a hole and slopped at the bottom. Satisfied, he turned and walked to the beheaded corpse sprawled in the middle of the barn. He shook his head, then grabbed Burl's bleeding skull and raised it before his face.

Jay's stomach lurched. He shut his eyes and gritted his teeth, but the sickness overcame him. He turned his head and vomited on the passenger's side door.

Hank looked to the pickup and panicked. He paled at the sight of Vance. He guessed that his cohorts were undercover cops. He was perplexed, however, as to why they held sporting goods instead of guns. Regardless, he had been caught red-handed. And it was all Paul's fault. He refused to take the bullet for a dirty pig.

Vance approached Hank, looking like Wolverine with the fisted wicket. Coren covered him with the lawn orb cocked back in shot put form while Jay regained his composure.

Vance quavered, his anger boiling in his throat. "Easy, Hank. I just want my -"

Hank hurled Burl's head. Vance and Coren ducked as blood drizzled on them. Jay looked up, reacted on instinct, and swung the mallet. He busted the head open against the side of the pickup. Brains and eyeballs squirted, dripping off the fender. Jay shrieked and dropped the mallet.

Hank snatched up the shovel and held it like a baseball bat. Coren launched the lawn orb. Hank swung and missed. The orb slammed into his chest and knocked him to the dirt.

Vance charged and pinned Hank down with a boot on his bruised chest. Hank seized Burl's shirt collar and yanked his corpse. Vance thrust the wicket and punctured the body shield. He withdrew his weapon and stepped back, grimacing as blood gushed from Burl's abdomen.

Hank staggered to his feet, still clutching the headless corpse. He barreled into Vance, who cried out as the body tackled him into the pickup's grill.

Coren rushed Hank. The farmer spun the corpse and performed the Heimlich maneuver. Greenish-yellow stomach acid and brown blood shot from the severed neck. The stream hit Coren in the face and he freaked, yelling and flailing as if covered with killer bees.

Jay twitched at the screaming, and then peeled his eyes off the head he had smashed. He had been doubled over for minutes chiding himself, disbelieving that he had committed such a heinous act. He felt more like a butcher than a reporter. His worries dissipated, however, when he realized that his counterparts were in trouble. Vance was slumped against the grill and Coren was covered in blood.

Jay grabbed the mallet, raised it over his head, and brought it down on the pickup's hood. It gonged and sprang open.

Hank tossed the corpse aside and choked Vance. He lifted his head over the grill and smashed his face into the engine. He held him there with his left hand as his right slammed the hood shut. Vance's body convulsed and blood seeped down the grill. Hank let go and Vance collapsed to the dirt, his skull crushed into the shape of a football.

Jay gaped as he realized the repercussions of his strike. His reaction had once again rendered a smashed head.

Coren collided with the Judas cradle, which killed his shouts. He wiped the blood from his eyes and turned.

Hank laughed. "What a goddamn mess. You pigs ain't gonna pin this on me, you hear me? I didn't kidnap no babies! You hear me?"

Coren clawed his drenched hair. The barn's bludgeoning insanity pinched his last nerve. "You're dead, MacDonald!"

Hank ripped the wicket from Vance's dead hand, and then approached Coren. "I know you. You're the newbie. I used to own your house." He pointed to the headless corpse that had soaked Coren. "So did Burl. Buried some bodies in the yard."

"I know. They've been locked up in my panic room. I bet Pritchard would love to know that you killed his daughters."

*"Burl murdered those brats! That dead man right there!"*

Hank lunged with the wicket. Coren sidestepped and the Judas cradle deflected the blow. Hank dropped the wicket, and then threw a left jab. The punch knocked out Coren's front teeth and he clutched his mouth, stumbling like a drunk.

Regardless of the blood Jay had spilled, he wasn't about to let the farmer kill Coren. He ran with the mallet over his head, yelling like an irate kung fu master. Hank spun and glimpsed his fate. The mallet came down and smashed the center of his skull. His forehead split a red fissure down through his nose and his eyes crossed. His face flushed and burst vessels. Blood poured from his nostrils and mouth. He crumpled onto the Judas cradle, dangling on the triangular point.

Jay let the mallet slip from his fingers and fall beside the wicket. The news bulletins bored into his brain. What had happened since they had entered the barn? He had been a reporter digging for a story. Now he was the story and the reporter had left the scene.

Coren approached him, bloodstained and weary. "The nutjob knocked out my teeth. Goddamn it. Let's get out of here. We don't need this traced to us. You have a family. They don't need that."

"Vance didn't need this. All he wanted was his daughters."

"And he went to all this trouble and still didn't get them." Coren shook his head. "This isn't our problem. It's just another story, right? Another news report."

"Yeah. This has been Jay Donovan for WNDY News."

*****

Pritchard felt as if he had been kicked in the face. Bound to three out of the four wheel wells were the Trammell triplets. Their tiny arms and legs were entwined with barbed wire. Their naked, purplish-blue bodies were dotted with bloodstains, as if the infants had been laid on a crib of nails. Their mouths were likewise gagged with barbed wire, which had been wrapped around their necks like umbilical cords. Even more disturbing were the blond wigs stapled to each of their skulls.

Pritchard wavered on his hands and knees as a torrent of images blinded him. He saw Henna, Loren, and Sylvia screaming in the wheel wells. He watched from a bird's eye view while Francine lynched his daughters with barbed wire from wood rafters. Then there was darkness and crying.

He shook off the prodding blackout and refocused his eyes. Vance Trammell's triplets, dead and defiled, were bound to the undercarriage of Francine Heller's Cougar. He released the knife and fished his Magnum out of the holster.

*She killed Vance's triplets and dressed 'em up like my girls. You gotta be kiddin' me. That sick bitch.*

He backed away from the bumper and stood. Edsel was right there, peering into the messy trunk.

Pritchard's glare was bloodshot and watery. His face was pale as a dead man's. "Post up. Now!"

Edsel turned without a moment's hesitation and hurried toward his squad car. Pritchard's arm dangled at his side as he clutched the Magnum. The Cougar's open front door creaked in the wind.

Francine yelled and thrashed. *"Take these cuffs off me! I didn't do anything! I didn't do a goddamn thing! I'll have your badge for this! You hear me? I'm not one of your pig daughters!"*

Pritchard's reply was curt; a single gunshot splattered Francine's brains on the dashboard and passenger seat. The glove box popped open on impact. A news clipping with the headline **Six-month-old triplets kidnapped, bloodied** tumbled out and soaked in the waterfall of blood.

Pritchard grimaced, lowered the Magnum, and then turned. Standing before him, silent and wan, was a group of ten to fifteen men; some were armed with shotguns while others held maps and flashlights. On his right, Edsel approached with his gun drawn.

Pritchard raised his Magnum and waved it at Edsel, signaling him to stand his ground.

Sam Emory glanced back at the search party, stunned as the rest of the men from having witnessed Francine's murder. He then met the sheriff's blazing leer and stepped forward.

"Paul? We found your daughters. They've been dug up in Coren Raines' backyard."

S.D. Hintz

# CHAPTER TWENTY-THREE

"So what are you going to do with the half-buried bodies in your backyard?"

Coren backed away from the kitchen sink, grabbed a dishtowel, and dried off his mouth. "What bodies? They crawled out and melted, remember?"

Jay shut the deck door. His gaze was fixed on the moonbeam that seemed to spotlight the graves as if connecting the dots. The tainted croquet accessories glinted on the table. "I don't know what that was about, but there's three skeletons out there. Even though we left the barn a mess, your backyard's a lot more incriminating."

Coren tossed the damp towel to Jay, who proceeded to wipe the blood off his hands. "Pritchard will kill me if he finds those bodies. I don't know, Jay." He kicked the garbage can. Table scraps and barbed wire littered the linoleum. "What am I going to do? I can't just leave them there! And how do I know Vance didn't tell somebody about what he found?"

Jay wrung the dishtowel in his hands. "Well, what if we drag them into the panic room? They're just skeletons."

"But I dragged them all in there once already!"

"Vance found them. I found them. They're still out there. I don't get all that zombie stuff, maybe it was some kind of warning from the grave, but it wasn't them. They've been rotting in that backyard for years and we need to worry about letting them rot somewhere else."

Coren nibbled his thumbnail and then nodded. "Well, let's do it. The night's still young."

A thump resounded behind them and the front door rattled in its frame. Several consecutive thuds followed, which Jay thought sounded like car doors slamming. Coren ran to the living room and peeked out the bay window. The doorbell dinged and dinged, oozing with impatience.

Coren turned and dashed back to the kitchen. "Pritchard and the whole town are at the door!"

Jay raised his hands. "Just calm down. We have to play this cool."

"He's been out to get me since day one and his dead daughters are in my backyard!"

A boom shook the front door, its hinges parting from the wall.

Coren seized Jay by the arm and yanked him down the hallway.

Jay attempted to wrench free. "What are you doing?"

Coren opened the sliding door. "This has nothing to do with you. None of this. You came here for a story, not to get booked for a triple murder." He shoved Jay into the panic room. "Don't come out of here until they've all left."

"There's no way -"

"Jay, you have a family of your own, remember? Don't screw this up. I don't have a thing to lose but alimony."

Jay bit his tongue as the door slammed and the darkness swallowed him whole. All he had was a small window to keep him in tune with the world. He saw Jeanette and the girls in its reflection. Tears trickled down his beard as he sat and succumbed to the silence.

*****

Pritchard's mind spun as fast as the squad car's wheels. The bumper trampled corner bushes. Curbs were checked and marked by the tires. Street signs shook in the wake. All the while the one-handed sheriff cranked the wheel back and forth, blinded by the past day's disillusionment as if a downpour drenched the windshield.

Francine's murder and the gruesome discovery of the Trammell triplets cowered in his subconscious. His twitching red eyes saw blurry images of oversights.

He saw his daughters bawling on a summer day after school, explaining how Francine Heller had clubbed them with her backpack. He regretted all of his past disciplinary measures. Even back then the recluse witch had been torturing triplets.

Pritchard bellowed as the tires screeched onto Inventory Street. It all made perfect sense. Raines and Heller were accomplices. They had probably considered burying the Trammell triplets in Raines' backyard.

The squad car jolted up the gravel driveway, jarring Pritchard's thoughts even more. He knew that Heller had threatened Raines, probably put a knife to his throat.

He saw the bloody Tribune headline.

He slammed on the brakes and parked sideways, blocking in the Suburban. He stepped out and scanned the premises. A light burned inside the rambler. He removed the Magnum from its holster.

He kicked the driver's side door shut as an approaching glare caught his eye. He glanced back. The cavalcade consisting of the search party and other nosy townies rumbled toward him. He turned and stormed up the front steps. He needed to handle business before the scene became a circus.

He removed his finger from the trigger and pounded on the door. He punched the doorbell and followed up with a boot. The door shifted as the hinges popped out. He kicked it again and it flew into the house as if it had been crashed into by a battering ram. He barged inside with his Magnum level.

Split second sound bites from Raines' mouth haunted him as his vulture gaze roved the house.

*There's no one here but me. Do you hear any babies crying?*

*I didn't kidnap anybody's kids!*

Pritchard's thoughts throttled as he crossed the vacant living room. *Yeah, ya didn't kidnap any kids, Raines. Heller did that. Ya just dug up my daughters, right?*

He approached the bright light. The kitchen was deserted. Garbage was dumped before the deck door.

"Ya got some explainin' to do, Raines! Ya hear me? Ya gonna quit hidin' and tell me why my daughters are buried in yer backyard? Huh? *Why are my daughters in yer backyard?*"

Coren tiptoed to the end of the hall and peered into the kitchen. "Ask Adler and Nelson."

Pritchard whirled, and then ducked moments later as a lawn orb hurtled at his head. It clipped his Stetson and shattered the deck door. Coren stepped out of sight and plastered his back against the wall.

"Yer dead, Raines! I nailed Heller for killin' the triplets! Now I find out my girls are buried in yer yard! Yer a goddamn accomplice!"

Coren dwelled on Pritchard's affirmation. Francine Heller had killed the Trammell triplets. The dead Blondies had been trying to warn him of that the entire time. But why? Had Francine killed them, too? Had she enlisted Adler and Nelson's help? Whatever the case, Sheriff Psycho had the wrong man and was either clueless or plain deaf to accusations.

"You're confused, Sheriff! Adler and Nelson murdered your daughters! Francine Heller probably helped, too! But I wasn't here fifteen years ago!"

Pritchard bellowed. Coren jumped as the kitchen table somersaulted into the living room and smashed through the bay window. He transferred the mallet to his right hand.

Pritchard spun around the corner. He then lurched back as Coren's swing breezed past his shirt. The mallet slipped from Coren's sweaty palms and thumped across the floor.

Pritchard growled while tears brimmed in his bloodshot glare. He charged Coren and jammed the Magnum in his mouth. *"Why'd ya kill 'em, huh? Why'd ya do it?"*

Coren gagged on the barrel, staggering back as Pritchard continued to charge. He heard shouts and pounding footsteps. The sounds became background noise the moment his head slammed into the hallway wall. He was inches from the panic room door with the Magnum tickling his tonsils and Pritchard's chest pressed against him. He had to lead him away.

Francine's voice screamed from Pritchard's pocket. *"Your daughters were pigs, too! All of them! You knew they were bullying me!"*

Pritchard's face was mauve and bulged veins from his forehead to his jawline. The tape recorder broke the dam. Fifteen years of pent up guilt spilled down his cheeks. *"Yer lyin'! My Blondies are dead in yer yard! Why'd ya kill 'em?"*

In his periphery, Coren glimpsed a crowd rushing into the living room. A crazy thought slipped into his head of his house being taken over by a frat party. He clung to the notion, hoping someone brought a bottle of Seagram's.

\*\*\*\*\*

The suspense was killing Jay. He knew Pritchard was out there beating Coren senseless. He was deaf to the outside world, though. There was only peace and darkness, where his conscience tortured him. While he thought of Jeanette and his girls, he also thought of Coren, who needed an ally more than ever.

He grasped the door handle without a second thought. Regardless if he was unarmed, he could not let an innocent man get cuffed by an insane cop.

S.D. Hintz

# CHAPTER TWENTY-FOUR

*Loren moaned as she came to. Her eyes fluttered and strained to focus through the blur. She screamed, stabs of pain raking her mouth. Blood streamed from her split lips between dangling teeth.*

*She writhed and wailed, wanting to run but paralyzed to the cold, moonlit floor. Henna's decapitated corpse was sprawled beside her in a coagulated pool of blood. Sylvia's dismembered body twitched nearby as if still coping with the shock. Loren couldn't tell if she was alive or dead. She looked down at her own body. Her legs had been mangled and her mouth destroyed.*

*She heard a door slide open. Hank stepped in the moonlight. His eyes locked on her. Her screams died as he crouched before her. She tried to speak, and then realized her tongue was gone.*

*Hank flashed a toothless grin. "You're a little trooper, aren't you? Got more spunk than your father. It's too bad you squealed. You might've just been grounded."*

*Sylvia rolled over and wept. Loren's heart leapt and her eyes lit up. Her sister was alive!*

*Sylvia rasped between sobs. "Please…Please no…Daddy made us…do it…He made us…bully Franny…Please."*

*Hank walked over to Sylvia. "He told you to kill the little girl that ripped off your stinking legs. You got what you deserved."*

*"Daddy hated…Franny's papa…He made us…be mean…to her."*

*Hank grabbed Sylvia's right stump and dragged her over to her sister. She hollered and thrashed. Before Loren could react, the sneering farmer smashed Sylvia's stump into her face. He pinned her to the floor with his cowboy boot on her chest. She squirmed, struggling to breathe. Her body soon relaxed, suffocated by her sister's bloody limb.*

*Hank threw Sylvia aside. She slid across the floor and collided with the wall. He then seized her hair. He slammed her skull against the steel until her screams died and blood poured from her eyes.*

*He reached into his overalls, and then eyed the three sheriff's badges. Pritchard was a sicko. He wanted the badges stuffed in their smart mouths for taking advantage of the fact that he ran the town and they got away with murder. Hank thought it was his way of burying the guilt even deeper.*

*After implanting the badges, Hank wiped his hands on his overalls and dragged Loren out of the panic room. As he shut the door, he swore that he caught a glimpse of Henna's eyes blinking.*

*****

Jay opened the door. A gunshot rang near his head. Blood sprayed his face. He stood still, befuddled, surprised by the explosion. His heart sank. He was too late.

Coren's body slumped at his feet. Pritchard stepped into view, staring at Jay as if he was a ghost, the Magnum barrel dripping brain matter. He pointed the pistol at eye level.

Jay's jaw slacked and he stepped back as a million thoughts zipped through his head. He was going to die. He was never going to see his wife and daughters again. He was going to be a news flash on every station in the state.

Movement caught his eye. A group of silhouettes turned the corner and rushed toward them, shouting and waving their arms. A frigid breeze tickled Jay's nape as recollections of the panic room haunted him. He saw the dead Blondies converging into one body and splitting apart to reveal Francine. The breeze seemed to wrap around his head like a scarf, filling his ears with raspy pleas.

He seized Pritchard's wrist and yanked him into the panic room. The door slammed and the Magnum fired. The shot reverberated, piercing the far wall. Jay stumbled backwards and hit the floor. Pritchard stood tall, took aim.

The panic room mimicked a meat locker. The Magnum glinted in the sliver of moonlight, trembling in Pritchard's hand. The cold rushed through his veins. Shivers rattled his bones. He trained the gun on Jay.

The darkness blinked out to crimson light that surged from the floor. Pritchard's trigger finger straightened and his head snapped. The steel walls peeled and bled. The throbbing muscles burst from every direction. The three walls that Pritchard faced dilated like giant eyeballs.

The maimed Blondies plopped out in rivulets of blood, and then crawled toward their father.

Sylvia towed her stumps from the right wall, speaking through a mouthful of maggots. *"Please no…Daddy made us…do it…He made us…bully her."*

Loren slithered from the left. *"Oohh. Oohh."*

Henna inched forth on her knees, holding her upside down head by the carotids level with her severed neck. *"You never…loved us…You beat us…You hated…hated…hated…you hated us. You killed us."*

Pritchard's nose bled. He bellowed. *"No! Get away from me! Yer not my daughters! Yer not my Blondies!"*

Jay crept back into the farthest corner. Pritchard had lost his focus. He was surrounded by his dead daughters, tortured by emotions buried in his black heart. The Blondies grabbed his legs and clawed at him. He reacted on instinct, unconvinced that the horrors were his girls. The Magnum sparked three times in a deafening echo. The Blondies toppled to the floor in unison. Their bodies smoldered and melted like candle wax. Left behind was a pool of blood and bones with three glinting badges.

The pocket door caved in. The crimson light extinguished. A flipped switch revealed Jay glued to the corner and Pritchard eyeing his smoking gun. Glaring steel walls and cardboard boxes surrounded them.

Nothing else.

They were alone in the panic room.

Pritchard turned to see a pair of Vance's buddies with shotguns linger in the doorway. His eyes glazed and he fell to his knees. The gun smoke burned his nostrils as he raised the barrel to his jaw. A trail of tears streamed. He pulled the trigger. His brains splattered the ceiling and he collapsed on the bloody floor.

Sam Emory entered the room. "What in the hell?" He spotted Jay. "Sir? You okay?"

Jay swallowed the shock and forced his legs to stand. "Yeah. Yeah, I'm fine."

"What the hell's going on here?"

"Hostage. He had me hostage."

"Who? Raines? He had you locked in here?"

Jay shook his head. "No. Pritchard did. Raines never knew I was here."

Sam furrowed his brow.

Wendell Wurtz stepped forward. "Holy cow! I thought I knew that voice. You're Jay Donovan, WNDY News."

Before Jay could reply, an elderly man in a red raincoat pushed out of the crowd at the door. "Sam! You gotta see this! We found something in the backyard!"

Sam turned. "We know, Charlie. Three bodies. Where have you been?"

Charlie frowned when he saw Pritchard's bleeding corpse.

"No, something else, that suddenly makes a whole lot of sense."

"Well, what is it?"

"You gotta see for yourself."

"Wendell, get the Chicago P.D. on the phone. Tell them we need the FBI down here."

Sam barged out of the room. Jay approached the crowd. Some of the men filtered in while most tailed Sam.

Jay stared at Coren's body as he followed the search party down the hall in a trance. His brain was scrambled. Nothing seemed real anymore. Had everything that night happened or had the haunted panic room cast a wicked spell?

He stepped through the shattered deck door. The moon shone bright and illuminated the backyard. There were men circling the well and prodding the grave near the scrap metal. Some of the townies were waving flashlights beyond the fence in the wetlands.

Jay stopped a man in a poncho at the bottom of the steps. "Do you have a cellphone I could use?"

The man nodded and reached in his pocket. "Callin' the tip line?"

"You got it. I'll bring it right back."

Jay dialed home as he approached the well.

"Jeanette? Jeanette it's me. It's me, baby." His voice cracked and the past days stress blurred his vision. "No. I'm alive. I know, I know. I'm sorry. It's a long story." One of the men left the well and ran toward the glinting scrap metal. "They did? They said I was missing? No, no. I'm still in Onward. I'll be home by morning. I promise. Jeanette? I love you."

Jay ended the call, dried his eyes on his sleeve. He stepped up to the well. Two men shined flashlights in the hole. They stared at the skeleton that protruded a foot down in the crumbled wall. Something glinted from within. Jay's stomach turned when he saw what they gawked at. He vomited in the hole.

Sam stood on the opposite side. His mutter echoed down the well. "They all got the same thing in their mouths…barbed wire and sheriff badges. Jesus Christ. We got six dead girls on our hands."

Jay's head spun. His thoughts dwelled on the three-day horror story. Both sets of triplets had been found dead. The murders of Coren, Vance, Hank, Burl, and Francine brought the death toll to eleven.

Eleven deaths traced back to one sheriff.

Jay walked away and headed to the front yard, which had been converted to a parking lot. The reporter in him was dead. He lacked the urge to join the frenzy and ask or answer questions. He wanted to go home to his family.

He stopped a man in a postal uniform. He knew he had to act the reporter one last time if he wanted to skip the godforsaken town.

"Hi. I'm Jay Donovan, WNDY News. Is there any chance you could give me a lift to Chicago? My car's dead and I need to get this story to the station."

Ray Ratner grinned as if he stared at a movie star. "Jay Donovan? You bet! Will I be on TV?"

"You and everybody else."

Jay followed Ray through the crowd as sirens sliced the night in the distance. He passed reporters he recognized whose smiles and comments were like bad reception. They thought he was there to cover the story. He was part of the story. They would uncover the details in due time. Right now it was all static. Every townie had a tale and three-fourths of them simply wanted to share the spotlight. They could have it.

Jay climbed into the rusty mail truck and gazed down the drive at the approaching line of police cars. *Please get me out of here.*

Ray Ratner turned on the radio as he waited for the parade to pass. "So, you ever done a story on mail carriers? I can tell you some tales. I remember this one time I had a letter -"

"There's a surprise."

"Now it wasn't just any letter, it -"

"Can we just get the hell out of here?"

Ray continued to chatter as he pulled away. "Our town motto says it all. Onward and upward, yes sirree. Onward and upward."

*"Would you just shut up and drive?"*

At that moment, Jay needed Coren's best friend Seagram. Maybe he would have Ray stop at a bar on the way to Chicago.

Ray scowled as he floored the gas pedal. "You're gonna be out of my truck! Damn reporters! You're all the same! All you want is your stupid story!"

"This has been Jay Donovan, WNDY News."

Jay laughed until he thought he would wet himself while the bloodstained town of Onward danced in the spotlight.

S.D. Hintz

# ABOUT THE AUTHOR

S.D. Hintz is the author of *Starvelings*, *Blood Orchard*, *Sacrificial Witch*, *Tales from an Undertaker*, *A Haunting on Eerie Street*, as well as numerous short stories is several anthologies and magazines. He is also the CEO/Editor-in-Chief of KHP Publishers, Inc. S.D. is married with two children and resides in Minnesota. Visit http://sdhintz.com to read more of his work.

www.ingramcontent.com/pod-product-compliance
Lightning Source LLC
Chambersburg PA
CBHW070354260626
47161CB00001B/136